A MILLS
Mills, Sam,
The viper w
R0024355639

SO-BZH-981

The Viper Within

THIS IS A BORZOI BOOK PUBLISHED BY ALFRED A. KNOPF

This is a work of fiction. Names, characters, places, and incidents either are the product of the author's imagination or are used fictitiously. Any resemblance to actual persons, living or dead, events, or locales is entirely coincidental.

Copyright © 2007 by Sam Mills

All rights reserved. Published in the United States by Alfred A. Knopf, an imprint of Random House Children's Books, a division of Random House, Inc., New York. First published in Great Britain by Faber and Faber as *The Boys Who Saved the World* in 2007.

Knopf, Borzoi Books, and the colophon are registered trademarks of Random House, Inc.

Visit us on the Web! www.randomhouse.com/teens

Educators and librarians, for a variety of teaching tools, visit us at www.randomhouse.com/teachers

Library of Congress Cataloging-in-Publication Data
Mills, Sam.
[Boys who saved the world]
The viper within / Sam Mills. — 1st American ed.
p. cm.
Summary: Bitter and angry after his parents' divorce, Jon joins a cult, The Religion of Hebetheus, at his high school and soon becomes embroiled in a plot to kidnap a fellow student and suspected terrorist, but their plans go terribly wrong.
ISBN 978-0-375-84465-2 (trade) — ISBN 978-0-375-94465-9 (lib. bdg.)
[1. Cults—Fiction. 2. Kidnapping—Fiction. 3. Religion—Fiction.
4. Conduct of life—Fiction. 5. Divorce—Fiction.] I. Title.
PZ7.M639837Vip 2008
[Fic]—dc22
2007031952

The text of this book is set in 14-point PrioriSerRegular.

Printed in the United States of America
June 2008
10 9 8 7 6 5 4 3 2 1
First American Edition

Random House Children's Books supports the First Amendment and celebrates the right to read.

The Viper Within

SAM MILLS

Alfred A. Knopf
New York

PART ONE

In two hours' time I—and the rest of the Brotherhood—will kidnap a terrorist.

Our code name for this terrorist is SNAKE. By kidnapping SNAKE tonight, we—the Brotherhood of the Religion of Hebetheus—will prevent a bomb from going off at St. Sebastian's Secondary School. If I lean out of my bedroom window and look beyond the jagged patchwork of rooftops, I can see its metal railings, waving treetops, green playing fields. I picture what might have been, papier-mâchéd out of TV images. Red blood sprayed across red brick. Parents hugging teenagers. EMTs lifting them into ambulances. Smoke spiraling up across a blistered sky. We will prevent all that.

I reach under my bed and pull out the wooden box, sifting through rustles of tissue paper. When Jeremiah first passed it on to me, I had this compulsion to just look at it. Sometimes two, three times a day. Just opening the box made my hands shake with anticipation. The virgin glint of the knife, arrowing through the paper, caused a firework to explode inside me; long after I'd put it back and tucked it under my bed, little sparks would fly through me for the whole day.

But over the last few days, whenever I've taken it out, I feel blank. I stare down at it now—nothing. Just a bit of metal trapped in a wooden handle.

I look at the posters on my walls and think: *Slash them!* Will that bring the knife back to life? Then I remember Jeremiah's words: *We must keep acting as though everything is normal. A slip by just one of us will destroy our sacred mission.*

I slice up air. Picture the blade held against a brown throat. How light or hard should I press it so as to provoke fear but not draw blood?

I hold it up so it catches the last of the sunset, narrowing my eyes until the silver blurs into a thinner knife of pure light. In its shimmers, I see all our faces: Thomas, Martyn, Chris, Raymond. And Jeremiah, our prophet, with his wise eyes and gentle smile.

"Jon! Dinner's ready!"

The knife slips and slices against my thumb, drawing a thin dribble of blood.

I hear a creak on the stairs and quickly shove it under my pillow.

"I've made lasagne—your favorite."

"Coming, Mum."

7:15 P.M.: ONE HOUR AND FORTY-FIVE MINUTES TO GO . . .

"Can you just finish laying the table, Jon? I forgot the serving mat. There. . . . Thank you."

This morning, when it was twelve hours to go, I forced my-self to eat a bowl of cereal, but it felt like eating stones and on my way to school I spewed it up in some bushes.

A red trickle has reached the tines of my fork. I quickly look at Mum, but she is engrossed in her own world. She eats like a sad bird, taking tiny little mouthfuls, as though eating is a lux-ury she feels she doesn't quite deserve.

I press my thumb hard against the fork to stanch the flow from the cut, but my blood laces the lasagne with a salty, metal-lic taste.

My eyes sweep across the table and I notice that she has done it again. She has laid a third mat. Even though it's been a year. Last night, she brewed up two mugs of Horlicks before go-ing to bed and then pretended that one was for me, even though I hate Horlicks. She still has dinner at 7:15 P.M., even though she's hungry much earlier, because that was the time Dad pre-ferred it.

I take another mouthful and stare out the window. Six months ago, we moved to a new suburban housing estate where every house looks the same. The same red bricks. The same double-glazed windows, outfitted with gray bars to keep burglars out. The trees look pale and anorexic, wilting at being stuck in such a dump. Over the fence, I can see lines of other houses, stick figures moving about, people sitting down to eat, families snacking in front of the TV.

I look at these people and I wonder how they can go through life living the way they do, not doing a jot to change anything. No, they're all too busy dreaming of getting onto reality TV for fifteen milliseconds of fame. I fantasize that my fork swells into a giant metal harpoon that I smash through each house like a missile—

"Was school okay today?" Mum asks.

"Yeah, it was okay," I say. "It's always okay."

Silence. Then—

An explosion.

Outside.

Green glitter lights up the sky. The stars shrink and the streetlamps pale away.

People gaze up, mesmerized.

"Guy Fawkes tomorrow," says Mum. "I bought some sparklers. And some sausages. We can have a little fun and a fry-up."

"Uh-huh." I try to thread my fork through another layer of lasagne, but my hand is shaking too violently. The explosion echoes through me, carrying warnings of burning flesh. I feel relief that we are going ahead with the plan, that tonight we will be saving our school. Our first step to saving the world.

I push my plate away. Mum looks up.

"Oh, Jon, I spent all that time cooking your favorite and then you take three mouthfuls—"

"It's good, Mum, I'm just not that hungry. Maybe later."

"Well, will you come with me to church tonight? We're helping to set it up for the concert next week."

"I hate church."

"You don't mean that."

"I do."

I used to be a False Believer too. Christianity seduced me like a purring snake. I was the good boy of my school, the guy who never got picked for games because his dad was the local vicar, the guy who got teased for singing in the choir every night. But none of that mattered.

None of that mattered because I was living in a fantasy. I thought that the Christian God would love me and look after me and answer all my prayers. At night I used to lie awake and imagine that if God suddenly scooped up water in his hand and hurled it at our country in a second flood, I would be like Noah. Me, Mum, Dad, our dog, and all the other Christians—we'd be warned. A sign would come, and we'd make boats and survive to watch the other sinners drown. I believed going to church every week and reading a book of lies and singing stupid hymns were like money in the Bank of God, a kind of spiritual life insurance that would always protect me. I thought I was special.

Then one day Dad came home and told Mum he was in love with the woman who lived across the road. He moved in with her the following week, and we spent our evenings eating and trying not to look out at them but doing nothing but looking out at them. We watched them eat their dinner, her fussing over Dad, smoothing his collar, kissing his cheek, laying out his food. It was as though we were being given a glimpse into a parallel universe we couldn't quite believe existed. Six months later, we moved. I've never set foot in a church since.

Tonight Mum will leave the house promptly at 8:30 P.M. Five minutes later, I will join Jeremiah and the Brotherhood. By the time Mum gets back, I will be long gone.

Right now, I am clearing away the supper plates. A text appears on my mobile.

7:40 P.M.: ONE HOUR AND TWENTY MINUTES TO GO . . .

It's from Martyn.

GOT THE KNIFE. R U READY TO HANDLE THE SNAKE?

It's like a conch being blown, like a tribal war cry. I punch the air.

7:50 P.M.: ONE HOUR AND TEN MINUTES TO GO . . .

I hate TV. I force myself to sit on the sofa with Mum for a short while. I watch without watching. Jeremiah explained to me how our minds are malleable and can be infused with any color. When we watch TV our minds are tossed between what the government wants us to think and what the big companies want us to think, until all our own color is leached out, leaving only a pastel gray.

I flick a glance at my mum, the images dancing across her eyeballs as though she's being hypnotized.

"Look at that," she says, pointing the remote at the screen showing black-and-white images of people waving placards. "You see, in my day, when people marched, things changed. Not anymore. People make a fuss and the government still goes to war."

I am suddenly gripped by a desire to tell her everything the Brotherhood is about to do. But that would be suicidal.

8:00 P.M.: ONE HOUR TO GO . . .

*What is the difference between the Catholic
Church and the Church of England?*

Another one of Mr. Abdilla's pointless religious studies questions.

It was because of my dad that I go to St. Sebastian's, a posh fee-paying school. I might have ended up at the public school, getting my head permanently stuck down a toilet, but Mum called up Dad every night for a week, insisting he pay the tuition. My first week here, I was amazed by how many people attempted to befriend me. I was no longer the Christian kid. I was almost cool. But I said no to movies, to football games, to party invites. I felt determined not to enjoy anything that was funded by my dad.

Even though I'd lost interest in Christianity, I was still a seeker. When I lay in bed peering at the night sky, I was convinced that only a divine intelligence could have created something as awesome and intricate as all the galaxies and black holes and planets in our universe. So I kept on searching. I was determined not to be sucked in this time; I wanted the ultimate truth. I dabbled in Buddhism; I went to a few classes on Judaism; I researched the Baha'i faith; I even tried and failed to persuade my mum to take me on holiday to India, where I could seek blessings from a guru. Nothing quite convinced me.

Ironically, it was Mr. Abdilla who brought me and Jeremiah together. Everyone else in his class was always yawning or doodling on their notebooks. But Jeremiah kept bulleting questions at him. *Why do you think there is so much suffering in the world, Mr. Abdilla? Why do you think prayers aren't answered?* By the end, Mr. Abdilla would be sweating and spluttering and shrugging. And Jeremiah would be sitting there surrounded by an aura of calm, as though he already knew all the answers but couldn't resist teasing his teacher.

It took three weeks for me to work up the courage to approach Jeremiah and ask if I could hang out with him. I was terrified he'd tell me where to go. But a tender smile passed across his lips. He said he'd been waiting for me.

What is the difference between the Catholic Church and the Church of England?

I pick up my pen and write out the truths of the Brotherhood. Even though I know them by heart.

THE TRUTHS OF
THE RELIGION OF HEBETHEUS

Hebetheus is a true religion that will correct the mistakes of past religions.

    Past religions are based on lies, corruption, and mistakes. Over time the purity of their teaching has been lost, subverted, and polluted. These worshipers follow a false figure, not God.

    The god that current religions worship does not exist. This is why there is still sickness, suffering, and famine in the world and why prayers go unanswered.

    The God of Hebetheus is the one true God. The aim of the Brotherhood is to understand him and do his work.

    Every man is both good and evil. But man is inherently weak and lazy, so he will tend to slump into evil. It is up to every member of the Brotherhood to constantly choose good in his day-to-day actions. Every member has a duty to expel evil and cleanse the world.

We, the Brotherhood, are fortunate to have been chosen by God to wipe out the false religions and bring ours to the people of the world. This has been verified by Jeremiah's dreams.

Every member of the Brotherhood shall be chosen by God through Jeremiah. Every member will undergo an Initiation to prove his worth and devotion to the Hebethean cause.

No member of the Brotherhood is permitted to drink, smoke, watch TV, or be beguiled by the sinful temptations of the opposite sex. Every member should spend at least one hour a day in prayer in order to cleanse his soul. In return, our God will listen to our prayers and perform amazing miracles. This has already been proven by the miracles Jeremiah has experienced and conveyed to the Brotherhood.

By doing good, we will inspire others to join the Hebethean religion. When everyone has joined Hebetheus, the world will be saved.

Therefore, to save one person in the name of Hebetheus is to save the whole of humanity. To do one good deed to protect people is a first step to saving the world.

I flit back to the religious studies question. What right does Mr. Abdilla have to set us questions, to judge and mark our work, when he clearly knows nothing? After we found out about SNAKE's terrorist plans, we approached him after school. He seemed to listen carefully, but then he shook his head and told us to leave SNAKE alone. He said we had made a mistake.

We went to the park, fizzing with pent-up anger, Raymond declaring he was ready to beat up bloody Abdilla for not believing us. That was when the idea came to take matters into our own hands. If Mr. Abdilla wouldn't listen to us, the police probably wouldn't either. It was up to us.

Tonight will be my Initiation into the Brotherhood. I've become impatient, ardent with waiting. For six months I've been a member, but not a full one. There are still secret pacts I don't know, prayers I haven't yet been taught to recite.

Jeremiah has been telling me for weeks that I will play a crucial role in the mission. But he says it's better that I find out the details when the time comes.

I admit that I'm scared. Jeremiah has such faith in me. What if I fail him? What if I throw it all away tonight?

I swallow. My pencil slips through my sweaty fingers onto the bed. My clock ticks away like a bomb. I gaze around my room. Eminem. Coldplay. Keane. I put these posters up six months ago. I feel strangely sad looking at them. I remember how excited I felt when I tacked Eminem to my wall, and tears fill my eyes. I flick them away, shake myself, check the clock.

It is time. Mum should be leaving now. I jump up, my stomach swimming in butterflies, and hurry down the stairs.

"Uh, Mum, you off now?"

"Oh, I decided not to go after all," she calls out. "It's all right, we can both just stay in and watch some TV."

8:30 P.M.: HALF AN HOUR TO GO . . .

It must be the Christian God. I've left his religion and now he's getting back at me. But he doesn't exist. So is it just me? Maybe Jeremiah was wrong in taking a chance on me. Maybe I should call Jeremiah right now, maybe we can arrange it another night. *Oh God, please don't turn on me, please help me, maybe this is a test, well, please help me pass it.* I run back into the living room.

"Mum," I say, "I really think you should go to church. I didn't mean what I said. I really think it could help you."

She looks surprised and then smiles.

"No, Jon, I think what you said earlier was true. For the last few weeks, I've been feeling as though I've just been singing meaningless songs in an empty building."

"But—but—I think it could *help.* . . ."

She checks her watch uncertainly.

"Maybe you're right . . . but I've left it too late now. I'll go on Sunday to make up for it." She frowns. "Are you okay, Jon?"

I can hear Jeremiah's voice in my mind: *We're all cogs in this delicate operation. If one of us spins out, then the whole thing jams.* I run out. I stand in the hallway. I stare at the paintings running down the stairs: prints of a willow draping a lake. I grab my jacket, get my mobile. I fling open the back door. Out into the twilight. Something brushes my head. I jump wildly—the police? Here already, tipped off? No—just a leaf, dead pieces clinging desperately to its skeleton. I press Jeremiah's number.

Voice mail. Jeremiah's voice, slow and deep as chocolate: *I'm sorry I can't speak to you right now. . . .* Why isn't he answering his phone at a time like this? I clear my throat to leave a message. Pathetic apologies flare and then splutter in my mind, dying into embers of shame. I hang up. I hear my mum calling, "Are you all right out there? Can you close the back door—it's getting cold." I could run now. But I've left my weapon upstairs. I go back indoors. I stand in the kitchen and send Jeremiah a shaky text:

TROUBLE GETTING OUT—MUM. WHAT
SHOULD I DO?

I stand and wait. A row of saucepans shines my face back to me in grotesque leers. My mobile beeps.

IMPROVISE.

8:40 P.M.: TWENTY MINUTES TO GO . . .

Upstairs in my room, I kneel down on the floor, clasp my hands together, and recite the rules of the Brotherhood out loud. It becomes a kind of meditation. As the words shake from my trembling lips, I forget the meaning of them. They become a monotonous hum. The hum becomes breathless whispers. The whispers fade into faint impulses, thoughts that are more colors than words. The panic ebbs away, leaving a cool, empty space in my mind. I realize, sitting here, that there is nothing to stop me going. I remember Jeremiah's words: *Our thoughts are our only boundaries, nothing more, nothing less.*

I'll just walk out. And if she tries to stop me, well, then I'll—my eyes fall to the glint of the knife, and I recoil—*I'll . . . I'd better pack.*

I stuff everything into my backpack, click it shut. My hands aren't shaking anymore. Not one tremor.

I tread down the stairs quietly. I hear the downstairs toilet flushing—perfect. I click open the door—

"Jon?"

"I'm going out, okay?" I say, without turning back.

"Jon! What do you think you're doing?"

"I said," I mumble, feeling the wind tease my face, blowing scents of freedom, "I'm going out."

"Jon! You know you're not allowed out on a school night."

She tries to grab my arm—and instead she yanks my backpack, pulling it off.

"Mum!" I cry, whipping round. I try to grab it back but she clings to one of the yellow loops. I see determination flash in her eyes, and suddenly I feel my cool certainty drain away. "Mum, I just want to go out for a quick walk."

"Where on earth are you going to go for this quick walk?"

I hesitate.

"Just down the road."

"Jon, we've had this discussion before. You're going to stay in and do your homework. Now."

She reaches out—

And I push her.

I don't mean to push her so hard. I don't know what gets into me; it's a lightning flash of anger and frustration that sends her stumbling back against the bottom of the stairs. Her hair swishes over her face; her hand claws the air.

I stare down at her, numb, my hands dangling by my sides. I wait for her to tell me off. Then I see it in her eyes—fear. At first I feel horrified. Then a whoosh of triumph supersedes it. My chest beats hard; I am a man.

"I'm going out," I hear myself say loudly. "I'm going out, okay? And don't wait up."

I turn to go when I hear the sound. It sears through me. Crying.

"Mum," I try to say, but the word is lost in a gulpy lump in my throat. "Mum."

"Please stay. Please." She reaches up to grab my hand, and the warmth of her fingers sends a shock up my arm. I realize it in a flash—I do want to stay. I want to put down my backpack and go in and watch TV, cozy against the growing chill of the twilight. Suddenly the autumn air that tempted me is scented with cold and danger, a world of darting dark shapes running in fear. But then my mobile beeps. It's Jeremiah.

WHERE R U?

I pull her up and give her a tight, quick hug. I close my eyes and think: *It'll be different when I come back. The next time I see her, she'll be praising me. She'll be saying, "This is my son, the hero."*

She clings so tightly, as though she's frightened she's never going to see me again, and it's the weirdest thing, because suddenly I feel like I am the parent and she is a child.

"Please don't go," she whispers. "You promised you'd be with me after Dad went. You said you'd stay in during the week. Please stay and keep me company."

I touch her hair. Before Dad left it used to feel silky; now it feels like dead grass.

"I'll be back soon," I say desperately, pulling away.

"Jon—" A sharpness returns to her voice, and I back off before she can become my mum again.

I dart out through the door. I slam it hard and it feels as though an invisible cord between us is severed. I run out into the twilit world, the streets roaring with traffic and mayhem.

I am late, and I pray to God to give me wings.

8:50 P.M.: TEN MINUTES TO GO . . .

I'm so late. Come on, get a move on, oh God, what's Jeremiah going to say?

I was supposed to meet them at the van at 8:40 P.M. Now it's 8:52.

I am changing in the bushes in the park by my house. I had to vault over the fence to get in. The playground looks naked without children, swings meandering eerily in the wind. I think of my mum, lying by the stairs. What if I hurt her—what if tomorrow she wakes up with ugly bruises? The park warden is whistling in the distance. *Oh God, please don't let him notice me.*

I rip off my school tie and stuff it into my backpack. *Come on, come on.* I undo half the buttons on my shirt, then yank it over my head. The wind lays chilly palms on my back. The black sweater scrapes against my face as I pull it on. I can leave my jeans; my black school pants will do.

Then I panic because I can't fit everything into my backpack. I didn't plan room for my school uniform, and my blazer won't go in. I decide to leave it under the bushes—but what if the police find it? On the pocket is our emblem, a griffin, with the school motto winding around it: Aim for the Highest. I take my knife from my bag and slice off the emblem in a jagged oval, stuffing it into my pocket. As I push my knife back into my bag, suddenly a voice pierces the night.

"What d'you think you're doing here?"

The park warden, a rusty old man with wispy clouds of hair, is peering down at me. No doubt he is a *raptor*.

"Nothing. I'm going, I'm going."

"I'll have to let you out."

"I can—" I dare not climb over the fence or create a fight and draw attention to myself. I lower my head and stare at the ground, waiting in torment while minutes race past as he goes through his ring of keys and finally slots one into the lock, undoing the padlock loop by loop. Hopefully, he won't remember my face. I don't think I have a memorable face.

The chain slithers free and I run.

I run and run and run and run. Pain in my calves; my lungs hissing pistons.

Up above, another explosion. Eerie spaceship showers of green tumble down the sky. *Faster, faster.* It's 8:57 P.M. now. I thought Jeremiah had deliberately chosen the day—as close to Guy Fawkes as we could—as an homage to a man who also dared to rebel against society. But Jeremiah said it was because people would be busy and distracted, the police busy with dumb kids shooting off their fingers. I replied that I thought we wanted attention. *Oh, we do,* he said, *but not tonight. Tonight we need to be men of silence and stealth. By tomorrow, it will all begin: we'll drop a boulder into the ocean of British consciousness and send ripples through it that will reverberate through history.*

Besides, he added, *I don't see Guy Fawkes as a figure of inspira-*

tion. Ultimately, he failed. What is the point of celebrating failure? We're not going to fail.

Nine P.M. now. It should have already happened. *Just cross the main road, ignore the traffic lines. Fuck, they're honking at me. Ignore them. Just get across. I just have to pass two small roads, Bennington Close and Ashleigh Gardens, and then I'll be there and maybe, maybe there will be a day celebrating us in a hundred years' time, statues of us in Trafalgar Square encrusted with pigeon shit*, and I am running running running running to the vehicle outside Jeremiah's house.

Jeremiah and Raymond are standing by the van.

Chris pokes his head out and stutters: "H-h-here he is!"

"At last!"

"I'm sorry, I'm so sorry." I can barely speak, but it's so important that I tell my story, that Jeremiah understands. The other faces may be angry or impatient, but the only face that carries any detail for me is Jeremiah's.

I expected him to be as cool as ever; I am startled by the touch of anger in his eyes.

"I'm sorry, I'm sorry—"

"You idiot!" Raymond bursts out. "I knew you were going to mess up—"

"Ray, it's fine," Jeremiah cuts in. "Let's not waste any time arguing. Get into the van. Come on, let's go, let's go, let's go!"

Raymond and Jeremiah get into the front of the van; Raymond is driving. I get into the back with Thomas, Chris, and Martyn. There are no benches; we have to sit on the metal floor, knees bunched up.

My Brothers look nervous. Even *Thomas* looks nervous. He's a year older than us and has the sort of accent and manners that make adults sigh and secretly wish they'd brought him up. His father is a famous surgeon, and his mother runs some fancy charity that seems to involve organizing ten-course lunches every other day. On the surface, Thomas seems to get on well with them. But the truth is, they're hardly ever around. They just leave Thomas to rattle about in their big fancy house and give him a huge allowance on the condition that he keeps on scoring A's.

Martyn and Chris have known each other since they were little kids, when they used to play in each other's back gardens. A few years ago, they were in the Army Cadets after school. Martyn is short and stocky and reminds me of a very fierce Jack Russell terrier. To be honest, he puts me on edge a bit. If he wasn't in Hebetheus, I think he would have given me a hard time, shoved me in gym class, demanded lunch money, and so on. But Martyn has a difficult time at home. Tonight there is a fresh bruise shining on his cheek.

Chris is thin and gangly and twitchy. He suffers from asthma, and even when he's not using his inhaler he's always fiddling about with it, checking it's in his pocket, tossing it from palm to palm. Because he stutters, a lot of people think that Chris is a bit of a twerp. But once you get past his layer of prickly shyness, Chris shines like a conker. He can surprise you with his wit, his intelligence, his spark.

They all ask why I'm late, and I retell my story, altering a few details. Even though we're supposed to share everything in the Brotherhood, they don't know about the divorce. In fact, I lied and said my dad had left home long ago, when I was just a baby. I just felt so embarrassed by what a bastard he is.

I tell them that Mum fell down the stairs and sprained her ankle and that I had to bandage her up and sort her out. I'm not usually a good liar, but they seem convinced.

I let out a breath and look round the van. Inside, it has been painted with symbols in white paint. A candle. A mandala with six inner circles. A tree with six branches. A swastika. Jeremiah explained that though the Nazis made the swastika a sign of hatred, originally it was an Indian symbol of peace. My eyes drink them in. I feel soothed.

All the same, Raymond's words keep echoing in my mind: *I knew you were going to mess up.* I wonder if he is slagging me off to Jeremiah right now, poisoning his mind against me.

Raymond is the oldest in the Brotherhood. His faith seems a bit flimsy at times. In my opinion he wouldn't even be a member if he wasn't Jeremiah's older brother. He's eighteen, two years older than Jeremiah. Jeremiah's tall and thin and leonine; Raymond's six foot two, with arms of heavy lard. He works in an electronics shop. Raymond looks like he wouldn't answer to anyone, but he answers to Jeremiah. Whenever Jeremiah speaks, he seems to shrink and his eyes become soft and intent. He always lets Jeremiah make the decisions.

Jeremiah and Raymond live on their own together. Their

parents died last year. I asked Chris once how they died and he clammed up and stuttered that Jeremiah didn't like anyone to talk about it. The only crumb he would give me is that Raymond is now Jeremiah's legal guardian.

"J-Jeremiah says before their parents died, they used to argue a lot," Chris explained. "But the H-Hebetheus brought them closer together."

I wish Jeremiah was my brother. I curse and curse Raymond and his piggy eyes and fat face. And then I stare at the swastika for a while, praying hard. I begin to feel better. God will make sure SNAKE is still there. He will find a way to delay SNAKE. Everything will be fine.

In fact, my being late is probably meant to be. If we had arrived on time, then something else would have gone wrong. A police car would have sailed by, or a glass bottle in the road would have cut its teeth into our tire. God is working in his mysterious ways.

I look round at my Brothers. The air is thrilled with excitement. Chris is listening to Hebethean chants on his Walkman; Martyn tries to tear it off him and they jostle, laughing. Thomas flicks his lighter, the flame pirouetting up again and again and again like an exhausted dancing girl. Then, slowly, everything becomes still. The longer the silence goes on, the more impossible it is to crack. From time to time, our eyes flick and hop off each other and there's a jolt of shock at what we're about to do.

I can't stop looking at the equipment. The roll of masking tape. The saw. The circles of rope. The sacks. Crates of mineral water. Boxes of food. Jeremiah warned us that we may be in for a long haul.

A long haul. The words thrill me. *I am in this for the rest of my life, and beyond.*

A pair of silver handcuffs is tacked to a metal rod lining the van. The loose cuff jangles and clatters to the rumbling rhythm of the vehicle. It looks like a silver noose, formed to kill a small, heartless doll.

Then the van shivers to a halt. I find myself wishing it could keep going for a while. We're here, and I can't believe how quickly it's all happening.

9:30 P.M.: THIRTY MINUTES LATER . . .

Something is wrong.

By nine-thirty we should have already grabbed SNAKE. For the last few weeks we have been taking turns to spy on her, suss out her routine. The spot had been chosen carefully: the bottom of Mabel Drive, sheltered by the leafy trees that border the park. She leaves her house at around nine nearly every night to see her best friend—normally with her mum's shouts trailing behind her: "Are you sure you've finished your homework? You know you're not allowed to see Michela before you've done your homework!" This Michela lives three roads away. We will intercept SNAKE on her stroll over.

Yesterday Martyn thwacked a cricket ball into the street-lamps curling overhead. Tonight the area is vague with gloom. We watch the front door of number 32 Mabel Drive. SNAKE should already be walking down the pavement to the bottom of the road, taking the sandy, muddy track that is a shortcut through the park. Chris and Raymond are hiding in the trees, ready to pounce. SNAKE will be brought back to the van, where we will use our silencing equipment. Raymond will then drive us and the hostage to the warehouse in Streatham.

But it is now 9:30 P.M. And there is no sign of SNAKE.

9:50 P.M.

Are we too late? Has SNAKE already left for the night?

The weekend, once magnified with anticipation, now shrinks, as though seen through the wrong end of a telescope. I will wake up in bed tomorrow, Mum's frying wafting up the stairs, suburban sounds screaming in my ears; I will drag myself through another day at school, learning lies; then Saturday will come and I will spend a lone day in the park, watching boys spray graffiti. Everything will slide back the way it was, helpless, pointless.

"Maybe we c-c-can come back n-n-next week," says Chris.

"Next week?" Thomas cries angrily. "We've been planning this for so long. We can't back out now—we *can't*!"

"Where are you going?" Raymond asks.

Jeremiah raises one hand and we all fall silent, watching him. This is part of his genius: improvising. When you improvise, he says, you jump off a cliff and wait for God to catch you. It's a test that cements faith.

My heart gasps when I see Jeremiah walk straight through the gate, past the rosebushes, and ring the doorbell of number 32. A few seconds later, the door opens. A warm slice of light, the silhouette of an Asian woman, her beauty wrapped in the blue sheen of a peacock sari. I am taken aback. I did not expect SNAKE's mother to look like this. But then I remember Jeremiah's warning words on appearances.

She steps forward, smiling, and I realize she is not a woman but a girl—way too young to be SNAKE's mother. I figure she must be her sister.

Jeremiah chats casually. His polite attitude seems to impress her, for she gives him a warm smile and rubs his arm.

Then my stomach churns. Jeremiah turns and walks back.

It's over, then. Oh God, why didn't I just leave the moment Mum said she wasn't going to church? Why didn't I just run?

"Oh well," says Thomas sadly. "God did not intend tonight to be the night, then."

"It's fucking Jon's fault!" Raymond turned on me. "He messed up—"

"God did not intend—"

Jeremiah cuts in angrily.

"Gentlemen, you know that we're above this bickering," he says. We all instantly fall into sheepish silence. That is the effect Jeremiah has on people: speak to him and you suddenly feel small and petty, as though he is living life on a higher level you can only hope to glimpse. In moments like this, I swear I can see the color of his mind: luminous, celestial, golden.

"SNAKE's sneaked out. She's told her mum that she's at Michela's for a sleepover, but according to her sister, she's gone clubbing. She only just left, so—"

"Hang on," Martyn interjects, "her sister could just be bull-shitting, making stuff up—"

"I told her that we were Michela's friends and we sometimes hung out together. She didn't look that shocked. Clearly SNAKE enjoys plenty of male company." His voice is thick with disgust. "Or maybe she's just meeting some of her terrorist contacts. So now we go. We go now, we go to the club. There's no time to waste. *Go!*"

In the back of the van, I daren't look at the rest of the Brotherhood. Thomas pats me on the shoulder kindly and says I shouldn't worry, but Chris and Martyn stare at me with silent animosity. I keep my eyes fixed on the swastika. My head is hurting. My heart is hot. I keep cursing myself. I am close to cursing God. This is all too much like the night Dad left. The night my faith caved in. I remember hearing the faint sounds of my mum crying in the bedroom next door. I wanted her to feel assured that I was asleep, so I lay stiff in bed, barely daring to move a millimeter, sweat seeping into the sheets. A picture of Dad was crushed in my hand, and I kept staring at the cross on my wall and praying over and over, until my jaw ached, for God to bring him back. But my prayers were like dead letters.

Now history is repeating itself. It's as though I'm holding my belief in both hands like an eggshell, but I can't help squeezing it in terror that it's not really real, and cracks are forming like little spiders.

The van slows down. I pray desperately, tears fierce behind my eyes: *Oh God, please let me be wrong, please don't let me down. I thought I'd found you in Hebetheus, thought I'd found an ultimate truth, please let this be true, please let this be real. . . .*

10:15 P.M.

Somewhere in Kingston, we stop. Jeremiah opens up the back doors. We're on a small side street. It is a tramp's heaven, a garden of putrid black trash cans. Distant music thumps beneath the pavement like underground thunder.

Jeremiah's eyes are glittering; he's relishing this challenge, this chance to work his divine magic.

"Chris, you come with me. Jon, you get into the front of the van with Raymond. Thomas and Martyn, stay in the back—be ready to attack. Once we bring SNAKE in, we'll need to act quickly. Get SNAKE into the van. Silence her with the sack and tape and then we leave. Fast. Got it?"

We all nod solemnly.

As I get out of the van, I feel Jeremiah's long fingers reach out and rub my shoulder. It's as though he eases out all of the stress like a splinter. I smile in weak relief.

I climb into the van beside Raymond. He folds his arms and won't look at me.

In the side mirror, I watch Jeremiah and Chris become silhouettes. I can hardly believe the risk they are taking. I know the club SNAKE is going to: it's a *raptor* haven. I tried to go there once myself when we first moved here, one lonely Saturday night when my mum thought I was at a school disco. The only underage kids they allowed in were the pretty girls. Every night, there is a crocodile queue of glamour and black suits and glittering dresses stretching out from under its pink neon sign. SNAKE will be standing there now, chatting and laughing, spreading sin. But how will Jeremiah possibly lure her away?

I start to hum nervously: *We plow the fields and scatter.* Dad always used to sing this hymn around the house. I catch Raymond's eye and he gives me a look. He thinks I'm taking the piss. I shut up quickly.

I find my hand slipping down and curling into the door

handle of the van. If everything goes wrong and the police turn up, I can make a run for it. Maybe that's why it's already gone wrong; maybe God is protecting me.

But then I think of how my life was before I met Jeremiah. Those first few weeks at my new school, when I lay in bed at night and thought about emptying the medicine cabinet down my throat. My fingers fall slack.

"What's going to happen?" I blurt out.

"It'll be cool. Jeremiah has God-given powers of persuasion," says Raymond. "He'll spin some story. SNAKE doesn't have a chance."

"He's so clever," I say proudly. I see Raymond's face and I look away, embarrassed by my show of emotion. "Of course, it's really God working through him."

Raymond doesn't respond. I frown. Sometimes I doubt Raymond. He hardly ever talks about God. During prayer sessions, I have sometimes opened my eyes and seen him staring vaguely into the distance.

I check my watch: 10:30 P.M.

Why did he take Chris and not me? Am I being punished? I've seen Chris around girls; he can't get past one stutter. What powers of persuasion does he have?

And then, suddenly, I see a glimmer in the wing mirror.

Jeremiah is with SNAKE.

The look in her eyes is puzzled, faintly bewildered. Jeremiah's arm is slung around her shoulders. Chris is standing a

little way behind them, hands scrunched in his pockets, looking awkward.

It strikes me how vile her beauty is, how deceptive. She's
dressed herself up for the night in glitzy trousers, a black halter-
neck top. Her beauty hits me the way it did when I first met her.
It was my first religious studies class, and I was aware of sitting
at an empty desk, staring hard at the graffiti carved into the
wood, trying to pretend I was doing fine. She walked in, sat
down next to me, smiled, and said she hoped I was settling in.
All though the lesson, my eyes kept dancing back to her chocolate skin and the ebony waterfall of her hair. When she smiled,
her cheeks creased in her dimples and little stars danced in her
cocoa eyes. When she worked, she poked her tongue into the
corner of her mouth and gripped her pencil as though it was a
knife. We nearly became friends, though I don't want the Brotherhood to ever learn about my error of judgment.

It was Jeremiah who discovered her plots. Who overheard a
conversation, who followed her, who listened in. And now he
has captured the fly and brought her to our web.

10:40 P.M.

It all happens so quickly.

Chris flings open the doors. There is a faint scream. Then silence. The slam of the doors. Raymond revs up the van. I keep

thinking: *Is she really in? Was it that easy?* Raymond backs down the side street. He slams against a bin. It spins, topples to one side, vomiting rubbish. He swerves out into the road, brakes squealing—or is that more screaming? He lets out a cry and slams to a halt as we come to a set of traffic lights. An old lady waddling across the road gives us a murderous glance, assuming we are crazy thugs. I feel like shaking her. My heart is beating oh so fast. I can't believe we've done it. I can't believe we've got her. *Oh God, thank you, God. How could I ever have doubted you?* The lights change. Raymond speeds on. Jeremiah tells him to keep to the limit. We pass St. Sebastian's. My heart surges with joy. *Oh thank you, God.* Moonlight pours over its jagged roof in sweet relief; a squirrel bounces over the gates, fixing me with a beady eye before we speed on, leaving our hometown behind us, out into roads that are dark and foreign. . . .

11:15 P.M.

I am vaguely aware that the present remains strangely unsatisfying. An hour ago nothing mattered but getting SNAKE. Now I want to whip time on, get to the warehouse, make our hostage video, ignite the TV stations. But will they listen to us? Believe us? I keep thinking about the old lady we stopped for at the lights. The way she instantly judged us. I hear Jeremiah's words echo in my mind: *This is a world of appearances. Our minds are shaped to think in stereotypes. We're all guilty. For example, think of a librarian. What do you see? A woman with a bun, glasses, and a grim face. Think of a nurse. Think of a fireman. This is the world we live in. Think of a terrorist and you see a young man with a beard. Not a beautiful girl. This is the challenge we face: convincing the world to see beyond the superficial.*

We're in the countryside now. Jagged landscapes, trees piercing the night sky.

"I thought it only took twenty minutes to get to the warehouse," I say to Raymond.

He ignores me.

"This isn't Streatham," I repeat.

Silence.

He's sabotaging Jeremiah's instructions! This isn't right. I have to do something—*now.*

I lean across and bang my fist against the horn. Raymond jumps and swerves the van over onto a grassy verge. He slams on the brakes.

"What the hell did you do that for! I know what I'm doing, okay?"

Jeremiah comes up to the front. I wind down my window with a trembling hand.

"This isn't Streatham!"

"It's all right, Jon," Jeremiah says calmly. "You go sit in the back. It's fine—let me lead the way."

I don't understand what's going on, but as long as Jeremiah

is taking charge, I don't need to worry. In the back of the van, I have no choice but to sit beside SNAKE. Martyn, Thomas, and Chris have already carefully positioned themselves opposite her, watching at a distance, as though they are in a cage with a dangerous animal. I am glad of the sack that hides her face and the cuffs that bind her hands.

As the van revs up again, SNAKE starts to thrash about violently. I recoil, narrowly avoiding a kick. She scrapes and thumps her heels against the metal floor. We all cringe up against the van walls. I look at the others, relieved their scared faces mirror my own. Then Martyn bursts into laughter.

Thomas and Chris join in, and suddenly their laugh stings with a tone I don't like. I force a smile.

Jeremiah was in the changing room on that fatal, fateful day when SNAKE thought she was alone. He'd sidled up close to her, listening as she said quietly into her cell phone that she had found a way to get revenge on the West for the destruction they'd caused in the Middle East.

She had discovered Web sites for making a bomb. She knew how to get the equipment. She would plant it in a locker. She'd come in early, at 8:15 A.M., before any teachers were about. The date was set: November 15. What if that locker had been mine? I picture the moment: opening the metal door, and then—

What would it have felt like? Would I have died at once? Or would I have found myself lying in wet darkness, aware that parts of me were missing, rubble clawing my face, hearing the ragged ribbons of my friends' dying cries around me?

Oh thank you, God. Thank you for guiding Jeremiah. A few nights before he overheard her conversation, he said, he had some black dreams about her. They put him on guard. He was ready for revelation. Thank you, God, for showing us your way.

SNAKE has stopped thrashing about. But now her stillness seems more ominous. Legs slack. Sack flat. What if she can't breathe?

Just wait a few minutes, I tell myself.

Sweat starts to seep through my skin in wet slugs. What if she suffocates to death? All of us up on a murder charge. We won't be heroes, then. We'll be her equals.

I stare at the others. I will them to notice her, to click, to say something, do something, so that I don't have to. But they're all engrossed in murmuring about where we are going.

She's not breathing, she's not breathing!

I have to do something. I decide that I will wait another two minutes. I'll time it on my watch—

But then my body acts with a mind of its own. I reach over and pull the sack off her head.

"Jon, what are you *doing*?"

"Put it back on!"

"She's dangerous, you idiot!"

"She c-can't b-breathe!" I stammer. "For God's sake, she can't scream with that tape over her mouth anyway!"

Then I notice her eyes.

The look in them makes me wish I hadn't taken the sack off. I turn away.

"She couldn't breathe," I repeat shakily. I say it again, more loudly. "She couldn't breathe."

As SNAKE struggles to sit up, I reach out a cautious hand to help. I am shocked when I touch her. I expected her blood to run with terrorist ice. But her skin oozes a honey warmth. What if I can catch her sin from her touch, like a disease? I quickly pull my hand away, curl it in my lap.

She sits upright now, gaining composure. Her eyes flick very slowly around the group. Retinal rage.

Chris looks down awkwardly, but Martyn and Thomas glare back. Finally, her eyes slide over to me. I feel anger rise in my chest. I thought she'd attempt to convey some sort of apology in her gaze; I thought the shock of being found out might have humbled her. But there is defiance. No doubt she was making plans in the nightclub, gossiping with other members of her cell, preparing the countdown. She is only sixteen years old and she is prepared to kill hundreds of innocent people, and she genuinely has no regrets.

I wish I had left the sack on her damn head.

I want to stare her out. I want to show that I am not afraid of her. That I am ready to fight evil. But her eyes spit the deadliest of venoms. Finally, I have to surrender. I look away, shaking my head in disgust.

As the van rumbles on, her head droops and her eyes close. I keep listening out for a siren, but none comes. I see her lips flickering. I wonder if she is praying to her god for forgiveness.

MIDNIGHT

Sleep seeps into my mind like black tea. My neck begins to feel spineless; my head tips forward.

I snap it up, blinking, eyes stinging with fought tiredness. I haven't been able to sleep for weeks. I concentrate on the tree symbol. It starts to twirl and dance; it becomes a baton, moving so fast it is a white blur. The baton is being held by SNAKE. She is walking down the school corridor toward me in a leotard, a smile leering on her face, her brown thighs bouncing with muscle. I crouch down and wrap my hands over my head. But it's too late and I hear the crack as she kills me.

Now I am running down streets, being chased by dark shapes. I wake up at home, in my own bed, sweating with relief. I look up at the familiar cross on my wall and think: *Thank God we didn't go through with it.*

Then I wake up, cold air swirling around me, tangy with night scents, sheep smells. The doors are open and SNAKE is being led down the ramp, struggling between Chris and Martyn. My heart crushes in on itself as I realize we are here and we did go through with it. For one split second I feel like a frightened child and I want to run home. Then I stagger up, coming to, my conscious mind waking up, taking over, slamming down a lid on my fears.

This is it. The Beginning.

I clamber down from the van, land in a muddy puddle.

"Where—where's the warehouse?" I ask.

"That was just a line to fool you," says Raymond, smirking. "You're new. Jeremiah felt you couldn't be trusted. We're in Suffolk."

The van is parked on a thin road outside a small cottage. The landscape is flat and barren. In the distance, a sheep's baa drifts across a field.

"But—but—what about my Initiation?" I stammer. *Did Jeremiah lie about that too?*

"You think just helping with tonight is all you have to do?" Raymond says, shaking his head. "This is the Brotherhood, not some lame fraternity. This is just the first part—then there's the ceremony, and a final test to prove you're one of us."

Is he winding me up?

"But—"

"Later, okay?" Raymond says roughly. "We have to get this terrorist slut indoors."

Part TWO

Day One

12:30 a.m.

Are you happy?

When I approached Jeremiah on the playground, it was one of the first things he said to me. I opened my mouth to reply yes, purely out of habit. I was so used to being asked questions by adults where they wanted and expected a yes: *Have you done your homework? Will you be in by ten? Are you happy? Yes, yes, yes. Yeah, yeah, yeah.* But when Jeremiah asked the question, I felt that he was really asking it—you know, looking into my soul and asking.

Later, Jeremiah made me realize how slippery words are. When adults ask questions, there is always a subtext—one of Jeremiah's favorite words. It's what things *really* mean. Like *What do you want to be when you leave school?* when really they mean *Are you going to be a good boy and get a good degree and then go work in an office pushing paper round a desk so we can feel you're suffering in our footsteps?*

And then what? Jeremiah pointed out.

You become a cog in the capitalist machine. You have to

spend most of your time doing a job you don't like and the rest of your time sleeping to have enough energy to do the job you don't like. Why? For money. But what do you need so much money for? Not for food, since God has created a world where we can eat and grow our own food so easily. But to buy stuff. Stuff—a key word. Stuff: the temptations of the advertising industry. We're told that we'll be happier only if we have shinier cars and bigger TVs and cooler labels than the guy who lives next door to us. And then what? You end up having kids and having to work even harder because your kids want better toys and bigger TVs and more clothes with the Right Labels than the other kids on their playground.

The advertisers plant the seeds in grade school. You wear the wrong sneakers and you'll be in the wrong crowd, or get beaten up. But what is a sneaker? Jeremiah pointed out. A swath of cloth with a lace threaded through it. Made by some poor kid in Taiwan who has to slave for eighteen hours a day in a sweatshop.

It's all a part of the Conspiracy of Darkness, Jeremiah explained. Trainers and cars are like sticky colored candy that feeds the soul while rotting it away. Since I joined Hebetheus, that empty feeling that used to gnaw my stomach all the time has gone away; my soul is getting healthier by the day.

It took me a while to understand. When Jeremiah first told me he'd dreamt that I was going to become a disciple of Hebetheus, I was suspicious. I'd been seeking for a long time and I was on the verge of becoming cynical, believing there was nothing out there at all. But then Jeremiah said, "You can ask me anything you like about Hebetheus. *Anything.* I guarantee I have all the answers."

And so I kept asking. Day after day, week after week. Questions on God, heaven, hell, sin, love, girls. Jeremiah didn't snap at me like my father or grow bored like Mr. Abdilla. He was endlessly patient. And then one day I stopped asking. I realized I didn't need to question anymore, because my mind was at peace. I had found it. I had found him. The ultimate Truth.

Now every day is a joy; every day brings a new revelation, a gem of his genius. Like the guys at school who used to scare me. One of them shoved me in football and I felt hurt all day, until Jeremiah pointed out that those guys are as pathetic as the rest of society. They think they're cool because they smoke ciggies underage, when in fact they're just the slaves of tobacco, video games, trendy clothing. In the end, Jeremiah explained, the rebels are really the biggest squares. For the saddest people on this earth, said Jeremiah, are the deluded: those who live their lives as an illusion.

That's the amazing thing about Jeremiah. I used to see the world as one light; then Jeremiah fractured it open and showed me a rainbow. Thomas once said to me, "It's no use trying to understand or define Jeremiah—you never will. There are too many permutations to his personality. He's infinite, like God."

On some days, Jeremiah is so grand and magnificent he is like Aslan in *The Lion, the Witch, and the Wardrobe*; yet the other day I saw him bend down, spot a bug on its back wriggling helplessly, and with a look of utter tenderness on his face gently flip it back over.

Now, as we walk up the path with SNAKE, Jeremiah leading the way, my heart swells with pride to be his follower. How often does God put someone on his earth to speak his message? How many things have to happen—the planets to shift into perfect harmony, the stars to align into a magical formation—for someone like Jeremiah to be born? And we are so lucky to be the first select few around him. In a few years' time so many thousands of people will be pounding on Jeremiah's door, desperate for a word of wisdom, a healing touch, that we might barely be able to see him. Is this how it felt for the wise men who sensed the birth of Jesus? I look up at the sky; it is black and starless, a void.

We stop at the front door of the cottage.

Jeremiah takes a key from under a stone. Who owns this place? How did Jeremiah get it? Jeremiah inserts the key in the lock. Our silence quivers.

As the door opens, I glance at SNAKE. Fear has crowbarred open her face, trembling in her eyes and lips. Good.

We enter into the hallway. Everything is cloaked in musty darkness, and it's colder in here than out. I press my hand against a dank wall and the vibe of the place seems to seep into my skin: a sensation of forlorn sadness, of lost ghosts, of wind whistling through empty rooms. There is a terrible smell in the air: of dirt and old newspapers, of pee and rotting meat.

A light is switched on, and I blink at the fading yellow-rose wallpaper. We pad in gingerly, our boots clattering heavily on the bare boards. The doors of the hallway are shut—except the one for the kitchen, which we trail into.

"Hey," says Martyn. "Food. Why did we have to go stealing food for the last week when there's stuff here?"

"Shut up!" Raymond whispers fiercely. "Look."

There are piles and piles of newspapers and magazines, but they seem to follow a logic: *Sunday Times* in one pile, *Women's Weekly* in another, *Daily Mail* another. On the shelves, there are rows of bottles: a scarlet sea of tomato ketchup, a brown sea of HP sauce. There are black sacks of rubbish waiting to be taken out, squatting like huge, rotting plums.

But I can't see what the matter is.

Then Raymond points.

On the table. A dirty plate. A knife and fork. On the plate is a greasy yellow swirl, a stain left from a fried egg.

I turn and look at Raymond.

"Someone's still here," he whispers. "God. If Ned has rented this place out to someone else—"

"SNAKE!" Jeremiah hisses.

She manages to scream for just a second before he gags her, pulling a school tie from his pocket. She breathes in and out thickly through her gag, shaking. The school motto, Aim for the Highest, bobs against her mouth.

"Ned said that nobody would be here. He must have let someone else come to stay!" Jeremiah whispers.

"Well, you know what Ned's like," Raymond replies. "God knows who else he might have told about this place."

Who is Ned? Then I notice SNAKE looking at me, digesting my confusion. I quickly look knowing.

"We should hunt—" Martyn begins.

"What we'll do is this." Jeremiah cuts in and we lean in closer, our breaths forming a hot huddle, leaving SNAKE to one side. "We'll go to the front and back and lock the doors. Whoever's in here is probably hiding. We'll move from room to room. We'll stay as a group."

"What about SNAKE?" Martyn cries.

"Keep your voice down!" Jeremiah whispers. "She stays here. Thomas, tie her to the chair. Now, the rest of us— let's go."

1:00 A.M.

What kind of person would live in this weird cottage? My imagination starts scuttling into dark corners, blowing up dust from horror movies that have polluted my mind, picturing some psychopath who just happens to enjoy feasting on the hearts of teenage boys. As we go out into the hallway, my heart starts to thump and I'm glad I'm tagging at the back of the group, behind the safe wall of my Brothers' backs.

Aside from the kitchen's, there are five doors in the hallway. All shut.

We approach the first one, opposite the kitchen. Raymond and Jeremiah exchange glances. Jeremiah gives Raymond a gentle nudge. Raymond pushes it open. I stand on tiptoe to see in. Empty. I exhale.

Just a living room with dirty white walls, very simply furnished. A TV is balanced on top of a crate, the aerial twisted into a weird shape, like a silver finger pointing toward some divine event beyond the window. A single armchair opposite, dotted with cigarette burns like liver spots.

The next door opens out into a bathroom. Mildew crawling up the walls in green rashes; a windowsill with dying plants covered in dust.

The third door reveals a den: two bookcases filled with curling spines and a single rocking chair with a worn seat.

A fourth door opens out into a room filled with odd bits of junk. Boxes, newspapers stacked up, an old lamp.

"This will be our Prayer Room," Jeremiah whispers.

But nobody really hears him because now we're outside the final door. Jeremiah puts his ear to the door, whispers, "God be with us!" and then opens it. He switches on the light. And we see her.

On the bed is an old woman, her gnarled face contorted in a grimace of distress.

Raymond turns back, swallows, and says, "I'll take care of her. Everyone outside—"

"Wait," Jeremiah cuts in sharply. He goes up to her side and whispers, "Hello?" He leans down, frowning, listening hard. Then he stands up, blinking. "She's dead." He looks down at her, his eyes tender with compassion.

"But who the hell is she?" Martyn bursts out.

"I think she's Ned's granny," Raymond muses. "Shit. Ned owes me this favor—I lied for him in court and gave him his bloody alibi. He *promised* this place would be empty! Said he was going to get old Granny Knickers himself and take her to his flat!"

Raymond tries to call Ned up, but there is no answer. He clicks off his phone with a snarl of frustration.

"Now we'll have to go find another house!" Martyn cries. "I can't believe you trusted a criminal!"

Panic flares in my stomach. Where the hell can we go? How can we find another house now?

"No," Jeremiah says, "we don't. Look, she's only been dead a day or so. It looks as though she just went to bed and didn't wake up. As for Ned's family . . . well, obviously, visiting isn't their forte—they all spend too much time in prison for that. I doubt anyone will come looking for her for another few days. For the moment, we stay here."

Jeremiah's eyes pass over each of our faces in turn and we all nod in relief. And yet, still, an unease squirms in the air. . . .

"Don't worry," he says. "This is life—unpredictable. We make our own plans but improvise when called for. We only need a few days. God will protect us. We have enough time to do this; we have enough time to do our duty."

Is there anyone more amazing than Jeremiah?

1:30 A.M.

Raymond gathers us back into the kitchen while Jeremiah speaks with SNAKE in the living room, which has now been re-named the Brotherhood Bedroom.

"Right," says Raymond. "First things first." He burrows through one of the boxes he has brought in from the van, pushes past the rows and rows of baked bean tins, and yanks out a roll of black sacks, ripping one off. "You've all brought your phones, right? Well, put them in here."

"Why?" Martyn asks warily, pulling his Nokia out of his pocket.

"Safekeeping," Raymond says abruptly.

All the Brothers put their mobiles into the bag. All except for Chris, who looks a little embarrassed to remind us he doesn't have one—his parents have banned them. Raymond tosses the bag on the floor. With his steel-toe-capped boot, he stamps on them! Beneath Martyn's yells of protests, there is a terrible crunching. I go cold inside.

Jeremiah enters the kitchen.

"It's all right, everyone—I ordered Raymond to do this."

There is a shocked silence.

"This is a new beginning for us all. We need to leave the tainted world behind us. It's the only way for us to experience a Soul Shift."

The Soul Shift. I've heard that expression mentioned in whispered conversations among my Brothers. It sparkles and flickers with mystery and beauty.

"Besides, the police could track the signals. Okay, Martyn?"

"Yeah." Martyn scowls.

"I guess it's for the best," Thomas agrees, a little sadly.

I know Thomas is right. I know that mobiles are another big evil. But a secret part of me has been planning to call Mum, let her know I am okay. It took me six months of paper rounds to save up for that phone; it had a picture of Lisa Hargreaves, a girl I once nearly dated, on it, now reduced to a twist of crushed metal.

1:45 A.M.

We turn the living room into the Brotherhood Bedroom, clearing out the TV and chair, carrying mattresses from the van and laying them out with sleeping bags on top. It's heavy, hungry work. Martyn starts making a joke that the old woman might not really be dead, that there might just be a whisper of breath in her lungs, and though we all laugh, in the end Chris gets sent to check, just in case. He reports back that her doomed soul has definitely left its body.

Our next big task is to turn the empty room into the Prayer Room. We haul out newspapers, old boxes, a broken lamp with a frilly pink shade like a pair of knickers. Raymond and Thomas scrub the walls vigorously. It's a beautiful thing to watch, as though they're washing away sins, returning the wall to its original purity. I bend down to pick up the last scraps of newspaper. *News of the World.* A blond lady with hard tits. I feel my blood stir, and I bend away from the others, peeling the page back for a better look. *Remember,* Jeremiah once warned us, *desire is a snake that winds itself around the spine.* I quickly crumple up her face, tear her body into pieces, stuff her dead remains into a sack. I fill another bucket and start on the floor, swishing with determined strokes. Martyn cleans the windows; Chris sweeps cobwebs from the ceiling.

After the room is pure, we are ready to paint our symbols on the walls. Raymond consults Jeremiah.

"We can't paint them white," he points out. "The walls are white now. They have to show up good and proper."

Jeremiah's message comes back thus: "Paint them black."

I can't help remembering that Jeremiah once said black was an evil color. But I swallow the memory; Jeremiah often mentions the paradox of the divine.

The paint ends up going everywhere. Black footprints on the floor, black handprints on the wall. Like war paint on our faces, like streaks of night in our hair. The final thing we paint is a large black circle on the floor, with symbols curling around the border. This is where SNAKE will stand.

✝✝✝

We are ready now to make the video, everyone buzzing with excitement—but then Thomas tells us SNAKE needs to pee.

"Jon can take her." Raymond volunteers me, ignoring my filthy look. "I'm going to park the van round the back—it looks too suspicious sitting out in the front."

I go into the kitchen. They've taken her gag off now; she seems to realize screaming won't help. Her eyes look dull and tired.

"Well?" she says as I go in after her. "Can't I even piss in peace?"

"Uh—uh—okay," I stammer, stepping back. "But don't lock the door."

I stand outside, feeling nervous. Raymond comes out of the Prayer Room.

"Why is the door closed?" Raymond snarls. "Jesus, she has to be guarded at *all times*. Get in." He shoves the door open and pushes me in.

"Hey!" SNAKE cries, drawing up her trousers with clumsy handcuffed hands.

"I-I have to be in with you," I stammer. "I'm sorry—it's a rule."

"Well, turn around. Don't stare at me!" she shrieks.

"Sorry, sorry." I spin around, staring hard at the wall.

"I know you won't take my cuffs off if I ask, so can you tear off some toilet paper and give it to me?" she demands.

I pass her some, taking care not to glance back a millimeter. As she heaves up her pants, though, out of the corner of my eye I catch a glance of her panties: white with red hearts. She goes to the sink, spins the taps, and awkwardly shimmies her hand under them.

"What's that?" She nods. On the windowsill are the long boxes of dirt that Chris and Martyn carried in.

"Oh, they've got *oasis* seeds planted in them. They're these spiritual seeds Jeremiah got. They grow up into plants that we can then turn into a potion—" I break off, seeing the sneer in her eyes. "Forget it."

"Can you just give me one minute in peace?" she asks quietly. "I've got my period. I've got to put a tampon in."

"I—" I've never seen a tampon before, and the thought terrifies me. "Okay. One minute. But I'll be timing it on my watch."

"Okay. Sure. Thanks." She gives me a sweet smile, trying to find a way into me. Impossible.

The moment I leave the bathroom, I worry. What if Raymond walks past again? I turn back, push the door open a nervous inch. But the tampon looms in my mind, becoming bigger and bigger until it's as tall as King Kong. Then I hear an odd grating noise.

"Can I come back in?" I call. I push the door and a blast of freezing air from the open window slaps my face. She's already halfway out of the window.

"*Stop!*" I scream.

She dives out into the night. I grab the frame, trying to shove it up, but the gap is only just big enough for SNAKE's lithe frame. I spin round, hurtle into the hall, banging into Raymond and Martyn. They gaze at my red face in amazement. I can hardly speak.

"She's gone, she's got away!"

"What the fuck?"

"Out the window!" I cry.

Raymond yells, "Stupid idiot!" and we all pile out the front door, running down the side of the cottage, the muddy grass sucking and slowing our footsteps. I whirl around. Where is she? The treetops drift lightly in the wind. Where is she? Grass; prickly bushes like giant prehistoric animals; fields; grass; trees. Where is she? *Oh God, she can't have escaped, can she, oh God, can she?*

"She can't have gone far," Raymond cries.

"We need a flashlight," I insist. My head feels hot and pounding and thick with panic. "We need—"

"There!" Martyn yells.

A bush breaks symmetry into two dark shapes; one tries to dart away. Martyn throws himself on her.

"I've got her!"

Raymond and Martyn lunge forward. Our terrorist turns into a hissing, spitting, screaming, scratching beast. Martyn has her left arm, Raymond her right, but I bundle in and grab a handful of her sparkly top and wrench, feeling the material stretch out of shape, and for a moment a wild desire comes over me to tear it apart, to grab flesh, to bite, to feast, to destroy. It's the adrenaline of fate thumping through me: it's black versus white, evil versus good. The universe quivers, the seesaw tips up and down, waiting for the balance to swing.

We conquer the infidel, shaking her until she curls into a defeated ball.

We pull her up and march her back to the house, where Jeremiah, Chris, and Thomas stand, gaping and wide-eyed.

"She bloody bit me," Martyn keeps moaning. "The fucking bitch bit me!"

"I just—she said it was her period and she needed to put in a tampon—" My voice breaks on the word, and I hear Chris giggle, and then Martyn chuckles too. "I just couldn't . . ." I trail off, feeling their contempt. Jon the new boy has screwed up again. Will they call off my Initiation?

Jeremiah clasps my shoulder.

"It wasn't Jon's fault," he explains. "He's too kind, that's all
Don't worry—your kindness is a virtue. You just need to be
more clear about who deserves that kindness. Okay?"

Immediately, the mood of the group shifts. Chris mutters
"Tampon!" and we laugh and everything is all right and I am re
united with my Brothers.

"Look." Martyn sucks his hand and shows us the wound
three red eyes gaping in the curve of his thumb.

I look at SNAKE, who stares back at me with sullen eyes
Her hair is mussed and the look on her face is shrunken, de
feated; I think we have battered a little of the evil out of her
Perhaps this is the reason this incident happened.

As we go back into the house, I find the glitter from her to
has come off on my palm, dusting my skin with tiny stars.
quickly go to the bathroom and wash my hands three times.

2:00 A.M.

"W-w-w-we are f-f-f-from the H-H-Hebetheus r-r-r-religion.
W-w-we have k-k-kidnapped a t-terrorist."

Chris breaks off, yanks out his inhaler, and breathes in
deeply. He opens his mouth to speak again and then screws up
his eyes, shaking his head.

"I can't r-r-remember it."

"You're doing fine," says Jeremiah softly. "Switch it off,

switch if off," he says, waving his hand at Thomas, who has balanced the camcorder on his shoulder. "We'll start again."

We're standing in the Prayer Room. It's empty now except
for a bookcase in the corner; candlelight flickers over ragged,
broken spines. We encircle Chris, our narrator, our voice.
SNAKE stands next to me, handcuffed, her ankles bound with
rope. Every time I glance at SNAKE, my heart twists with a flash
of hot hatred.

I'd thought Jeremiah was going to ask *me* to be the speaker
for the video; he'd dropped a few hints last week. I thought my
main rival was Thomas, with his posh voice, who sounds like he
ought to be reading the evening news. Instead, he has chosen
the one member of our group who will splutter out our glorious
slogans in bits of broken sentences and drools of saliva. Martyn
is trying not to laugh; it's putting Chris off. But Jeremiah just
softly instructs Chris to let God take him over and speak
through him.

Poor Chris. Once after school I went back to his house.
Chris asked his dad what they were having for dinner and his fa-,
ther said, "W-w-we're h-having b-burgers." It was such a perfect
imitation of Chris's stutter that it took me a minute to twig that
he was mocking his own son. Then he winked at us as if to say,
Can you believe this idiot is my son?

Chris tries and fails again and wastes two more takes. I feel
frustration heating in my chest. I feel like putting my hand up
like some stupid kid in class and pleading, *Let me do it, let me.*

Then I let out a deep breath. I must be patient. None of us can fully understand why Jeremiah does as he does: he works in mysterious ways.

I just hope he's not still angry with me.

"Chris," said Jeremiah in his liquid angel's voice, "I think you should try again with more feeling. Just let your heart open up with love for God, let him trample away your stammer. Okay? Good."

Jeremiah steps back. The camera rolls. Chris starts again.

"We are from the Hebethean religion." A good start; he smiles in relief, close to tears, and Jeremiah nods intently, twitching with excitement. "We h-h-h—" A pause, and we wait for the house of cards to blow apart, but then he keeps going, gaining momentum. "We have kidnapped a terrorist! A *terrorist!*"

And then the noise comes out of nowhere. We all look round in confusion.

Singing. Beautiful singing. In a language I don't understand.

Chris's voice meanders into a squeak.

"What the hell?" Jeremiah turns on SNAKE, and I am shocked by the fury blazing in his face. "It's not your turn yet!"

Her singing fades. She looks at us with pleading eyes.

"You!" Jeremiah points a finger at me like a bullet. "Shut her up."

"Be quiet—okay?" I say sharply.

"He means gag her, you idiot," Raymond whispers.

I scan the room helplessly and then Raymond gives me another sharp look, so I quickly improvise. I walk behind her, pull
her against me, and clap my hand over her mouth, like they do
in the movies. Chris starts again, but he is lost again, a twitching huddle of hunched shoulders and mumbles. SNAKE's lips
are damp against my palm. I picture their kiss imprinted against
the skin. Chris tries again and again, but her singing lingers in
the air like a poisoned perfume. I press my hand tight against
her face. She will not make a fool out of me a second time.

"Okay, Chris," said Jeremiah, drawing him away. "You did
well. Really well. Thomas will take over now. But you did good.
We're all proud of you."

And suddenly we are. Even Martyn. Everyone smiles at
Chris, pride beating in our communal heart. Thomas gives him
a punch to let him know he'd rather not take over really, and
Chris ducks his head and smiles shyly, relieved, pretending to
be regretful.

Thomas fluffs his first take, then turns to Chris and says,
"It's hard, isn't it?"

Finally, this is how the video is done.

3:00 A.M.

PLEASE NOTE:
THE PARTS OF THE VIDEO IN BRACKETS [ ]
ARE TO BE EDITED AND CUT FOR THE FINAL VERSION.

THOMAS: We are from the Religion of Hebetheus.

The camera pans over our faces, except for Jeremiah's.

[**MARTYN:** Jeremiah, why can't you show your face?

JEREMIAH: I want to avoid being a figurehead for the group. What if people begin to idolize me instead of God? Carry on, Thomas.]

THOMAS: We believe that peace *can* be real—that we can live in a world without fear. In our quest for peace, we have taken matters into our own hands. We are people who will act, not speak pretty, meaningless words. We have captured the terrorist Padma Laxsmi, who was about to plant a bomb in St. Sebastian's school. This is the girl *your* country, *your* police force failed to stop.

The camera pans to a close-up of SNAKE's face.

[JEREMIAH: Come on, SNAKE. Admit to the world what you were planning to do, the lives you were about to destroy. . . .

SNAKE: I don't know what the hell you're talking about.

JEREMIAH: We suggest that you cooperate with us. Look, don't be afraid. Be open about what you believe in. Say it now—loud and clear. We're going to put this video on the Internet, we're going to e-mail it to the Houses of Parliament, to every MP in the country, to the chief of police. Now is your chance to proclaim your message.

SNAKE: I want to go home, I want my mum, you're all insane—

JEREMIAH: Okay, enough, we'll speak for her. Jon, gag her properly. Martyn, it's your turn to speak.]

MARTYN: The police didn't bother to do anything about SNAKE, they're just lazy bastards, but we're not. We'll take action, we'll do anything to save hundreds of lives, so you should all listen to us, right? Now, listen to our demands and take them seriously. One, we demand that the police investigate SNAKE and make sure none of her terrorist friends are planning to bomb our school. Two, we want the Prevention of Terrorism Act changed. It's too lame. We need to get *tough* on terrorists! It's not enough to increase the period they can be held without trial from fourteen days to twenty-eight days or even ninety days! Ninety days is *nothing*! In the U.S. they can hold someone they suspect is an evil terrorist for *as long as they like.* This is what you call being tough on terrorism. We demand that our wimpy, weak-willed government change the law again so it's the same as the U.S.'s.

[**JEREMIAH:** Good, good.]

MARTYN: Three, we want the government to recognize that the Hebethean religion is a new religion and in turn give us one million quid—

[**JEREMIAH:** Say "pounds," it sounds better. Say we want them to acknowledge our help.]

MARTYN: We want the government to acknowledge our help and give us one million q—pounds so that we can build a temple in London. Then we can begin to spread the word of Hebetheus so that everyone will be able to live in a safe world free from terror.

[**JEREMIAH:** Now say what happens if they don't take us seriously.]

MARTYN: If you don't meet our demands, we will torture our hostage—

[**JEREMIAH:** No, no—just say we will respond with extreme measures.

MARTYN: But that sounds so lame.

JEREMIAH: No, because they'll have to imagine what those measures might be— maybe they'll think we're going to kidnap more people, and so on. The power of the imagination, Martyn—it's an amazing tool.]

MARTYN: If you don't meet our demands, we

will be forced to respond with extreme measures.

[JEREMIAH: Good, good. Enough. Where's our very own hacker, Chris? You're sure you can do this?

MARTYN: Can Chris do this? Can he? Is the pope Catholic? Chris once hacked into a bank, I saw him—he hacked right into Barclays, but he wouldn't take any money, he was too scared—

JEREMIAH: In the meantime, we need to put SNAKE somewhere.

RAYMOND: There's always the cellar.

JEREMIAH: Yes! Perfect. Just for the night.

MARTYN: I'll take her down. Hey, shouldn't we turn the video off now?]

End of tape.

5:00 A.M.

I'm half awake, half asleep. A nightmare uncoils and slowly slithers through my mind. I'm back in the bathroom. The spiritual seeds have sprouted like Triffids, a wall of thick choking stalks, flowers hissing poison nectar. Somewhere in the middle of them is SNAKE, but they are protecting her and I cannot find her. I try to fight my way through, and my heart is pounding because I must not let Jeremiah down—I must not let him down—but then a strand of vegetation coils around my throat, choking me, and I drown in a sea of poisoned green and as I go down I see SNAKE's eyes, two laughing black orbs. . . .

I wake up, breathing hard. *Where am I? Where's home?* Then I remember.

My breathing slows and I lie still. Martyn is snoring hard; Chris echoes him lightly. Jeremiah sleeps in silent serenity, hands flat across his chest, as though resting in peace. My heart throbs. I feel funny watching him while he's sleeping, and I quickly look away. The sounds around me are comforting. I always wanted to join the Boy Scouts or the Cadets, but I never had time because of church. Being here feels like a taste of it.

What a day. So much happened, so quickly. Fragments spike my memory. It feels good just to lie here and think it all over, digest it, so I am ready for what is to come next.

I wish I'd a chance to speak to Jeremiah alone, but it seemed selfish to demand his attention when there were bigger things to deal with. I don't mind if I have to pass another challenge to show my devotion to our cause. But those words—*Initiation ceremony*—shiver through my mind. I keep picturing horror scenarios: being locked in a coffin, having to eat cold baked beans. Stupid, childish stuff. I know Jeremiah would never be so crass, but . . .

I keep trying to ignore my bladder, but soon the pain becomes too intense.

I get up, pad through the bodies on tiptoe, and slip out into the hallway. The bathroom door is shut. My nightmare rears. I pause outside for five minutes, feeling like a scaredy girl, before I finally get the guts to open it—

It's empty. Of course. I remind myself: *Don't be afraid, you're surrounded by the protective shield of your faith.*

Even so, the boxes of spiritual seeds make me feel squirmy, and I piss quickly.

When I come out of the bathroom, I pause in the hallway. The bedroom door beckons. It feels as though an invisible hand presses onto my shoulder and pushes me forward, envelops my hand, and makes me twist the handle and go in.

The dead old woman. The moonlight shines in through the window, lies in pools in the wrinkles and furrows of her face. Beside her, a collection of china animals seem to dance in the moonlight, as though they might come alive; their eyes gleam, mocking me, as I step forward.

I've always wondered what it would be like to touch a dead person.

I am surprised by how dry her skin feels. Like old leaves. There is a photograph of a pretty young girl by her bed. It's her. One day I'll be an old man with a photo on my bedside table of me looking like I do now. Suddenly the woman seems human, real, as though she could have been my granny, and pity cuts my heart. I bleed with sadness that we didn't get to her in time. Jeremiah could have read the Book of Hebetheus to her. We could have saved her soul.

Before Jeremiah saved me, I used to be scared of death all the time. But now I know I'm safe, because the Brotherhood will all go to Manu when we pass on.

But this poor woman—she'll go nowhere. Her soul will leave her body, and it will search and search for the light. But it will find nothing. It will soar up to the clouds and howl in despair; it will appeal to the moon and sun, crying out for salvation, but its screams will echo and fade among the stars. Then, without the nourishment of God's love, the soul will starve and grow weak. It will find a dark place, a graveyard, a cobwebbed corner, and huddle into a ball, slowly seeping away into a smudge, into air, until it becomes nothingness.

As I go out in the hallway, I think of SNAKE below. Even though she got me into trouble, I feel glad that we found her in time. Maybe we can save her from the same fate as the old woman's. We'll see.

✚✚✚

Back in the bedroom, Thomas is awake. For one odd moment I
fear he might be crying, but he turns away, hiding his face. I lie
down and close my eyes. I feel too excited to sleep; tomorrow
everything will really begin. Eventually, I make myself drop off
by reciting part of the Book of Hebetheus, the words slowly
floating away from me like driftwood as a wave of sleep washes
over me: *A million years ago, the Earth was a void. Colorless, tasteless:
it was nothingness itself. Then one day, a tiny spark, a shimmer of energy, tickled the void. The tickle rippled through its nothingness. A par-
ticle was formed, a piece of blackness curled and took shape. A crow was
born, and that crow was God. . . .*

*The first people to live on Earth were the Hebethean race. The mo-
ment each baby breathed its first breath, that breath swirled into its
lungs and a divine alchemy took place; the baby instantly experienced a
Soul Shift and became God in human form.*

*Back then, no Hebethean had to strive for a Soul Shift the way that
a Hebethean Brother has to today. There was no path to God beset with
thorns or snakes or deceptive undergrowth, for there was no path. People were God and life was lived in pure and perfect peace.*

*They lived simple lives, side by side as Brothers and Sisters. All
loved one another, but not in the sinful way; they never touched each
other, never swam in the putrid bath of sex. When a woman reached
fourteen years of age, a crow would visit her in the night and touch her
forehead, and in the morning she would be round with child. There was
no curse on women and hence they did not have to suffer the pain of*

carrying a child for nine months. A child was begotten and was born a day later.

Everyone who lived on Earth knew and understood their place. They were all flowers and plants in a beautiful garden of God and each knew what perfume they should waft. The men were hunters. The women were mostly blond. They served the men, cooked their food, and were devoted slaves to them; they brought up the children; they . . .

Day Two

Noon

"Wake up—we're on!"

A face above me: Martyn. He punches my shoulder, a little too hard. I let out a yelp.

"They've got our video!" Martyn cries exuberantly. "Chris sent it and we're on TV! *Now!* Come on!"

His words strike a match inside me. I bounce up and rush into the kitchen, where everyone is huddled round the small black-and-white portable.

SNAKE's image, flickering on the screen, slaps me fully awake. It's a school photo that makes her look all demure and innocent, her soft face framed by a wave of hair caught neatly in a kirby grip. Underneath her photo, the caption screams, "MISSING."

"Holy shit!" Martyn cries.

"Jesus, this reception is terrible!" Raymond roars, banging the TV jubilantly. "Where's Jeremiah? Jeremiah, get your arse in here *NOW*!"

"Where's Thomas?" I cry, seeing Jeremiah come in.

"Just coming!" Jeremiah cries breathlessly. "Come on, Thomas!"

"Shh!" Raymond cries as Thomas thunders in. "We're missing it!"

We stare up with wide eyes, TV light falling on our faces as though we've been mesmerized by an alien spaceship.

"Yesterday Padma Laxsmi, a sixteen-year-old schoolgirl, went missing from a club in Kingston." The newsreader is an Asian woman with a very English accent. "However, a video sent to the police and the Houses of Parliament reveals that she has been kidnapped by a group of young Christian fundamentalists. . . ."

"*Christian!*" Raymond shrieks.

"They can't be serious—"

"Shh!"

". . . the video conveys their intentions."

A clip of our video: Thomas saying that we will act, that we are not people who use meaningless, pretty words.

"They cut it short, there's nothing about our message, about Hebetheus—"

"*QUIET!*"

"The six boys disappeared from their homes yesterday evening. It is thought that they abducted Padma at around eleven o'clock that evening before disappearing to an unknown location. . . ."

One by one, our faces appear behind her head. Each photo seems to have been handpicked to make us look as sullen and dysfunctional as possible. Even Chris, with his red hair and freckles like a blast of autumn sunshine, looks wan and evil-eyed. When my face flashes up, I jump. It's a passport photo, the one my mum forced me to have taken just after she forced me to have a horrible haircut with a square fringe at SuperCuts R Us. Jesus. Then Raymond's photo appears.

"The leader of the group is ex-convict Raymond Gibson, age eighteen. He is the elder brother of Jeremiah Gibson, another member of the gang; both boys lost their parents in a tragic fire."

I look at Jeremiah, my heart hammering with intrigue, but Jeremiah's face is a blank.

"Raymond Gibson was released a year ago from the juvenile detention center where he served a sentence for stealing firearms. He is the only member of the group who is not studying at St. Sebastian's school and is thought to have led the impressionable schoolboys astray. He worked at Fixons Electrics for one year before disappearing, taking with him some stolen electronic equipment."

Stolen? I glance over at Raymond, who shrugs bullishly.

A man wearing a white shirt and thick black glasses appears on the screen. He has a fat paunch and a mustache sits on his top lip like a black caterpillar.

"Raymond was always turning up late and smoking in the nonsmoking area of the canteen. I always thought there was something suspicious about him. . . ."

"Oh fuck off," Raymond hisses at him.

"The parents and teachers of St. Sebastian's are extremely concerned about the boys. . . ."

Chris's parents flash up on-screen. His mum is very fat, with carrot-colored hair and buck teeth, and she is clutching a rabbit to her chest. His dad stands beside her at an awkward angle, like a bent stick.

Funny how Chris's parents change their tune now. One minute he's the family embarrassment, but now that he's gone, they want to claw him back. Maybe they're worried about what their neighbors might say.

"Chris, we miss you," his mum says, sobbing. She holds out the rabbit. "Dixie misses you too, and Pixie. Please come home. . . ."

We all laugh, yelling, "Dixie! Pixie!" and Chris turns a violent red, shaking his head. Next up is Martyn's dad, looking like a bouncer with his tattoos and bald head. My heart flips a beat. What if my dad is up next? Oh, I'd just love to see him up there. First the embarrassment of being the wicked vicar who had to leave the church 'cause he can't keep his dick under control. Then playing it all down and getting himself a management job with a respectable sheen and a briefcase he can swing to work every morning. I can just see his fancy new boss and colleagues all whispering and prodding: *Did you hear about his son and what he did? What kind of a father would let that happen?*

"Martyn, we're worried about you," says Martyn's dad, though he looks as though he'd like to tear Martyn apart.

Martyn gives the screen the finger but his shoulders shrink, his eyes flashing with fear.

I turn back to the screen, dreading, hoping, waiting for Dad's face, but—to my shock—Mr. Abdilla appears on the screen. He's dressed in a suit, our school a benign silhouette in the background.

"Boys—Jon, Jeremiah, Thomas, Chris, Martyn—I'd like to appeal to you. Padma Laxsmi is not a terrorist. I realize you probably feel frustrated and think we don't understand or that we're being naive. But I have honestly gone to the police and checked up on your suspicions. I've spoken with her family and friends, and I can honestly say that she is innocent. I'm afraid you've all made a terrible mistake. There was never any bomb. Please come back safely. If you bring Padma back now, I promise you that you won't be arrested or charged. I've spoken to Padma's mother and she won't press any charges against you."

Padma's mother appears on the screen. Her eyes are

swollen and her voice snags with snot as she begs us to bring her precious daughter back. We all shift uncomfortably. Suddenly I feel panic rising in my stomach. My mother's voice hisses in my head: *Come on, Jon, why don't you ever bother to think things through properly? You never look before you leap!* I hadn't thought at all about whether SNAKE's mum might press charges. After all, she'll never be able to accept the reality that her daughter is a cold-blooded killer, will she? What if *we* all end up in jail? SNAKE might be guilty and we might be innocent; she might be the murderer and we might be heroes; she might be black and we might be white—but what does it matter in the end? I always thought only bad people went to prison. Then I remember what happened to my dad before he left me and Mum. The vandals who broke into our church one day, smashed the stained-glass window, looted the church funds. When they were arrested and taken to court, they got off with counseling and threatened to sue my dad for keeping a church locked when they needed a holy place to seek peace. I remember him saying in a bitter voice that didn't belong to him, *We're a nation who worships the god of PC at all expense. There's no justice in this country anymore. . . .*

But it's different for us, I tell myself. We are protected by the God of Hebetheus.

"The Asian actors of Michael Winterbottom's film *The Road to Guantanamo* were arrested yesterday," says the newsreader, "under the Prevention of Terrorism Act. . . ."

We wait a few more minutes, but it's over: our story is done. I feel oddly empty. That's it? Why wasn't my dad interviewed? Did he just shrug and say, *No comment, not my son anymore, nothing to do with me?* Bastard.

Still, we were on TV.

But—*bastard.* He doesn't give a toss about me. Even Martyn's dad—who beats him up—gives a toss. But no—my dad is too busy screwing his blond bimbo to bother fretting about his precious son.

Raymond switches the TV off. He looks around, his lips thin.

"Well?"

"Christian fundamentalists!" Martyn breaks the silence.

"They've only just got our video," says Jeremiah, frowning. "They probably watched it very quickly, rushed out the news. We'll see what they say on the six o'clock edition. The point is, we made it on!"

"We did," Martyn says. "We were on, Jeremiah, we were on!"

He gives Jeremiah a light punch, and Jeremiah laughs, and suddenly the euphoria hits us. We were on TV. And even if Dad wasn't on it, I can't believe he wasn't *watching.* Mum would have called him, I know she would.

We were on TV! We jump around and punch each other and then Martyn scrunches up a piece of old newspaper. He kicks it to me, yelling, "Goal!" I stare down at it doubtfully, then attempt a kick. Martyn cries, "Nice one!" and dribbles it to

Chris. I look over at Jeremiah. For a moment he looks as though he might object—but at the last minute he bursts into a grin.

We play with raw, sweaty exuberance. I've never liked football, but I find myself scoring three heart-pumping goals. Only Thomas stands on the sidelines, his arms folded, looking bored.

Finally we collapse onto the floor and talk dreamily about what we will do when we've saved the world, the temples we will build, the souls we will save.

We pray together. We bow to the east, to the north, to the south, to the west, to give thanks for our publicity. We pray that our message will spread far and wide until we touch every soul in the world.

And then comes the knock at the door.

12:30 P.M.

"Hello?"

A voice, floating through the wooden door. "Hello?" A female voice, with a Suffolk twinge.

"Shit!" Martyn cries. "They've found us, they've found us!"

We all make for the hallway, but Jeremiah calls us back.

"Martyn—you go," he whispers. "Just go and look through the spy hole."

Martyn returns and hisses: "There's a woman at the door."

Raymond splutters.

"We'll just ignore her," he whispers. "There's nobody home."

We all stand still. My eyes are level with Raymond's Adam's apple. It seems to roll under his skin as though a finger is rotating a marble.

We wait for another knock, but there is none. Our ears tingle, acute; we hear a sigh, a mutter, and then the crunch of footsteps.

"She's gone," says Martyn.

"Wait," Jeremiah cuts in. He darts to the window, peers through the net curtain, then whirls back. "Jesus—open the door, open the fucking door!"

"What!"

"She's going round the back! You open it!" Jeremiah cries at me.

"Me?" I cry palely.

"You go, Jon—"

"I can go," Thomas volunteers.

"No, it's got to be me."

I run out into the hallway. I pray to God to speak through me in a calm and deceptive manner. I will not let Jeremiah down again. Ever. This might be my last chance.

Raymond darts across the hallway into the kitchen; the others draw back quickly into the Prayer Room. I open the door. Nothing. Nothing but grass and stone and an empty road and a bitter skyline.

"Hello? *Hello?*" I call out. The blowing wind steals the

sound of my words. "Hello?" I call more loudly, stepping out onto the gravel.

"Oh—there you are!" The woman, who is just about to veer round the side of the house, comes waddling back. I quickly regain my territory, stepping back into the door frame.

"You must be Ned," she says, smiling up at me.

I don't reply. I just look her up and down. She is wearing dirty jeans and a checkered shirt and one of those green coats posh country people wear. Her face looks as though it's made of bacon and her hair as though it belongs to a Scottie dog.

"So, Ned, did Walter get back from the home?"

"Er, no," I mutter awkwardly.

"Surely Brenda's here with you?"

I glance back at the Prayer Room. Chris's face peers out an inch; he looks on the verge of hysterical laughter. His eyes bulge and he shrugs at me.

"I could drop by later," she says.

"No," I cry. Her blue eyes widen, and I gulp, heart pumping. What would Jeremiah do in this situation? *Improvise.* "Brenda—oh—Nan, you mean! Nan's ill, so I'm—I'm just looking after her."

"Right." She knows something's wrong but she keeps on smiling, showing off teeth like chunks of bad apple. Her gaze flickers to the hall, trying to crowbar past my shoulder, but I fill the doorway. "Tell Brenda she can come over for a cuppa as soon as she's better."

"Sure, I'll tell Brenda—Nan," I say, the sweat in my voice cooling. "I'll tell Nan you came by. It's cool. I'll tell her."

"All right, my love. Well, bye."

Raymond hisses for me to shut the door, but I know that Jeremiah will want to be told every detail. So I watch her walk down the road, a brisk but wobbling stroll in her Wellingtons. I watch her pass another farmhouse—she is diminishing into a stick now—and then turn up the path to a cottage. As she opens the gate, she seems to look back at me. I pull back and quickly close the door.

Raymond emerges from the shadow of the kitchen door frame, holding a piece of piping. My eyes travel from the tip, gloved in his meaty fist, to its jagged black end. What would have happened if the woman had barged in?

Raymond. Doesn't he remember the part of the Book of Hebetheus that says that we shall always act in peace and never harm another human being?

Has he even read it?

How can a prophet be related to this thug?

1:00 P.M.

We congregate in the kitchen for a group discussion.

At first, it's impossible to hear anything. Our group is like a mirror dropped onto the floor: our communal heart smashed to shards, voices shattering and splintering over each other. Then Jeremiah bangs the table with his fist and yells, "Quiet!" We fall silent, breathless, settling.

"The next time I see Ned, I'm going to give him a bloody piece of my mind!" Raymond cuts in. "God, I don't know. I could call Matt, see if he can suggest somewhere—a warehouse, somewhere safer, where people won't come knocking on the bloody door."

"And how reliable is Matt?" Martyn snaps. "I mean, Ned wasn't. What if this Matt calls the police?"

"Matt and I go back a long way," Raymond says sharply. "He'd never do that, nor would Ned. Look, he can find us somewhere safe, I know he can!"

"What, and move our hostage?" Jeremiah cries. He sits down on a chair, presses his hands into a steeple. "She's a Muslim terrorist. She's highly dangerous. Now that we've kidnapped her, her other terrorist friends might well start looking for us."

We all pause in shocked silence, considering. What if they've found out all our addresses? I think of my mum, how I left her lying at the bottom of the stairs.

"Furthermore, our faces have been on TV—we'd risk being spotted. No, we stay here."

"But we can pray to God to protect us from her friends. I mean, we just can't stay here!" Martyn interjects. His face is very red, his fist curled around a chair top. I feel uneasy. My eyes flit around the group. Thomas is always calm and balanced whenever we have a group discussion but, like Chris, I tend to curl up and remain silent. It's not that I don't have ideas or that I can't think for myself, but I'm just not very good at putting them into words, so I tend to swim with the current of the group.

At St. Sebastian's Martyn always got picked by teachers to lead debates. Once we had a debate on whether immigrants should be allowed into the country; it was obviously one of the PC debates manufactured so that the evil viewpoint would lose, but Martyn spoke so persuasively that he won by fourteen votes to ten. Our teacher, Mrs. Kay, was flushed with embarrassment.

"Jesus, this whole thing is a farce!" Martyn cries. "People think we're mad Christians, nobody has given one toss about our message, we have a dead old grandma in a bed, and now madwomen are knocking at our door!"

We all fall silent, stung by the truth of his words. I look to Jeremiah. He stares at Martyn steadily.

"Let's take this one thing at a time. We need to be patient. The government is no doubt considering the point we made about the Prevention of Terrorism Act. They're probably discussing it right now—"

"Oh, yeah, sure," says Martyn.

Jeremiah recoils, frowning, and I feel my heart tense. Martyn shouldn't be challenging Jeremiah. To interrupt Jeremiah is to interrupt the flow of God.

"Martyn does have a point," Raymond cuts in as Jeremiah bristles. "We thought that we'd have some kind of response right away—even if they just said they were debating it. All right, we weren't sure if they'd give us the money for our temple. But we all thought they would debate the Prevention of Terrorism Act immediately. We need to do something more."

"I mean, what if other members of her cell actually go and set off the bomb in retaliation?" Martyn blathers on. "I mean, they're crazy and ruthless, that Al-Qaeda lot."

"S-s-someone," Chris tries to interrupt.

"Let Chris speak," Jeremiah says.

"I w-w-watched this T-T-TV program about t-t-terrorism," Chris says, the spotlight tangling his words up into even tighter knots. "And—and—it w-w-was about th-these A-A-Americans who sh-sh-shot a t-terrorist—b-but as soon as the t-t-terrorist was d-d-dead, a-another m-man took his place, s-s-s—"

"Yes, we *did* discuss this," Jeremiah says.

"Yeah," Martyn cries, "you said they'd be too intimidated if we kidnapped one of their own, but, I mean, these guys aren't pussies!"

"But—"

"*And*," Martyn cuts in, "she might be part of a whole network. If a bomb bloody well does go off, then it'll serve them right—"

"It won't serve anybody right!" Jeremiah shouts.

"But—"

"No, you listen. We are warriors for peace. I mean, have you ever thought about, really thought about, what happens to people when a bomb goes off? It's not like in the movies, you know. People don't just die. They lose bits of their bodies; they lie under bits of brick and metal, with blood streaming over their faces. You know, my uncle was part of the cleanup operation for the London bombings, and he said it was like hell in that tube station. So don't *ever* say it serves *anybody* right."

As Jeremiah finishes his speech, I feel my heart burn for him. He's put Martyn in his place, and nobody else, not even Mr. Abdilla, could ever put Martyn in his place. He's put emotions into words in a way I could never do. I can feel the good coming off his heart in blazes of purity that blast into my heart and make me feel small and selfish and make me wish I could understand the world the way he does.

Martyn ducks his head and mutters a sorry. But it's a slightly offhand one.

Chris says sorry too. He sounds as though he means it.

Raymond nods, rubbing his beard.

"Brothers," Jeremiah repeats, "all we need is a few days. The woman's not going to do anything extreme just yet—she thinks Brenda's resting. Jon handled that well." He nods at me and my heart sings. "And in the meantime, we'll have guard duty: someone at the front, keeping an eye on the house. We'll take it in turn."

I nod, relieved. Everything will be all right, everything is still going according to plan. Only Martyn looks upset, almost as though he doesn't want everything to be wrapped up so easily.

"But what about the fact that nobody got our message?"

"Look," says Jeremiah, standing up. "D'you know how many people just watched that program? Ten million, fifteen million, maybe even twenty. Maybe more. *Twenty-five million.* Think of that."

For a moment the figure dazzles us. Twenty-five million is a number I can't begin to fit into my head.

"But twenty-five million people now think we're Christian fundamentalists!" Martyn cries.

"Come on, Martyn," Jeremiah snaps back, "did you really think they would shove aside all the other news and devote a twenty-minute slot to outlining all the aims of the Hebetheus and conclude by telling everyone to join?"

"Well . . ." Martyn glances around, satisfied to see that we all look bewildered. "Well, yeah, I mean, what else was the point?"

"Look, when Jesus first came down to Earth, many people thought he was crazy. All he had was a very small band of followers. How many men turned up at his birth? Three. Not hundreds, just three. And how many believe in him now, thousands of years later? Millions of people! All over the world. Even though we don't believe in Jesus, the story serves us well. Because this is the way new ideas get introduced into society. They trickle in slowly, slowly, slowly. . . ."

His voice rises with every word, like a tidal wave gaining momentum.

"People can't digest complex things at first. The media is very black-and-white. Everything has to be in sound bites. Look—it's like the Hebethean religion is this big jigsaw, and we have a lot of the pieces, but they can only see one piece at a time. There will be people who understand us right from the start—the chosen ones, whom God has blessed. Then there'll be people who come round slowly, who will keep wondering and keep questioning us but, in the end, will wake up one morning and know this is the truth. And then there'll be people who never understand. They'll go to hell, and it's very sad, but there's nothing that can be done for them.

"But don't say our first TV appearance was a failure. It's the start of something wonderful. We are doing God's work. We are great!" His voice crashes over us, leaving us singing with a sweet wash of relief and new hope. "So let's be happy! Let us speak to God one more time and give our thanks!"

We are uplifted. Even Martyn looks appeased. We go into the Prayer Room and pray for protection. Somehow it feels as though the invasion has tightened the invisible threads that bind us, woven us into one firm rope. As I bow and my nose touches the floor, I feel—I'm embarrassed to use the word, but this is how it feels—as though I love them all. My dear Brothers. My dear Brothers.

✟✟✟

As we rise, we hear the siren. We all freeze, eyes mooning. Jeremiah's shoulders slacken before the rest of us realize it is a distant threat.

Leaving the Prayer Room, there is a sense of fragility among us. A sense that time is short and we have so much to do, and may God help them to understand us before it is too late.

3:00 P.M.

Raymond lightens the mood by putting on an apron that must have belonged to the old lady, white plastic with ducks waddling across it in yellow rows. He cooks us up some beans on burnt toast.

It's only after we've eaten that Chris points out that SNAKE might be hungry too. The thought surprises me; I'd secretly imagined she must live off hatred and rats' tails.

"So," Jeremiah asks pleasantly. "Who would like to volunteer to take SNAKE her food?"

An awkward silence. We all avoid each other's eyes.

"Jon." Jeremiah's eyes rest on me. "Raymond told me you had a few questions about your Initiation. Well, before we proceed with the ceremony I feel you should undergo a few more challenges."

"Of course." I gulp and take the tray. There is a glass of water and a plate of bread and butter.

"Hang on," Martyn says. "I mean—she's been really, you know, *quiet* since we put her down there. Shouldn't he take his knife?"

I grip the tray tightly, my heart thudding, visions of SNAKE flashing across my retinas.

"No," Jeremiah reflects. "We checked the cellar last night; there's nothing she can use as a weapon. Actually, this reminds me of a point I must make to all of you. At first not everyone is going to believe us about SNAKE; not everyone is going to appreciate and understand our behavior. We need to take care that we never stoop to her level. On some occasions—such as last night—we may need to use force to keep her under control. But otherwise we will never inflict any harm on her. Understand? We must be whiter than white, purer than pure. We must show her our compassion. Our aim, ultimately, is to save her soul, to introduce her to Hebetheus, to bring her onto our side."

"Of course," I say, my voice quivering. The tray is beginning to weigh heavily in my hands.

"In the meantime," Jeremiah says, "if you can find out anything more about her plots and plans, that would also be useful. Befriend her, even. But never get too close, Jon. You'll be good with her—you're gentle with women. But remember: she is a snake."

I slowly tread down the steps, aware of all eyes on me. *Gentle with women.* I could never tell Jeremiah that girls actually scare me. I'm still a virgin. The closest I ever came to a girl-friend was Lisa Hargreaves. I danced with her one night at the school disco. The next day, I punched her number into the phone over fifteen times before I finally had the guts to pick up the receiver and connect. She said, "Who? Who?" and I had to repeat my name. Then, finally, she remembered me. I asked if she wanted to go to the movies, but she laughed softly and said, "I'm sorry, Jon, but you're just not my type—you're too nice."

Since joining the Hebethean religion, I haven't had to worry about girls anymore. Jeremiah says they are a distraction from the Path. Even when one of Lisa's friends later walked up to me and said, "If Lisa would say yes if you asked her out, would you ask her?" I ignored the flutter in my stomach and said I wasn't interested. She kept asking me, over a number of weeks—it was almost as though my every no fed Lisa's desire for me. But in the end, she gave up on me. I have lived like a monk for the last six months—except for some private moments when I have relieved my ugly desires swiftly, with a sense of shame.

In truth, it was a relief. I find expressing myself hard enough as it is, but talking to girls is nearly impossible.

As I climb down the steps to see SNAKE my heart begins to quiver. *Oh God*, I pray, *make me brave.*

I put down the tray and unlock the door. It's pitch-black; I walk forward blindly.

"SNAKE?" I call out gently.

No answer. My fear rises. What if she's lying in the shadows, ready to spring and attack? I quickly put down the food and kick the door shut behind me; at least she can't escape, even if she pounces.

"I've—I've brought you some food."

My eyes begin to adjust to the dark: smudges take on line and form. The boxes. And a figure, crouched in the corner, eyes flickering. She is afraid too.

"Would you like some water?" I say. "Anything?"

"Which one of them are you?" Her voice sounds strange: thin, as though it comes from a spirit, not a human. "I can't see you."

"I'm Jon. You—you know me . . . so . . . I'm here to help you," I say loudly. I sit down on the floor, cross-legged, folding my arms. "I'm here to tell you about the Hebethean religion and why you should turn your back on your wicked ways, so that you can understand why you should join us. But first you can eat."

The shape shuffles forward. I steel myself and resist the urge to pull away. To my surprise, I see that her eyes are wet.

"Are you hungry? Please eat."

"I—I can't with these on."

I don't even know where the key is. Then I stop myself. *Oh yes—I'll take off her cuffs and then she'll embarrass me again.* There are limits to the compassion I can show her.

"You have to just try. Bend down, use your mouth. It's fine."

She sniffs and leans down. Her hair falls forward; she shakes it back. She takes the bread in her mouth, trying to chew a bite off; half of it breaks away and the other half hangs from her lips. I make a mental note to cut it into small pieces next time.

She chews and chews, quickly, swallowing it down hard. As she leans down to eat the other half, emotion seems to overcome her. She sits up, tears falling in cascades, trickling into her hair, dropping onto her cuffs. A little bit of bread is still hanging from her mouth.

I guess that for all her evils, she is human too.

"Don't worry," I say. "I know this is all—this is—I mean—look." I gulp. "I . . ." What should I do, what should I do? *Improvise.* I'll speak the words of Hebetheus; that will cleanse and reassure her. " 'Hebetheus is a true religion that will correct the mistakes of past religions. . . .' " The sound of her crying hits my heart like hailstones. " 'Past religions are full of lies, corruption, and mistakes—' "

She reaches up to wipe away her tears, then realizes her hands are cuffed. She lets out a wail of frustration and wipes her face against her sleeve, sniff-hiccuping.

I can't bear it anymore. I crawl up a few more feet.

"Please don't cry," I beg her desperately. "Look, we really do want to help you. This isn't . . . Look, I know you think this is some sort of weird cult and that we're all crazy, but I promise you we're not. When Jeremiah told me about the Hebetheus, I was a bit uncertain at first. But once I'd asked loads of questions and he'd explained everything properly, I suddenly realized that this—this was *it*. And I can't tell you how amazing that felt! So we're all prepared to talk it through with you, SNAKE, to help you understand what we're about." She has, at least, stopped crying—but now she is staring at me so intently that I break off, feeling my cheeks warm.

There is a brief, burning silence. Why is it so hard to translate my feelings into words, to explain what the Hebetheus has done for me? I've forgotten what it's like to be a lost seeker. A frustration kicks inside me. How can I make her *see*?

Then I remember the very first words Jeremiah said to me.

"Are you happy?" I ask her. *Stupid question, Jon.* "I mean—before you—"

"Why do you call me SNAKE?" she interrupts.

"It's just a kind of . . . code name." I pause nervously, wondering if I'm allowed to tell her that.

"So what's your code name then? Dickhead?"

I splutter in shock.

"We're here to help you—"

"*Help me?* Just look at how you've helped me." She shows me her wrists. The cuffs have rubbed against the skin, forming raw red bracelets. "You've kidnapped me!" Her voice begins to rise hysterically. "I mean—what is this? What d'you *really* want? Money? Is that what this is all about? 'Cause my parents don't have any, we're not rich, you picked the wrong girl!"

In my anger, I forget to be compassionate.

"Yeah, right," I cry, "just deny everything! Just pretend we're some evil guys who want money. We don't care about money. You know why you're here, SNAKE!"

"What? I *don't* know why I'm here! *You* tell *me*. God, you are going to be in so much trouble. My dad—when I get out of here—he'll *kill* you. You'll be arrested."

"No, SNAKE." I shake my head firmly. "You're the one who's going to be arrested."

"How the hell will I be arrested? You don't get arrested for being a kidnap victim."

"No, but you *do* get arrested for planning to put a bomb in the school." SNAKE stares at me with an open mouth. "Jeremiah overheard your conversation. We know everything. So there's no point in lying." I spit the words at her.

A long silence. Tears fill her eyes again, but she blinks them away fiercely.

She shakes her head incredulously. "*What* conversation?"

"The one you had in the changing room when you thought nobody else was around. He heard *every word.*"

"When? When was this supposed conversation?"

"I—I can't say that exactly, but listen, SNAKE, we know *every* detail. You were going to plant that bomb on November fifteenth, at eight-fifteen A.M., in someone's locker. You were going to come in early, before school starts."

There is a burning silence while SNAKE ponders. Then she

cries, "You bloody idiots! I *said* I was going to come in and put a textbook in Sarah's locker before school started. She needed it for chemistry! You can ask her."

I shake my head, appalled. I can't believe SNAKE has come up with such a lame excuse.

"Though how the bloody hell you could twist that into me leaving a bomb, I don't know. For God's sake, where was I supposed to hide this bomb? In my pencil case? 'Cause, yeah, sure, I had an exploding pencil sharpener. Had it made especially. God!"

"It's not a laughing matter!" I cry. "These are people's lives we're talking about—how you can *joke*—"

"I'm not bloody joking! You know those attacks on London? The bus that blew up? My cousin was on that bus. She lost her legs, she's stuck in a wheelchair now for life, and so, no, I don't find this one bit funny."

This isn't going the way I'd imagined it; I had anticipated a gradual unpeeling until finally she would spill a confession that I would then carry out to Jeremiah like an offering.

She almost sounds genuine. But then I remember Jeremiah's words of warning: *The most dangerous thing about SNAKE is not that she lies. It's that she's deluded. She thinks she's doing good. This is the nature of evil. Nobody who does evil can ever imagine, can ever digest the fact that they are doing it—they always persuade themselves that it is the right thing, that they have no other choice.*

I open my mouth to try another tack, but she says, "Have you ever thought about why someone would want to become a terrorist? Can you think of why?"

"Well—I mean—you'd know best," I say without thinking. She gives me a look of such deep fury that I hurry on, humoring her. "I mean—they're evil, aren't they? They're a long way from undergoing a Soul Shif—" I break off, realizing such concepts will go over her head.

"Crap," she says emphatically.

The word hangs in the air, diffusing a nasty smell. I feel my cheeks burning; I can't believe she's getting the best of me.

"Don't you even watch the news? A typical terrorist is some young guy who's lost someone he loves and is burning up with rage against the West. Well, what do I have in common with that? I'm happy. I *was* happy. I was enjoying life, I was doing my homework, going out—I mean, I don't have any drum to bang, I don't want to harm anyone, I wanna get good grades and go to Cambridge to become a doctor, so why the fuck would I become a terrorist? I *like* the West. I love my country. And as for bombing St. Sebastian's—as for killing my friends, my teachers, the people I love—well, that's just insane. I'd never do anything like that."

"But—but—well—you're a Muslim," I point out.

"So now you're saying all Muslims are terrorists? I mean, how prejudiced is that?"

"Well—no—but—"

"I'm not a Muslim."

"*What?*"

"I am not a Muslim."

"So what are you, then?"

"I'm a Hindu."

"Oh."

"Yeah. Oh. But even if I was a Muslim, I would still be innocent. God."

"Well . . . I . . . Tell me about Hinduism, then," I say quickly, still shocked by this new twist. *Is she lying? Is she playing me?* "Isn't that the one where you have lots of funny gods?"

"No. We worship *one* God, only our God expresses himself in different forms." Suddenly she withdraws, turning in on herself. "You're so clueless. It's all just so pathetic. . . ." Her voice breaks.

"I—" I feel upset at our broken connection. "Have—have some water." I pick it up.

"How am I supposed to drink out of that?"

"Well—here—I'll hold it," I say.

"D'you remember?" she suddenly says. "About a year ago, when you were new at school and you were falling behind in religious studies? And Mr. Abdilla asked me to help you out with some homework about ethics, and I came over to your place and I helped you?"

She remembers. What would my Brothers think if they knew I'd once fraternized with this terrorist?

"And then we watched *The Simpsons* and we sat in your room listening to music. We had such a good time."

A flash of memory: sitting on the sofa together. Padma suddenly rolls up the *Radio Times* and playfully hits me and I tickle her and then Mum comes in and thunders, "What is this noise?" and we both crack up. After that night, she gave me her number and I always meant to call but I was never sure if she just wanted me to call about homework or if she wanted to be friends or something more and I was too shy to risk finding out.

But that happened in the past, to a naive and deluded and sinful Jon.

"I've forgotten," I say quickly. "Just have a drink, okay?"

I am about to let her drink when she whispers something.

"What?"

"Kiss me."

My eyes dart to her lips. A deep red rosebud. Then I realize that my mouth is hanging open and I quickly snap it shut. I get up, walk a few feet away, and sit down cross-legged.

"I'm going to tell you the ten truths of the Hebethean religion."

"Okay." Her voice is pale, but there is almost a singsong in it. "But I'm thirsty. Can't I just have my water first?"

I pick up the glass at arm's length and hold it to her lips, letting her drink. I watch the water bead on her lips, the pink flick of her tongue as she licks it off. *If she tries to kiss me, I'll teach her a lesson.* She drinks a little more, then lifts her eyes to mine. *If she tries to kiss me, I'll . . . I'll throw the water right in her face.* All the hairs on my skin seem to quiver upright with static energy. It almost feels like that day when we went on a school trip to a National Trust property and Martyn eyed up the sign saying DO NOT TOUCH THE ORNAMENTS and the teacher said, "Martyn!" but we all knew he would do it, as he always breaks the rules. Just before he reached out to stroke them, I felt my stomach tickle with a kind of angry pleasure.

"How can you do this?" she asks me. "How can you take away a person's freedom? Isn't there any love for other people in your religion?"

I stumble back in shock, tipping over the water. It flows across the floorboards, reaching her thigh. I step back, then forward, pick up the glass, set it upright. Only a little remains.

I tread back to the center of the room and sit cross-legged. I stare at a patch of wall and I recite for what seems like hours, my eyes blinking in strain, my voice becoming scrapy. As the words flow, I feel as though I am coming home, as though I have been venturing out into a forest, pricked by thorns, and now I have found my path again; all is well. My voice becomes cracked and hoarse, but I will not drink her water.

Suddenly—a loud bang at the door. SNAKE and I both jump. I rise, my legs shaky with cramp. Martyn peers round the door at her, as though peeking a thrilled glance at a dangerous creature in a cage. Then he and Chris pull me out, quickly closing the door.

"So have you found anything else out?" he hisses.

"She says she's not a Muslim," I whisper. "She claims she's a *Hindu*."

Chris frowns, but Martyn shrugs.

"So what? It doesn't matter what religion she is. She can belong to the religion of golliwogs for all I care. A terrorist is a terrorist. Is that *all* you found out?"

"Well—well—"

"Jeremiah says we can have a go now," Martyn cries excitedly. "We need to get her to confess stuff, so we can use it in the next video!"

"But . . . ," I trail off, looking at the teeth marks on his hand, now a faint blur of bruises. I feel irritated; I shrug it off. To be honest, SNAKE was tying my mind in knots, and it's a relief to escape. "Okay," I say. "Sure. See if you can learn anything from her."

"Oh, we will," Martyn says, nudging Chris, who blushes and chuckles. "We will."

I take one last glance in—to reassure her Martyn and Chris will treat her well—but she is huddled in a corner like a spider, her face a vague smudge.

They go in, slamming the door behind them. *We will . . . we will . . . we will . . .* singsongs behind me. I turn back uneasily, then shrug and hurry upstairs to see if Jeremiah wishes me to take more divine dictation.

4:00 P.M.

"Is that someone coming?"

Thomas frowns and screws up his eyes.

We are in the front garden. The landscape consists of fields of hard brown, anorexic trees, sinister packs of forest. We can just about see the humped back of a local farmhouse, a spiral of smoke wreathing from its chimney. And then—a black shape. A figure? Heading our way?

"No—it's just a crow," Thomas says. "Look."

The black shape spreads and soars into the clouds. I feel my heart follow it.

"It must be a good omen!" I say.

We continue laying out the stones.

When Jeremiah passed us a heavy brown sack and told us to fortify the cottage, I pictured metal mantraps with big fierce teeth that will snap an ankle like a twig. I felt ashamed when he drew stones out of the bag, each painted with a Hebethean symbol.

"I want you to lay them out in a circle. You must make sure each stone is touching the other one. That's very important, d'you see? This way we'll create a Sacred Circle, a linked chain of God's blessings. Nobody will be able to touch us."

It is a joyful task, simple and neat. Back and forth we go,

laying them out, stone on grass, stone on grass, stone on ear-wig, stone on dust. Suddenly, for the first time since we've arrived, I feel a sense of real usefulness. The mental splinters SNAKE left in my mind are slowly eased out. For the past few weeks, I've felt like an actor playing a part, waiting to be here, to become my true self. Now my heart sings; I relish the pain in my muscles, the ache of my back as I stoop and stoop and stoop. Every stone I lay is a stepping-stone closer to God; every stone is a bridge toward peace for all mankind. As each stone chinks against its brother, I feel shivery inside. I can almost see the sparkles of magic leaping and fusing.

"Thomas, did you have to undergo an Initiation?" I muse.

A few weeks ago, I made the mistake of asking Martyn what his Initiation had involved, and he mysteriously replied, "I can't tell you, but I can guarantee yours will never be as testing as mine was." Chris too was secretive about his. But Thomas's kind nature gives me hope that he might reassure me or reveal something.

Thomas doesn't reply. He is staring at a patch of earth in deep fascination. He pushes his finger in, twists it, frowns deeply. He lifts his finger to his mouth and licks off the crumbs of earth.

"It tastes like God," he whispers.

I laugh in faint confusion.

"D'you know anything about Jeremiah's parents?" I change the subject. "About how they died in a fire?"

No reply.

Maybe Jeremiah has ordered Thomas not to talk to me because I am not yet a proper member of the Brotherhood. Maybe I am tainting his higher purity in some way. But Thomas has been chatty in the past. I stare at a whorl of earth. It looks like a mountain; the spray of a dead feather above it forms a cloudy backdrop. Is this what the world looks like to God?

Thomas shifts beside me. I get up too, following the circle round. I am dismayed to realize that the line is jagged, looping out too far on the left side of the cottage. At the back we have a gap about a foot wide—and no stones left to fill it.

I turn to tell Thomas—but he has disappeared.

I hurry back to the front garden. Has he gone back inside the house?

Then I catch sight of him. *He is walking down the road.*

"Thomas—Thomas—where are you going?"

Thomas doesn't look back. He shoves his hands in his pockets, whistling.

"Thomas!" My whisper becomes a hiss. *"Thomas!"* I risk calling out. *"Thomas!"*

"I'm going for a walk," he declares, still without looking back.

What's he playing at? Scenes from this morning's celebration flick-flack through my mind like a set of playing cards. Thomas not joining in with our football. Thomas's weird, sad smirk. And what about last night, when he seemed to be crying? What if he's a mole? Like in those movies where a criminal pretends to be a policeman or a policeman pretends to be a criminal? What if he's going off now to update the police with a report about us? To collect a reward? I turn, ready to run into the house and tell Jeremiah.

But what if Jeremiah told him to walk off and leave me here? What if I go and tell on him and leave the house unguarded and then Jeremiah tells me Thomas has been sent on a secret mission and then just at the moment I leave the house vulnerable someone comes along and catches us out?

Why am I always the one left out, the new boy, the one whom nobody tells anything?

Minutes pass. Oh God, what should I do? Improvise. But how? *Please give me a sign, God. Please guide me.* I crouch down and pick up a small, blackened acorn. If it lands with its green cap facing me, then God is telling me that Thomas is on our side. But if it lands with its acorn facing me, then God is telling me that Thomas is a traitor.

Just as I toss the acorn, I suddenly see through the bushes someone walking by. I duck down sharply. It's that woman again.

She looks at the house. She stops. Looks at the house again. This morning we closed the curtains so that nobody could see in. She frowns. I tense, ready to raise the alarm.

She walks on. My heart slows but refuses to settle; Thomas's absence keeps itching away at it.

Finally, I see him coming back.

He crouches down beside me behind the bushes. His cheeks are ruddy, his breath short. He grins at me. Will I hear the sound of sirens soon?

"Here." He uncurls a red palm. A squashed fir cone.

"It looks like God," he says. Then, as I blink, he checks his watch, suddenly switching back to being normal Thomas again, brisk and together and in charge. "Hey, our time's up." He checks that the road is clear, gets up, and walks to the house. As I get up, I suddenly notice the acorn. It landed sideways.

9:00 P.M.

A close-up of SNAKE. The bottom half of her face is hidden by a white bandage. Her breaths sound raggedly muffled. Her eyes roll.

MARTYN (voice-over): This is the terrorist, SNAKE. Take a good look at her. We have interrogated her at length and learned that she planned to put a bomb in a locker at St. Sebastian's school. We have intervened and prevented SNAKE from taking this line of action, saving the lives of hundreds of innocent boys and girls. We have also learned from her

own confession that SNAKE is part of a whole
network of forty-five planning these acts in
schools across Britain.

A close-up of the swastika symbol on the wall.

MARTYN (voice-over): We belong to the
Religion of Hebetheus. We believe in peace
for all mankind. We are watching the news on a
daily basis. We are waiting for your swift
response to our demands. We demand that the
government immediately hold a vote in the
Houses of Parliament to amend the Prevention
of Terrorism Act and make it tougher! We
demand that the police investigate SNAKE
and smash her cell of forty-five terrorist
friends. We demand a million pounds to build a
temple to spread our message. Time is running
out. If we do not hear of these actions
happening within the next two days, we will kill
SNAKE.

　　This is not a threat. We will act in the name
of peace to wipe out all terrorism on the
planet.

11:00 P.M.

I feel weirdly close to crying, but I won't cry, I won't, because then I'd be like a girl and maybe being too much of a girl is why I'm not allowed in.

I pull on my school shirt, my pajamas substitute, and lie down in the Brothers Bedroom, alone in a sea of musty mattresses. I open up the Book of Hebetheus and try to focus.

The rest of the Brotherhood are in the Prayer Room. Jeremiah told me I couldn't join in because I wasn't ready for the knowledge they were discussing. Because I hadn't been initiated yet. I nodded and smiled and said, *Sure, fine, I understand.* But I don't understand.

Be patient, I tell myself. *Jeremiah knows what he's doing. Just read.*

> *A member of the Brotherhood of Hebetheus should avoid reading books, watching TV, or reading newspapers. Books encourage us to enjoy evil as entertainment. Examine the hypocrisy of our nation. On his way to work a man will buy a newspaper that details on the front page the horror of a child's murder. He will express inner dismay and then, a few minutes later, begin reading and enjoying a*

novel about a child killer. We express dismay when terrorists blow up our buildings, then run to the cinemas to watch disaster movies. All art is evil, because it feeds on our lower and baser instincts, telling us to extract pleasure from pain, thrill from fear, security from watching others suffer while knowing we are safe. Too often, art encourages us to worship villains and blurs the boundaries between good and evil, creating complex moral messages that cause audiences to feel confused about what is good and what is evil. But the Hebetheus states that good is good and evil is evil and all art is evil for suggesting black may be white or white may be black. Read only the Book of Hebetheus; all else will pollute and confuse the mind.

Why am I not ready yet? What's wrong with me? Is it because I messed up and let SNAKE nearly escape? When I first met Jeremiah, he told me that I was special. The word seemed to stretch out in my imagination like a beautiful gold cloth I wrapped around myself, and whenever I thought of my dad and Celine, I'd remember: *Jeremiah thinks I'm special. God thinks I'm special.* But a few weeks later, when he was teaching about the dangers of women, he told me I was fragile. "What I mean is, Jon, you're sensitive. The world is too harsh for you. In this survival of the fittest, you're not going to go far." I was stung. Did he mean I was weak? A wuss, a girl? But then he shook his head and explained: "Those who thrive in this survival of the fittest are those who are cruel. Look at the richest and most powerful people in the world. They deal in arms; they make huge profits by running sweatshops and forcing children to work twenty-hour days. People get ahead by trampling on the weak. To be weak in this world is to be noble. But I didn't use the word *weak*. I said you were fragile." There was Jeremiah again: pulling words out of a hat like a magician, turning lead into gold, helping me see the whole world in a different way.

Are they discussing SNAKE's shocking links to a network of forty-five other terrorists? When Martyn announced he'd extracted this confession from her, Jeremiah acted as though he'd performed a bloody miracle. He's been treating Martyn like a deity ever since. Martyn's triumph feels like my failure. I keep trying to push my jealousy away but I can't help it. Why didn't she confess this to *me* in my interrogation? I think I felt too sorry for her. I was *too* compassionate. I let her weep all over me. I am not just fragile, I am weak.

Shut up, Jon, shut up. I pull my sleeping bag over my head and bury my face in my pillow and eventually I sleep.

Dreams come. Hot, sensuous dreams. Dreams of SNAKE . . .

†††

I wake up suddenly, shuddering. My first thought is: *Oh God, I'm going to have to wash my sheets without Mum noticing.* Then I remember.

The bedroom is still empty. I reach down and feel my spent cock, limp like a dead sea horse.

In the gloom I become aware of a figure at the door. He beckons me gently, puts a finger to his lips.

I rise, glad of the darkness to hide the damp shame of my pants. I come closer; Raymond smiles. Then, suddenly, he grabs hold of me.

At first I think he's play-fighting and I kick him gently, feigning a tussle. Then Jeremiah comes at me. A black bag veers toward my face. Wham! I am in darkness and the cloth soaks up my screams.

Midnight

"It's okay, Jon. It's all right." His voice is very close, tickling through the stitching of the bag. "Trust me, okay? Trust me."

I feel his hand slip into mine. The feel of his long, cool fingers reassures me for a moment before the panic flares up again.

"Walk forward."

I'm being punished. Was it the wet dream? Because I let SNAKE escape? Are they going to hurt me? Are they going to—my hand splays out, feeling the painted brick of the wall. Are we going forward, toward the front door, or backward, toward the cellar? A breeze—a door opening? A feeling of space. We are entering a room. I can smell fresh paint and incense—the Prayer Room?

"Sit down."

I collapse onto the floor, my palms feeling a coating of paint, the dried texture of brushstrokes. Yes, the Prayer Room. Surely they wouldn't hurt me in the Prayer Room.

"Can I take off the bag?" I try to say, but the cloth slurs my words into a drunken-sounding spool.

"Trust me, Jon. Be still and be calm. It's all right. This is the first part of your Initiation. Be still."

A trickle of sweat slithers down my cheek, soaks against the cloth, dribbles back salty onto my lips. My Initiation; thank God. *Thank God!*

Footsteps; whispers; the flare of a lighter.

"Take off your clothes."

"What?"

"Take off your clothes. It's all right. Trust us."

I pull off my black school pants. My fingers brush my boxers, then flit to my shirt, feeling my way down my buttons. I take off my shirt, the cool air caressing my chest. No command is spoken, but I can feel it heavy in the air. I pull off my boxers.

"The Hebethean God . . . He waits and . . . Time for . . ."

Whispers, too low for me to decipher.

Fingers, skin against my skin. I yelp and hear their laughter. Are they laughing at me? Did they ever mean to—

Someone pulls the bag from my head. My eyes wince, then widen, flitting around the room.

Jeremiah is kneeling in front of me, a candle and a small saucer of water by his side, a knife—*my knife* (they must have taken it from under my pillow)—in his hands.

The others sit in a circle, cross-legged, their faces smudged with shadow.

Goose bumps prickle over my skin; I feel more naked than naked.

"Relax," Jeremiah whispers. "You're ready now for your Initiation ceremony." He looks at me with eyes of pure love. Then, with the tip of his forefinger, he pushes my head back down and wields the knife.

I freeze in terror. I think of Abraham, whom God asked to kill his son as a test. Am I meant to die now before God? *I must accept my fate.* I think of my mum, the way I left her crumpled on the stairs before I ran away, and my heart cries a silent apology to her. I think of Dad too, but I feel only hatred for him.

The knife slides against my scalp. I screw up my eyes tight. With a strange, detached curiosity, I think: *So this is what the moment feels like just before death strikes.*

I wait for the pain.

But there is none.

Just a light scrape. A dark lock of my hair falls like a feather.

I realize I have been holding my body taut, every muscle stretched to the screaming point. I sag; my muscles turn to trembling jelly. As I feel the cold knife coming down again, the words sink in. *My Initiation ceremony. My cleaning. I am not worthless; I have not failed him. Jeremiah feels I am ready, that I deserve to belong. Oh thank God, oh thank you.*

Every scrape of the knife causes a warm bubbly feeling to break a path through my heart. The fingers on my skull pause, as though sensing the feeling. Tenderness seeps from his fingers back into my skull. My heart beats and swells.

Jeremiah begins to chant softly as he bathes my shorn head with water.

I silently echo back each word until my body is a choir of singing cells. His voice becomes hypnotic, and at times I almost pitch forward into the cradle of his lap. I open my eyes and watch the last fluff of hair separate and swirl to the ground. I notice a few splats of blood on the floor. I relish them; I want him to cut me, to cut himself, to feel my blood mingling with his.

"Jon?" Jeremiah says.

Water trickles from my hairline, dampens my eyes.

"Yes?"

He hands me something. I recoil, thinking it's a snake. It drops to the floor.

He picks it up, laughing, and I laugh, and then our eyes meet and he holds my gaze steady. I feel unspeakably touched, as though I have just received a medal. As though Jeremiah has cut away all my sins and worries. As though some inner war that has been raging inside me is now over. My past is truly past. I am a new Jon, and our God is my new father.

Jeremiah sits upright, his face a beautiful mix of sternness and serenity, and I know then that his soul has opened to God and he is about to impart some knowledge of great profundity. His voice is so light and cool it seems to float through the air, ephemeral as the candle smoke.

"You helped to kidnap SNAKE; that was the first test of your faith to the Brotherhood. Now your ceremony has been performed. And now it is time to reveal what your final Initiation will involve.

"What is an Initiation?" Jeremiah asks. "It is a step into the Sacred Circle of the Brotherhood. A door opens and you enter it. But then the door closes behind you. Once you enter, you never leave. Are you sure you're ready for this, Jon?"

I nod.

"In order to open the door, you need a key. You've been waiting for this key, Jon. And now, finally, you're holding it." He points to the coil of rope I'm holding. "This is your special key."

I nod.

"You understand, Jon, that we would never ask you to do something small or trivial. The whole point of an Initiation is that it should be a challenge. It should stretch your soul to its very limits. Expand the soul and allow God to fill it."

"Yes."

"If you want to be great in the eyes of God, if you want to prove your love for him is great, then you must do something great. Something that will change your life forever, will change others' lives, will change the landscape of the world around you."

"Yes, yes, I want to be great."

"Our hostage, SNAKE, is a threat to humanity. But we must also show her compassion. She is, after all, a human being, nearly. As you know, a soul as ruined as hers cannot go to Manu. And yet there is hope for her. There is a way we can save her soul, a way *you* can save her soul, Jon. You can do this. You can release her soul."

"Can I . . . I can?"

"This will be your Initiation—to release SNAKE's soul. Are you ready?"

"D'you . . . d'you want me to pray for her?"

A faint ripple of laughter, fading into the darkness.

"Jon, God wants you to act, not just talk about acting. Millions of people all over the world pray every day. For them, prayer is the lazy opium of the human soul. They treat God like a servant; they expect him to rearrange the whole world to meet their needs. No—God wants us to be *his* servants, to act for him. To pray—and then to do! And you have the answer. Right in your hands."

I look down at the rope.

"I . . ."

"It's the kindest thing to do, Jon."

"You mean . . ."

"Jon, look at me. We live in a terrible world. All our values are upside down. Including our ideas about good and evil. Yes, the Bible says, 'Thou shalt not kill.' But the Bible is full of lies—we know it to be the deluded ramblings of spiritual wannabes. Think about it. What's right? That SNAKE should be allowed to walk free and a hundred people die as a result? And think of the pain that spreads from that. The boy who never gets to grow up and become a doctor. The woman who loses her precious daughter. It could happen to you. It could be one of your family."

"But if the government responds to our terms . . ."

"Yes, they may respond. And if they respond, we may think about allowing her to live—if we feel that we can convert her. But though we must show her compassion, we must also face up to reality. Sadly, her heart is possessed by a *raptor*, and it has coiled its tentacles tightly around her heart, so tightly that whether or not we can remove them remains to be seen. Martyn spoke to her for over four hours today and she would not back down or apologize once or show the slightest sign of remorse. Instead, she bragged of her other plans, of her fellow *raptors*, as you well know. However, there may be hope for her. If in the next few days she shows signs of being receptive to a Soul Shift, then we may respond with a different course. *But*—she may not. And then, Jon, we will call on you to be great. Are you ready to answer this call, Jon?"

"I . . . I want to be."

"Jon, each of us is put on this earth for a purpose. Sometimes it takes us a while to discover what that purpose might be.
I remember that when I first asked you to join the Brotherhood,
you were surprised. You didn't think you could be a special chosen one. So humble, I thought. You told me you weren't sure
what you wanted to do after you finished school, that your
grades were average, that you didn't feel God had given you any
talents. But this was because your ambitions were more noble;
you told me that all you wanted was to find the truth. I knew
then that you had a purpose, a great and grand role to play in
God's divine plan. That you were destined to be a hero. To save
innocent people. To slay evil. To be great! Are you ready for
this, Jon? Are you ready to be great?"

"Yes—I . . . I . . . want to be great, I do want to be great!"

"Jon, you may feel it is a sin to kill, but let me tell you it is
not. God kills all the time, every day. Earthquakes erupt; rains
fall; waves wash entire nations away. Death is a part of life. We
cannot shy away from it. And why should the evil be allowed to
live when so many innocent and sweet souls die? We live in a
twisted society that says every person should be allowed to live,
even if he or she plans to spread destruction across the globe. It
is not a sin to stop this! It is not a sin! It is a *duty*. A responsibil-
ity. Because if SNAKE lives and people die as a result, then
every single one of those deaths will forever be a bloodstain on
your conscience, and your chances of a Soul Shift will wither;
perhaps you will not even reach Manu. . . .

"Remember that it is not *me*, Jeremiah, asking you to do this. It is God.

"You are not alone, Jon. We will all be with you when you perform this great duty. You will act for all of us. Can you do this, Jon?

"Can you do this, Jon?

"I asked, can you do this, Jon? If you cannot, you should leave this house tonight and you will have failed our Initiation.

"Can you do this, Jon?"

"*Yes,*" I say.

Yes.

1:00 A.M.

My sneakers thwack and drum against the road. My lungs claw air. I turn, look back at the cottage. Did they see me run? A yellow light gleams in the window; the cottage looks so cozy, as though it belongs in a fairy tale. I push on a few more feet, but the stitch biting my side sinks its teeth in too deeply. I double over, clutching my ribs and spitting. I run my hands over the bristle of my shorn head, feeling the nicks where the knife cut too deep. I hear myself moan lightly. *Oh God, what am I doing here?*

I'm a coward. That's my problem. I'm too kind, I'm too girly, I'm too whatever, because all of them could do it but I can't.

I can't do it.

To kill her will crack me open like a nut; I'll splinter, fall into pieces.

I run a little further. I wonder if there's a phone box nearby, where I can call home. What will my mum say? What if the police pull me into an office like they do in movies and shine a spotlight into my eyes and force me to give them all the details of our secrets? It will break my heart to betray Jeremiah; I can't do that, I can't.

There's a light ahead: a farmhouse. I creep along a line of hedge, peering through the gaps. A woman comes out of the door, her white hair shining in the moonlight. She whistles and calls, "Here boy, here boy!"

I could ask to borrow her phone. I could just say I'm lost. And when my mum tries to take me to the police station, I can refuse to go; I can lock myself in my room and tell her I'll starve myself if she makes me go.

"Here boy, here boy!" A collie comes bounding up and she pats it gently.

A smile breaks open on my face. I remember the dog I had, a red setter called Isaac. I loved Isaac and he loved me. When I was fourteen and turned against Christianity in a period of doubt, my dad took him back to the pound. I didn't speak to him for a week, until he persuaded me that it was God's punishment, not his.

The woman goes back into the house. The door closes and

the lights go out. I sit by the hedge for a while and look up at the stars with bitter sadness. I've been waiting so long for my Initiation. I'd always pictured it as the happiest night of my life—and now this.

I don't make a conscious decision to go back; I just find myself getting up and slowly walking. My legs feel weak and every so often my body breaks out in a shaking fit. When I get to the gate, I hesitate. Nobody seems to have noticed that I ran; I guess they're all asleep, thinking they're safe with me on guard duty. I feel a sudden rush of shame; my Brothers are counting on me. And I just nearly betrayed them.

The moon is almost full. I think of God looking down on me and feel a rush of comforting warmth.

Thanks to Jeremiah's compassion, SNAKE has been brought up from the cellar to the den, now known as the Hostage Room. A light shines from the window. It tempts me. With a shudder of fascinated revulsion, I find myself going up to the window to peer in. I hope I don't catch her at work. I keep worrying that she might find something, some little thing in the room—a knife or a fuse—and make a bomb or weapon during the night. I wouldn't put it past her; I still feel stunned by Martyn's revelations. I realize now that I've underestimated just how dangerous she is.

She's awake. Her skin glows in the bright moonlight. An echo of my wet dream sings through me, and I flush.

She looks up at me. When I look at her, she drops her eyes.

Almost as though she's—ashamed? Maybe Martyn's interrogation did some good. Maybe by being forced to admit everything, she had to face up to who she is.

I know that I should hate her. I know that I should crave her death. But when I search my heart for blackness, I can't stop thinking instead of the night she helped me with my homework. I remember feeling a little sulky about having a *girl* bring me up to speed. But she didn't patronize me once. She explained everything clearly and kept telling me how intelligent I was, how quickly I was learning. How did she change from that kind, fun-loving girl, who tickled me and told me she had a silly crush on Bart Simpson, to this—this *animal*, whose head is churning with explosions, who is hungry for bodies to burn?

Her expression suggests she is becoming human again. Maybe she is remembering the girl she was before she got sucked into terrorism. I wonder who recruited her. Maybe it was some charismatic, older guy who had a way with words, who encouraged her to go against her heart and deny her nature.

And doesn't shame imply regret? Doesn't regret imply the desire to repent? No—not repent, that's a wicked word. To *revow.* Doesn't revowing imply the beginnings of a Soul Shift? Doesn't a Soul Shift imply she should be forgiven?

A sudden noise in the distance.

I tense, searching for an interruption in the darkness. But— nothing. I think, I hope. Just the wind, cool on my cheek. And a feeling I am being watched.

I turn and look at SNAKE.

Our eyes lock.

Self-consciousness drops away. Her eyes rake my face. For a moment it feels as though I am the predator and she is the innocent victim. Then I shake myself and smile awkwardly.

A grin breaks across her face. Her eyes become huge and luminous. Her cheeks apple. Her smile has a goofy crook to it, with pokey front teeth.

This smile hooks my heart. I find myself laughing, my eyes on her, feeding from her, and she giggles too, and for a moment we connect.

Her laughter dies out before mine. Her face sinks back into sadness, her lips pinch. She stares at me with terrible eyes.

Then she starts crawling toward the window, moving in sideways undulations, a cross between a snake and a crab. Her head pops up at the window. She can only balance by leaning on the ledge, her nose squashed up against the glass. I squash my nose up too, trying to make her laugh again. But she just stares at me. I drink in her face. I hadn't noticed how she has freckles, or thick eyebrows, or dark circles of misery under her eyes.

She breathes on the glass and reaches up. I see her struggle with her bound hands and I reach instinctively, my fingers banging the glass. She pokes one finger at a stiff angle and writes:

Help me

What can I do?

I picture myself putting the rope around her neck and kicking away the chair. The gurgle of air squeezing out of her throat. I feel sick. I stare down at my trembling hands. I can taste bile in my throat. I start to chant silently in my head, trying to make it go away. Her gaze feels like a laser and I want to shout at her to stop.

I'll speak to Jeremiah. That's the right thing to do. First thing tomorrow, I'll tell him that SNAKE seems different, that the *raptor* in her heart is dying.

I look up at her and see that my yes or no is a cliff face that she is clinging to. When I nod, tears fill her eyes. I mouth, "I'll try." I nod again, each nod a rub of her shoulder, a wiping away of her tears, a smile. I mouth, "Good night" and go to join my Brothers in sleep.

DAY THREE

9:00 A.M.

I realize that people might classify our religion as extremist. But those are the type of people who don't really understand what a religion is. Jeremiah explained to us that the word *religion* comes from the Latin *religare*, which means "to bind one's soul back to God." For most people religion is about tweaking their souls as a little hobby—half an hour singing pretty songs on a Sunday to make themselves feel better for the rest of the week. But our Brotherhood believes that *every minute* matters to God. Every single minute is a chance to soar or to sin, to save the world or to chip away a little more at it.

The word *extremist* is really just a way of putting us down, making us all sound like loonies. If we're extremists, then they're all smallists.

When I was fourteen years old, I had a crisis of faith. This was even before you left home, Dad. I remember asking you about the word *repent* and what it really meant. And you said it wasn't just about saying sorry. You told me it came from the root word *metanoia*, meaning "to change one's mind" or "to change one's direction." So *repent* wasn't really a black-and-white term but one with shades of meaning. In fact, it might not have anything to do with being sorry at all. And I said to you, "Dad, what about all the other words in the Bible?" And you said in a vague sort of way, "Don't worry about it. They're the words of God."

That was when I began to doubt everything. If just one word can be twisted in translation, surely the Bible is just the echo of an echo of an echo of a once clear and sweet religious song? Later, you persuaded me that the Bible was God's message and I should trust it rather than question it. I came back to Christianity. But now I know better. I don't want to worship the religion of a dead man, whether he is holy or not. I need—we all need—a voice of God who is alive today.

And that voice is Jeremiah.

He might only be sixteen. But Buddha was once sixteen; so was Jesus. Age doesn't matter. We think a prophet ought to have gray hair and look wise. But God could have chosen anyone to speak his message. He could have chosen a young girl with blond hair—not that women are allowed to be his messengers. But he could have. The point is, people only really respect great leaders once they're dead, and then it's too late.

Last night Jeremiah said that I may have to kill SNAKE to save the world from her evil. But now we are sitting in the Prayer Room, blessed by a beautiful morning, fragile as an eggshell, and I feel ashamed that I ran. Jeremiah has to be strong in order to slap awake all these stupid people out there. But if I look at my Brothers, I know they wouldn't really kill someone.

And Jeremiah is right that we should aim to do great things for God. Smallism pollutes every area of society. A few months ago, for example, Mrs. Kay called me in for a career advice session. She said, "What do you want to be when you grow up?" I said a rock star. I just blurted it out because I couldn't think of what to say. And she said, "Don't be silly, Jon." So I said an astronaut. And she sighed and said, "Try to think a little smaller, Jon." What she was basically saying was: *Be an accountant or work in a bank.* Because that's what adults all seem to think becoming an adult is about. Giving up on greatness. Being practical. Not being disappointed. But I tell you, God is GREAT and life is about BEING GREAT and DOING GREAT THINGS and that's why guys our age are best suited to being God's messengers. We, the New Generation, the next generation, will be the ones who change the landscape of this world.

I'm trying to focus on prayers but instead I find myself talking to you, Dad. I don't know why I keep doing this, keep letting you into my head. But I'm talking not to the bastard you are now but to the dad you once were. Don't think I've forgiven you. And don't think I'm doing the wrong thing now. I don't need to defend myself to you. I know I am right. I had a vision this morning, on waking: a vision of a beautiful *zepor*, with flowing fair hair. She slipped into number 10 Downing Street, into the prime minister's bedroom, and gently whispered into his ear, her voice as sweet as the sound of the sea. So he will respond to us. He will. . . .

1:30 P.M.

After lunch, Thomas and I are sent to continue SNAKE's education.

The moment we enter the room, Thomas thumps himself down on the floor, opens his exercise book, and begins to read aloud from his copy of the Book of Hebetheus. I feel frustrated; I hoped I might be sent to educate her on my own.

" 'Imagine for a moment that human beings are in a cave. From childhood, they have their legs and necks shackled so that they can only stare straight ahead of them at a light reflected on the wall—which comes from a fire burning far above and behind them. On the wall, they see dancing patterns of life like shadow puppets.' " Thomas's voice sounds like a spring tightly compressed into a jack-in-a-box; at any point it might break open and burst into laughter or tears. Padma too senses something is wrong and looks at me.

She looks beautiful this morning.

" 'Imagine that one of these men was released from his shackles. He's compelled to stand up, walk, and look up at the real light above him, outside the cave. His eyes are dazzled and he cannot trust what he is seeing. He wants to turn away from the light and put his restraints back on.

" 'But then someone drags him by force toward that light. The man might shout out in protest, but still he is dragged. Then the light shines onto him and he can't see anything.

" 'But slowly, slowly, his eyes grow accustomed to the light. And then he sees the true nature of things.' "

The sun gleams through the window, forming red fireflies in the dark sea of her hair.

" 'But imagine if that man were to go back into the cave.

" 'Now he is a stranger among the other prisoners. He knows the truth about the fire and shadow patterns on the wall, but they will only laugh at him. Perhaps they will say that if he went up and came back with corrupted eyes, it wasn't even worth trying to go up.' "

I look at the brown curve of her neck, imagining the harshness of the rope against the silk of her skin.

"ARE YOU LISTENING TO ME?" Thomas suddenly shouts at Padma.

"Yes," she says quickly.

Thomas puts down his exercise book. He stands up and walks around the room, then stops and stares down at a patch of floor. I slide his book over and read quickly, " 'If they were able to get their hands on the man who had released him and led him, perhaps they would try to kill him.' "

"Have you read any of these books?" Thomas shouts.

Padma's eyes widen and she presses up against the wall. Thomas gestures angrily toward the bookcase. He pulls out a random book, thumping it.

"Have you?"

"No, how can I—"

"You know that reading's evil, don't you? How can we purify you if you read?"

"How can I read with these stupid cuffs on?" Padma asks. "Besides, there's nothing wrong with reading." That note in her voice again, that sound that unnerves me: defiance. "Reading is fun. It helps you learn stuff."

"In the Hebethean religion we don't agree with books. Books are dangerous," I explain, giving Thomas a nervous glance. "They give people ideas. It's like—imagine if nobody had ever told you about the word, say, *hate*. If you didn't have the word for it, would you feel it? It's only because you see a film or read it in a book that you're tainted with it. Sometime in the future, when we've taken over everything, the word *hate* will be banned, you see. Because it just won't be needed."

"But . . ." Padma shakes her head. "That doesn't make sense. Sometimes you can feel an emotion and it's such a mix of all the other emotions—like all the colors in a paint box mixed together—that there isn't a word for it. But you still feel it. And books make you think—"

She breaks off, looking at Thomas. He is staring at her as though she's the most terrible *raptor* he's ever seen in his life.

Then he reaches into the bookcase and lobs a book. It hits the wall. Slams to the floor. Pages flutter by her feet. Padma catches her breath, appealing to me.

"Thomas," I begin, "what are you doing? Violence isn't our way. You remember what Jeremiah said—"

A book arrows in my direction. It skims my ear and hits the wall. Another book sails toward Padma, hitting her foot; another yelps against the ceiling. Pages roar through the air; spines rip; Thomas howls. I go to him, begging him to stop, to calm down, asking him what's the matter, but he screams in my face, "There're *raptors* in the bookcase, little *raptors*, screaming and jumping up and down," and I grab his arm as he reaches for another book and he smacks his fist against me, banging me back against the case. Pain zigzags down my spine; I cry out. Books tremble, as though drawing in a shaking breath, then topple to the floor like broken buildings. Thomas falls among them, loose pages taking flight like birds, his hands clawing his face, tears soaking his cheeks, his mouth a black hole of howls.

The door bursts open. Chris and Martyn pile in, gaping. Raymond enters, then steps aside for Jeremiah.

"He just went crazy!" Padma bursts out.

"You shut up!" Raymond orders. He stands over Thomas. "What the hell's the matter?"

"He's cracked," Martyn says in an awed voice. "He's—"

"He just lost it," I say.

"Let me." Jeremiah cuts through us, kneeling down by Thomas. He tries to remove his hands from his face, but Thomas claws them back.

"Get them off me, get them off me!" Thomas screams.

"It's all right, it's all right," Jeremiah shushes him in his angel voice. "It's just me, it's Jeremiah, you're okay, you're okay."

I look at Chris, who looks at Martyn, who looks at me.

"She's put a bad spell on him," Martyn whispers, and nods at Padma. Padma scowls.

Jeremiah finally succeeds in taking his hands, and Thomas rolls onto his side, sobbing. He looks like a little boy. I feel frightened. What's happened to him?

"I think," says Jeremiah, a benign softness warming his face, "Thomas may be on the verge of a Soul Shift." He smiles down at Thomas and gently touches his face. "Go—all of you," he commands. "Leave him alone."

We all hang about in the kitchen, talking, trying to work out what's gone wrong with Thomas, whether it's madness or divine illumination, though Raymond jokes there's a fine line between the two. Jerk. But I feel confused and, I admit, a bit jealous. Why is it that Thomas, with his good grades and fancy house and nice parents, has all the luck with God too? I'd thought that a Soul Shift was all about being happy, which shows how far off I am.

Some time later I hear a creaking and Jeremiah's soothing voice becoming loud and then distant. We edge to the kitchen door, peering surreptitiously into the corridor. Before Jeremiah leads Thomas into the Prayer Room, I hear him say, "It's all right, I can see you need them. It's all right, I'll sort it out for you. . . ."

Jeremiah shuts the door and then turns to me and instructs me to tidy the books up.

2:00 P.M.

Padma is crying again. I quickly shove books back into the case. I never know what to do when she cries. I turn Plato up the right way, then the King James Bible. The cover is white, the letters gold italics, the paper fine as tissue. It fits snugly into my hands like a white dove. And suddenly I am overcome with the strangest urge to open it up and read one of the proverbs. Just as I used to when I was feeling troubled.

I take a deep breath. I walk up to her, intending to stop at a safe distance, but my heart compels me forward and I find myself kneeling by her side. I reach for a tissue—but I have none. I offer her my sleeve and she laughs through her tears.

"Sorry about Thomas," I say. "He's just going through a Soul Shift. You see, a Soul Shift is when you—you know—you go into this, like, amazing state and you're with God." I don't know why, but my words only increase her weeping.

As she looks up at me, I can't help picturing those huge wet eyes blank and glazed. Every time I've played out a fantasy of killing her, my mind has vomited at the sheer thought. But now, in reality, with Padma flesh and blood beside me, it suddenly seems . . . My heart thumps with the shock of it. *I could do it,* I realize in excitement. *If someone passed me a rope now and said do it, I almost feel I could.*

Like a snap of the fingers, the revelation vanishes. One of her tears hits my arm in a salty trail; suddenly she is human again. I feel ashamed, and I find myself speaking to her in a sharp tone.

"When you spoke to Martyn yesterday, you told him you had a network of forty-five other terrorists. Can you tell me more about their plans? I know you don't want to grass anyone up, but if you can just give me some details . . ."

I will her with all my heart to confess. I don't care how long
t takes. I won't make the mistake of being too compassionate
his time. I'm going to keep chipping away until I get *something*,
ven if it's one bullet of information that I can carry back to
eremiah.

"What do you care?" she says in a choked voice. "You just
vant me dead. You're all animals. . . ."

"*Animals!* No, that's not true. I don't want you dead—none
of us does!" I cry, flushing, wondering if she used her evil pow-
rs to see into my mind. "It's not like that!"

She shakes her head, sniffing, tears falling and plopping
nto her lap.

"I've been thinking . . . that I want to convert to the
Hebethean religion," she says. "I don't want to be a Hindu
nymore, I want to join Hebetheus." She lifts her liquid eyes
o mine.

"Are you serious?" I ask.

"Well, I've heard your rules, I've heard passages from the
Book of Hebetheus. I might be new to it, but it really—it fasci-
ates me. I'm really, really interested. I think you may all be
ight about a lot of things."

"Well—that's great." I feel an odd disappointment. Does
his mean it's all over? But then I am excited. I was right: she
does want to revow. Perhaps I was her inspiration. Jeremiah will
be so pleased!

"If you go and tell Jeremiah now, will he let me go home?"

I hesitate.

"Yes."

She suddenly kicks the floor with an animal sob of rage.

"He won't, though, will he? He'll never let me go. None o
you will just *LISTEN* to me. Why won't you just all *BELIEVE* me
Instead I have to *PRETEND* to be interested in your *BULL
SHIT.* . . ." Her words disintegrate into moans.

"Maybe you're not ready for a conversion just yet, then,"
say sadly.

"So which one of you is set to kill me?" she sobs.

"I—well—I was," I begin, then stop, for her eyes enlarge
with horror and a fresh film of tears. "But I—I—"

She wriggles up next to me and squeezes her fingers into m
arm so hard it hurts.

"Please," she begs. "I'm seventeen next week—my mum'
organized a party and everything, and you know I haven't don
anything wrong, and I know you won't do it, right? You're nice
you're good, I can see your goodness." She looks me in the ey
fiercely. "You are good, aren't you?"

My eyes hold hers, then slide to her lips, then swiftly jerl
back up to her gaze.

"Yes, I'm good," I say, but my voice sounds weak. I frown
remembering. "I'm a member of the Brotherhood of He
betheus. Of course I'm good. We do good. It is our role in life
to bring peace to mankind."

She moves in even closer, her arm hot against mine, and

an feel the faint brush of her breast against my elbow as she
orces me to look up once again.

"You know I'm not a terrorist, don't you?"

"I . . ." I drop my gaze, but the ferocity of her attention
orces me to look at her.

"Come on, Jon—" Her voice rises with a hysterical edge,
ind I shush her quickly, nodding at the door. "This is my life
ve're talking about. I mean, for God's sake, I've never even spo-
ten to Jeremiah the whole time we've been at school. The *only*
ime he ever paid me any attention was when we got our essays
pack in English and I came top and his mark was just below
nine. I remember he turned and gave me such a dirty look. He's
iad it in for me ever since. I don't know, maybe I pissed him off
io he made up some story about me talking about a bomb on my
mobile when—"

Suddenly I frown, pull away from her body heat.

"No, Jeremiah's not like that," I say sharply. "He'd never do
something so petty."

"No—of course not, I know that, he's really amazing. But
you know I'm not a terrorist. I never, *ever* planned to plant any-
tl ing anywhere."

"Well, well—I mean, maybe." I try to ignore the panic
thrashing about inside me.

"Please don't kill me," she repeats. "Please."

"Look, the reason your death sentence came up is because
of your confession to Martyn. The thing is, if you could just tell

me about wanting to turn things around, get out of your terror ist cell, *really* convert to Hebetheus—not with just a few word so you can escape, but *really* understand what we're tellin you—"

"I'm trying, I'm trying," she sobs, "but how can I leave a ter rorist network I don't even belong to?"

"But yesterday you told Martyn that you did! Don't lie t me. You're playing games now. I'm not stupid, you know!"

"He *forced* me to say it," she cries. "He put his hands on m and he hurt me!"

"*What?*" I cry. "You're lying. Martyn wouldn't do that! He's member of the Brotherhood of Hebetheus, and we're not al lowed to—we don't—we don't put our hands or our attentio on women," I recite.

"Oh really? So this is just my imagination? I mean—jus look at my shoulder!" She wriggles angrily in her cuffs, swivel ing around to show me a ring of nasty bruises.

"You might just have—you might have banged yourself. . . .'

"No—he *forced* me! He *threatened* me!"

The word *force* echoes in my mind, with whispers o thrilling fear.

"Wh-what happened?"

In a quiet, dejected voice, she tells me the whole story. A first I am not sure whether to believe her. But as she goes on certain details ring true: Martyn's signature bullying, his ag gression. I feel instinctively that she is telling the truth. By the end of her tale, I look down and realize my hands are fists; I feel ready to smash his face. *For God's sake,* I cry inside, *she's just an innocent girl and we've—*

I look at her bruises again. I feel a sudden urge to hug her, to hold her tight and say, *Sorry, sorry, this isn't what we're about. None of us will hurt you again, I promise.*

"Right. I'm going to tell Jeremiah about this right now."

"Okay," she whispers, and a ghost of a smile passes across her lips. A pause. "Thank you."

I am about to get up when she digs her fingers into my arm again and nuzzles her head against my shoulder like a pussycat.

"We're friends, aren't we, you and me? We're friends?"

I am about to give a formal yes, for we in the Brotherhood are friends to all humanity. But the pleading in her voice touches me.

"Yes," I say, "we're friends." And we grin, and in that moment it's as though we've just shared another homework session and might watch TV or spend the afternoon slouching in the swings, swapping CDs. "I'd better go and speak to Jeremiah now."

I stand up. I feel unsteady; I press a palm flat against the wall. My head is reeling with confusion; suddenly I am desperate to leave the room, breathe my own air, close my mind to her thoughts. What if she's lying? If she's realized that she's in the wrong and now she's trying to paint over her past? Does that make her good or evil? Oh God, I wish there was

a test for goodness the way there is for lies, a detector we could
strap around her wrist to measure precise recordings of her
heart and conscience. Then I might know if she deserves to die.

3:00 P.M.

A fly is buzzing in the Prayer Room, lashing angrily against the
windowpane. Thomas is lying on the floor, dreamy-eyed. His
body looks limp and exhausted. Jeremiah is sitting in the middle, on the ring symbol, still and serene as the Buddha. He
beckons me forward.

I kneel and look into Jeremiah's cool blue eyes. In the black
hole of his pupils I have a sudden vision of myself laying the
noose around her neck, like some ancient virgin sacrificed to
the gods. Can he really want me to, can he really mean it? Is it a
test? Is he sorting the *zepor* from the *raptor* in my heart?

"Yes?" Jeremiah prompts me gently.

At first I can't get the words out. I stutter and stumble like
Chris, until Jeremiah puts a hand on my shoulder.

I explain everything to him.

Well, nearly everything. I do leave a few things out, I admit.
I keep telling him that I know it all sounds crazy but it really is
the truth. To my surprise, he accepts it all. He calls for Raymond to bring Martyn in. I rise to go, but to my horror Jeremiah
orders me to stay.

"Sit." Jeremiah motions. "Martyn, Jon and I have just been talking about you. . . ."

Martyn gives me a conspiratorial glance. As though we've just been called in to see the head at St. Sebastian's and we have to make sure our stories tally.

"Jon has interrogated SNAKE just now and he informs me that not everything you say is correct."

"What?" Martyn jumps. He swivels an innocent, injured gaze to me. "What?"

"Let me explain. Jon interrogated SNAKE at length, and SNAKE confessed that she is a terrorist. She is not only the head of a network of forty-five other terrorists across this country but the mastermind behind a worldwide organization of forty-five *countries*." I open my mouth to object, but Jeremiah flickers a sidelong glance at me and I play along. "So, what do you think about that?"

Martyn shifts uncomfortably.

"Well, that's really bad," he says. "She's, like, really evil."

"So you do think that SNAKE—a sixteen-year-old schoolgirl—could really mastermind a worldwide terrorist organization?"

"I dunno. Maybe. I mean, she could use the Internet, couldn't she, and that sort of thing."

"You don't think that Jon might be exaggerating?"

Martyn twists his lips up to one side, then lets them spring back.

"Yeah . . . I suppose he might be."

"What do you think the difference is between exaggerating and lying?"

The fly buzzes incessantly in the background.

Despite his casual shrugs, I sense Martyn's guard is up.

"Well, they're kind of the same, only one's a bit worse than the other. Lying's telling something that's false, whereas exaggerating . . . I mean, that's just adding a little extra bit on, and everyone does, all the time."

"So you don't feel guilty about the fact that yesterday you exaggerated SNAKE's confession?"

"I didn't!" Martyn's voice is close to shattering into a shout. "I didn't—she said—" He breaks off, clenching his fists and jumping to his feet. "That fucking fly is driving me crazy!"

He strolls over, but Jeremiah's voice stops him.

"Leave it. None of us has a right to kill God's creatures. Sit down, Martyn," he says gently. "This isn't a trial." He spreads his hands. "I'm your leader. It's not my place to judge or punish. I am merely a conduit for the God of Hebetheus. If SNAKE didn't really say the things you claimed, then you can tell me in all honesty. I'm not going to throw you to the lions." Almost parental now, almost tender, as though Martyn is an errant child. "You're one of us."

Martyn fixes his stare on the floor.

"I wasn't *lying*," he says flatly.

"So, Jon, why do you think SNAKE is telling the truth? What makes you think you can trust her over Martyn?"

I jump as though he's suddenly shone a light into my face.

"Yeah, Jon," Martyn spits out acidly.

"I—I—" I swallow, still trying to blink away confused patches of light. "I just think she can open up to me a bit more than, say, Martyn, or . . ."

"Why's that?" Jeremiah asks.

Suddenly I feel a cool sweat sticking to my brow. I thought Martyn was in the dock. Or is this all just a test to probe me? Is Martyn just the decoy?

But I've done nothing wrong. I have nothing to hide.

"Look, Padma likes me," I say.

"Padma?" Jeremiah mocks me. "But I thought our terrorist's name was SNAKE."

"Yeah, of course, I mean, SNAKE trusts me."

"Ooh, SNAKE *trusts* you. SNAKE *likes* you," Martyn singsongs under his breath.

"I think she trusts me," I burst out in a temper, "because I don't go around threatening to rape her!"

My words burn the air.

"Martyn?" Jeremiah's voice is cool with astonishment. "You threatened to *rape* her?"

"I—no," Martyn says, but the blush on his cheeks suggests he may be "exaggerating."

"Chris was there at the interrogation, wasn't he?" Jeremiah says sharply. "Raymond! Call in Chris."

Silence fills the room like choking smoke. Jeremiah's aura becomes arctic cold. The fly reaches a pitch of hysteria. I can feel Martyn shooting me furious, sidelong glances, silently screaming: *Traitor! My Brother the traitor!* I sit up very straight. I'm in the right, Martyn's in the wrong. Then, at last, the door opens.

I can tell Chris scents trouble the moment he enters. Martyn gives him a Brother's look, but Chris doesn't return it.

"Chris, did Martyn threaten to rape SNAKE yesterday?" Jeremiah asks.

"Y-y-yes," Chris admits at once. "But it w-w-was h-his idea, n-n-not m-mine."

"You bloody—" Martyn curses him, then breaks off. "Okay. So I did. But how else was I going to get her to tell us? I wasn't really going to. It was just a threat, right? I didn't lay a finger on her!"

"Chris, I want you to tell me exactly what happened," Jeremiah says. "Without any exaggeration."

Chris nods frantically. Martyn—I am glad to see—is in torture.

"At first, we j-just tried to get her to talk, but—" Chris breaks off to suck from his inhaler, and I can hardly stand the waiting. "She j-just kept denying everything. So th-then Martyn said we had to make her talk and so he told her we'd rape her if she didn't c-c-confess and then she confessed really quickly, but the p-p-point is, we didn't mean it, because none of us in the Brotherhood is allowed to t-t-t-touch a w-w-woman or even think about th-that."

There is a silence.

"But SNAKE did admit that she was going to plant a bomb in St. Sebastian's?" Jeremiah asks.

"She—" Chris breaks off. "W-w-well, we—didn't t-t-t-t-talk about th-th-that."

"Well, everyone knows that anyway!" Martyn says sharply. "You told us! So what was the point in asking?"

"True," Jeremiah says. He turns to me. "But she did admit it to you as well?"

The truth is, she says she's innocent. She says she never planned to plant a bomb. She swears she's not a terrorist. But if I say that—then what? It's too much for them to take. They'll think I'm in cahoots with her; Jeremiah is already suspicious. It could undermine the victory I've just scored for her. And besides, even if she did deny it, she must have planned to plant the bomb, or else what are we all doing here?

"Yeah," I say quickly, "of course she admitted that. But that's the *only* thing."

It seems strange to lie for the sake of holding up a bigger truth. For a moment I feel snagged in confusion. Why does it seem so hard to be white, to be good, to always tell the truth? Why can't things just be black and be white? Why does the world keep on smearing the two colors together?

"But," I confess, "she says she's not a Muslim. She says she's Hindu."

Jeremiah looks taken aback for a moment, then shrugs.

"Whatever her faith, her roots are still in the East; I heard her say in the changing room that she wished to declare war on the West."

"But even so, I think she's sorry. I honestly do. She seems really different over the last few hours. She actually said to me that she's interested in repenting, in coming over to the He-betheus Brotherhood—"

"As a woman, she could never be part of our Brotherhood," Jeremiah says coolly.

"Well, what I mean is, I think she wants to change, and I don't think she deserves to be . . . to be . . . you know . . ."

"But we've sent the video out now!" Martyn cries. "If we back down, we'll look weak and stupid. They'll think the He-betheus is a load of shit. . . ."

"You see the position your lies have put us in?" Jeremiah asks coldly.

Martyn quails. Chris tears off his nails with his teeth. He looks as though he's about to cry. Jeremiah stares at them stonily.

"I'm sorry," Martyn mutters, picking at the stitching on his sneakers.

Jeremiah makes another steeple with his hands and rests his chin on them. Behind him, the sun breaks through the floating clouds and arrows white rays through the curtains, falling on his hair in divine sparkles, shadowing the thoughtful curve of his brow.

"SNAKE must die," he says at last.

"What!" I cry, jolted. "But . . . but . . ."

"As you say, she has confessed to planning to bomb our school."

"Well, she *seemed* to say that, yes." I squirm in hot entrails of panic. "But she might have been intimidated by me interrogating her. I mean, I know you lot think I'm in cahoots with her, but I'm not. I was tough with her—I really—"

Jeremiah lays a hand on my shoulder.

"Jon, you have a compassionate heart. But we knew before we came here that she was going to plant a bomb."

"But you said that her soul could be saved! And we've been reading to her, and today she said she was close to coming round! We've done all this good work on her soul and now we're just going to kill her? That's not very compassionate!"

"Ah, but it is," says Jeremiah. "Because even though we have educated her, her soul is black in its very core. It simply cannot be redeemed. Look at the dissension she has caused among us. Besides, we have not just kidnapped an *individual*, Jon. You have to see beyond that. SNAKE is a *symbol* for all terrorists, a symbol of the ignorance of the government and the police who allow people like her to thrive. And how we deal with this symbol will show how we will save the world." He sighs, and a sadness seeps into his voice, as though he is weary of trying to save an ignorant world. "We'll give them until tomorrow to see if they respond. SNAKE's life will depend upon the enlightenment of this country."

"And . . . what about us?" Martyn asks unsteadily.

"You must be punished," says Jeremiah, to my surprise. "You will undergo a Sacred Cleansing."

He and Martyn stare at each other for a minute.

"You may go," Jeremiah says.

"Okay, fine," Martyn snaps. "Come on, Chris. We'd best go now, since we're in the doghouse."

Chris stands up, gangly and uncertain. Martyn suddenly spins back, saunters over to the window, and with a fierce *thwack* kills God's precious creature. Thomas lets out a faint moan. The bluebottle thuds to the sill, its wings moving stickily. I wonder how much pain an insect might feel when it dies; if, in its own small world, it suffers as much pain as we do.

Martyn stares at Jeremiah, waiting. Jeremiah doesn't respond. Martyn leaves. Chris trails behind him.

Jeremiah lets out a sharp exhalation.

I feel as though I have taken a knife to the protective sheen of our Brotherhood and made a tiny incision: just a hairline crack, but dangerous enough for it to split and spread into a chasm. "I'm sorry. . . . I'll talk to Martyn, I'll tell him I'm sorry," I tell Jeremiah.

"There's no need," says Jeremiah. "Tomorrow morning he will undergo a Sacred Cleansing and things will be different." He sighs. "You know, Martyn was initiated a long time ago, long before you, Jon, and yet he has so far to go in his under-standing of the Hebethean principles. You, Jon, have sur-passed him."

I feel as though I've just scored a goal or a piece of home-work has landed on my desk with the grade A plus slashed across it.

"I want you to watch him," Jeremiah continues. "Record in your notebook everything Martyn says or does. Be subtle; no need to trail him. Just note things down and report back to me."

"Of course," I say, with a thrill of excitement.

I get up to go—then turn back and kneel once more.

"Jeremiah, I just—I just wanted to ask about Padma—about SNAKE, I mean. You said you overheard her on her mobile talk-ing about her bomb plot. But what if—what if you didn't hear it, you know, completely? What if you got the wrong end of the stick? Because she says she was just talking about leaving a text-book in a locker. . . ."

Jeremiah stares at me for a long time. I look at the symbols on the wall, at Thomas, at the dead fly, at the symbols. I'm aware of my cheeks growing very hot.

Finally, Jeremiah says, "Jon, I think perhaps I've overesti-mated you. I can see you're not capable of killing SNAKE and you're not ready yet for your Initiation. Perhaps you'd like to go home."

"No, no, no," I cry. "I can do it, I can—I can do it. I just—it's fine. I can do it."

"I want you to know, Jon, that I would never lie. *Never.* Not to you or any of my Brothers."

"Yes. I know, I know. . . ."

"Good. Now sit with me awhile." Jeremiah smiles.

I open my mouth to tell him Padma is waiting for me to return, to reassure her. But then I close my lips. I obey him. Jeremiah's anger has seeped away; his expression is tranquil now. Just to sit with him is as soothing as listening to the sound of the sea. Slowly, my worries dissolve away. I realize that the best thing to do is avoid Padma from now on. I can't cope with her mind games, so it's best not to speak to her. I don't need to worry about her anymore, about right or wrong, black or white. It's not my place. Jeremiah knows best; I just have to put my decisions in his hands.

6:00 P.M.

The six o'clock news.

First: a suicide bomber has killed sixty-five people in a blast in Iraq.

Second: a boy has been murdered in a knife fight in a school in London.

Third: us.

"Police are still searching the country for the missing girl, Padma Laxsmi, who was kidnapped from her home three days ago by a group of young extremists," the newsreader says.

Then a detective, with a plump face and a silly brown mustache: "We are doing everything in our power to track down these boys. A woman in Kingston has identified the van the boys were traveling in on Kingston High Street last Thursday. Our CCTV footage suggests the van headed in an easterly direction. I'm afraid I can't give you any further information at present, but I assure you we will find them."

A rapid flash of our photos again, though there isn't time for all of us: Raymond's and mine are missing. Then Martyn saying we will kill her if our demands aren't met. Then Mr. Abdilla saying Padma is innocent. The weather girl concludes that temperatures are expected to drop in the evening, with a possibility of snow in the southeast.

Jeremiah lowers the sound until her voice is reduced to a murmur.

We all stand about with slack shoulders as it sinks in.

The government hasn't responded to us. Our slice of the news pie is shrinking every day, nibbled by newer and fresher horrors. The wild shock, the slam-punch, of our actions has gone; the repetition of the news has diluted the pain; this report will only bruise people's minds faintly, fading quickly as they return to cooking and putting their kids to bed and sinking back into their selfish lives of cozy houses and cars and careers.

Rage kicks my stomach. Just how far do we have to go to get ourselves taken seriously? Just how much more do we have to do to shock them awake? How many other terrorist suspects do we need to kidnap before they'll care? Isn't one life enough?

Oh God, I don't want to kill her, but what else can we do? It will be their fault, they'll have driven me to it, only I can't do it, can I, I can't?

Such indifference. So much suffering in the world, and yet still they drift through their lives oblivious. Suddenly I see how truly selfish we all are. We're all heroes in our own blockbuster films; everyone else just has cameo roles. No wonder the world keeps on churning out suffering. But how can I change it, *how*?

Martyn opens his mouth as though about to pontificate, then quickly snaps it shut.

Jeremiah is locked into a tense pose: shoulders hunched, fingertips pressed to his lips, brow furrowed. He flicks the sound back up, skipping channels, showering us with blasts of sin: a blond sex temptress cajoling us to buy butter; a program telling us how to improve our homes, inflaming capitalist greed; a celebrity singing contest feeding the hollow thirst for fame. The Houses of Parliament: a debate. Or maybe it's the PM's question time. Everyone's heckling and shouting clever things at each other. It reminds me a bit of school.

"Look at them," Jeremiah jeers in disgust. "When we sit and discuss problems, we work together. But all they do is score points off each other. It's not a debate, it's an ego circus. And they're running the country!" His voice rises to a shrill pitch. "We're going to *make them* listen to *us*. Martyn, it's time to get the noose."

7:00 P.M.

A close-up of Raymond.

RAYMOND (voice-over): We were amused to see that the police are planning to come after *us*. This just demonstrates why terrorism will never be wiped out. You decide to condemn a group who are trying to do good and write them off as a bunch of Christian fundamentalists—which, by the way, we are not. But when it comes to a real terrorist, you decide she's innocent—without even bothering to properly investigate her.

She planned to plant a bomb in the school, and there are many out there like her. At this point, we don't know the full extent of the network.

It is time to declare a true war on terror. Suspects should be held indefinitely. Furthermore, we believe that if someone is proven to be a terrorist, they deserve to be hung.

[**CHRIS (whispering):** I th-think this sounds too e-extreme.

JEREMIAH: The terrorists are extreme! We have to fight fire with fire. If they are prepared to end human lives, we have to show we can match them!]

RAYMOND (voice-over): All terrorists must be hung in Trafalgar Square. This bill—which we christen the Peace Bill—must be voted on in Parliament right away. We *must* hear action is being taken, or SNAKE dies tomorrow at midnight.

11:00 P.M.

Notes on Martyn's behavior, day 3

8:00 P.M.: Dinner. Jeremiah asked M to say thanks to God before eating and M did so. We're running out of tins of beans so we saved some & just ate toast. Raymond had to cut the moldy bits off the corner of the bread and it tasted stale. Martyn made a remark about being tired of toast, toast, toast. Thomas was not present; T was in the Prayer Room. M asked if he should take him some food. Jeremiah agreed and thanked M for his kindness.

8:05 P.M.: M was in the Prayer Room with T. I stood by the door, listening, but I couldn't hear what they were saying. Then Chris came out. C mentioned he feels bored.

9:00 P.M.: A phone started ringing. We all went crazy at first. Then we realized it came from the dead woman's bedroom. We stood outside, listening to the message. The voice was cheerful— maybe the woman who knocked on the door? Then I ordered R to tear the phone out of the socket and destroy the wires so nobody could call in. "Or out," M added—cheekily, I thought.

10:00 P.M.: Glanced into the bedroom while others were meeting in the Prayer Room for evening Love to God. Noticed a sheet of paper sticking out from under M's pillow. Had a cartoonish picture, looks like a zepor, only you can't get male zepors. Is M suffering from lustful thoughts?

There's something else that I feel I ought to write down before I show this to Jeremiah. Something I have to confess:

10:30 P.M.: I found myself briefly going into the Hostage Room and removing the Bible, telling SNAKE we planned to burn it. Then I went into the bathroom. I felt like some alkie nourishing a bottle of gin in his hands, begging his body to obey him, to put it back down. But I drank. I polluted my mind with some proverbs. I don't know why I did it. I guess sometimes when I read the Book of Hebetheus I feel as though my soul is being squashed into one of those Russian dolls and the more I read, the

*smaller and smaller the doll becomes. The Bible made me feel
fluid; I felt I could pour through it, let it pour through me. I
savored Proverbs:* My son, do not despise the Lord's
discipline and do not resent his rebuke, because the
Lord disciplines those he loves, as a father the son he
delights in. *I sat there, the words settling softly in my mind,
and I thought of my father without hate, but with a kind of
sadness. Then I felt rotten inside. I remembered that Jeremiah
had once warned me:* "There are those who lurch from one
religion, one belief, one New Age claptrap to the next. Those
people are not desperate for the truth. They just want to believe in
something—anything—that they can lean on like a crutch." *I
quickly shoved the filthy book away. The Hebetheus might be a
hard and narrow path, but it is the only one to God. And I want
the truth, the real thing, not an easy substitute. I must be strong,
I must be true.*

I read through my words and then tear off the bottom of the
sheet and flush it away before I take the report to Jeremiah.

MIDNIGHT

I wake up suddenly in the night, heart pumping. *Tomorrow you're
going to have to do it, tomorrow you're going to have to kill her, you
realize that, don't you, you realize that the government isn't going to
respond and then you're going to have to commit murder—*

They will respond. They will.
You're going to have to kill her.
You're going to have to kill her.
You're going to have to kill her.
You're going to have to kill her.
You're going to have to kill her.
You're going to have to kill her.
Shut up, shut up, let me sleep, let me sleep—
You're going to have to kill her.
You're going to have to kill her.
You're going to have to kill her.
Let me sleep. I'm too tired, I'm so tired, just leave me—
You're going to kill her.
You're going to kill her.

You're going to kill . . .

You're going to . . .

Day Four

10:00 A.M.

At the end of morning prayers Jeremiah asks Martyn to sit beside him at the front. We all sit upright; the air is rich with the
scent of danger.

Jeremiah just sits there, as though he wants the silence to
build up until the room screams with it. Finally, he says,

"Martyn, we all want to help you reach a Soul Shift—we're your Brothers. So now we feel you should undergo a Sacred Cleansing. We've discussed this and we're all going to help you with this. Aren't we?"

Jeremiah nods at us and we respond with a chorus of nods, though Chris shoots me a quick bewildered glance.

Martyn isn't fooled, though. He sweeps a glance over us and his shoulders droop a little.

"Martyn, why did you first come to the Hebethean religion?"

Martyn looks startled, then says quickly, "Because God called me to be with the Brotherhood. Because this world is totally fucked up and we're gonna save it." Silence. Martyn carries on hastily, "You were the one who told me I should join—you said you'd had a dream about me. . . ."

I start; when Jeremiah first told me about the Brotherhood, he said that God had spoken to him in a dream about *me*. Is this how he found all of us?

"Don't you feel, as a member of the Brotherhood, that you should tell the truth at all times?"

Martyn's mouth bunches up tight and he digs the end of his lace sharply into his trainer.

"Oh, because you're doing such a good job as our leader, aren't you, and only you know the truth, right?" Martyn snarls.

Even Jeremiah looks taken aback.

"And it's all going so well, isn't it?" Martyn carries on. "The government has responded to our demands, haven't they? You said it would work. *You* said the God of Hebetheus would go into the politicians' dreams and guide them. And that woman who knows the dead old woman keeps passing by the house, looking in; sooner or later she's gonna want to be let in. And Thomas's sick—he needs medication and you know it."

Shocked, I stare at Jeremiah. He looks . . . helpless?

"Look," he says quickly, "Thomas is undergoing a Soul Shift and he's not here with us in prayers this morning because he needs to rest—it's a big adjustment for his body to make."

"Because he's a schizo!" Martyn shouts. "And he needs his medication! And you told him before we came to stop taking it, so he didn't bring his pills, and now he's sick and look how much good you've done him!"

Thomas? Thomas a *schizo*? Schizos are those guys in movies who hear voices and have six different *raptors* in their bodies, fighting for their soul. *Martyn's lying, isn't he, Jeremiah? Isn't he?*

"Thomas is . . . mildly schizophrenic," Jeremiah says, turning to us. "But he is still one of our Brothers. We don't discriminate against schizophrenics. We all need to pray for him—"

"Pray for him?" Martyn cries. "One of us has to go into town and break into a pharmacy and get some—"

"No."

"*Yes.* It needs to be done."

"*Martyn, I have asked God what to do and I am waiting for an answer. Now is the time for your Sacred Cleansing.*"

"But how come you're the only one who God can talk to?"

Martyn yells. "What if I had a dream and God said I was the one he wanted to speak to? How can you say your dreams are any more special than mine?"

"Either you undergo a Sacred Cleansing now or you leave the Brotherhood."

Martyn turns to face us, his eyes narrowed.

"Who here thinks I should undergo a Sacred Cleansing?"

There is a silence. Jeremiah's eyes hold mine like a laser.

"I do," Raymond says.

"I do," I say quickly—anything for him to stop looking at me like that.

Jeremiah's spotlight spins to Chris. Chris flushes the color of a tomato and quickly nods.

Jeremiah lets out a sharp breath. Briefly, his expression looks almost stricken—but it quickly smooths out into normalcy.

"Good," he says. Martyn gives Chris a murderous glance. Then he swallows and mutters, "Okay, I'll do it then. . . ."

"So let's go back to when you first joined the Hebetheus." Jeremiah's voice is gentle. "Do you remember the dream I had about you? And at first you didn't believe me—you doubted me, d'you remember you told me that? No, don't bristle—you don't need to defend yourself. Your doubt was understandable. It would have been strange if you hadn't felt doubts. But do you remember the words I said that touched you, that made you believe?"

Martyn starts and looks slightly nervous.

"I saw your father in my dream," says Jeremiah slowly. "He was a *raptor*. I told you he was evil and you suddenly went quiet because you realized that if I knew that, I must be telling the truth. He is a *raptor*, isn't he, Martyn?"

Martyn nods slowly. His anger has dissipated now; he looks wary, vulnerable, almost boyish.

"And do you remember when you had to perform your Initiation? Yes, I know the details are always to be kept secret, but for once we will share them with your Brothers. I told you to burn his clothes, didn't I? I told you to take all his liquor bottles and pour them out into the ground, didn't I? To release him from his suffering and his anger?"

Martyn nods.

"It was a test," says Jeremiah, "and you suffered for it. You knew from the beginning that you would. But it showed, it proved, that you would do anything for the Brotherhood; it proved your love for God. You were so brave, Martyn, so brave, and I felt so proud of you."

Martyn gives a gruff, lopsided smile, his face dreamy with memory.

"What did your father do when he discovered you had burned his clothes and poured away his drinks?"

"He hit me," Martyn says lightly, shrugging as if to say, *So what?*

"You were black-and-blue. He put you in the hospital."

Black-and-blue? I can't help shuddering . . . but then I remind myself that Jeremiah was only being cruel to be kind.

"But that wasn't the first time he put you there, was it?"

"He doesn't mean to do it, he's not a bad dad, he just drinks too much," Martyn says, frowning. "It's just like you said—he's nice, but the *raptors* in his drink take over and he turns nasty and . . ."

My heart burns for Martyn; this is like watching him undress. I almost feel I shouldn't be here. But then again, he has seen me naked, and we're all Brothers, aren't we?

"And your mum . . . ?" Jeremiah coaxes him.

"She left three years ago."

"She left you a note, didn't she?"

"Yeah, on the table . . . she left a note . . . and my lunch money for that week, but Dad took it, he went down to the local bar . . . and . . ."

"Or maybe you drove your mother away and your dad to the bar?"

"What?"

What? we all echo in silent shock.

Jeremiah's face suddenly twists into a sneer. It looks so unexpected, so out of place on his features, as though a *raptor* has wriggled into his face and taken hold.

"Maybe your mum and dad were happy together, and then she got pregnant, you came along, and you put a strain on the family, and then your dad started to lose it and to drink, and you drove her away."

"I didn't drive her away!" Martyn's voice rises. "You're say-ing I'm a liar, a liar who drove his mum away! My dad did it, it was him, it was him, you should have seen the way he treated her—beating her up—I wanted her to go, I TOLD her to go, to be free of him—"

"But you wanted her to stay too, didn't you? You still felt deserted when she finally did leave?"

"What is this?" Martyn's voice breaks; his whole body is stretched taut, his fists perched on his knees like grenades. "I don't want to talk about this; I want my Sacred Cleansing to be-gin." He sniffs, jerking his palm across his face.

"And your father? Didn't you feel as though you'd failed him too?"

Stop, I want to shout. *Stop this, Jeremiah. What are you doing to him, what is this?*

"Failed him?" Martyn's eyes flash.

"Come on—you tried to convert him to the Hebetheus that night he beat you, but you couldn't bring him onto our side. Now he'll never reach Manu—you failed your own father."

"You try telling him!" Martyn screams. "You don't know what it's like. He won't even listen when I ask him to give me my lunch money. I can't go home half the time—I haven't got a home, he's not even a real dad—I don't have—you—fucking—" He sees another sneer on Jeremiah's face and *wham!* He thumps Jeremiah across the face, sending him flying back onto the floor.

The silence blazes. Raymond jumps to his feet, shaking. Chris is white. I half stand, then collapse back onto the floor.

"Jeremiah?" Raymond whispers in an icy voice.

Martyn goes to stand up, poised to fight. But Jeremiah sits up, rubbing his raw cheek, and—to our amazement—he laughs softly. Martyn stares at him, appalled—and then, as though cut down, he suddenly breaks and starts to cry. Raymond blinks. Martyn goes to strike out again through the blur of his tears, but Jeremiah leans in and hugs him. At first Martyn struggles in shame and fury, but then Jeremiah says, "It's all right, you don't need to care about that bastard, we're your family now, we're here with you and we're never going to let you down," and Martyn lets go, lets the tears flow, though he's probably never cried in front of anyone in his life before. My heart ties up into a knot and I feel as though for the first time I understand Martyn, I've had a glimpse into his soul, and I say silently: *I'm so sorry, Martyn, I'm so sorry.*

"We can't all be leaders," Jeremiah says. "We can only have one, but Martyn, this doesn't mean you don't have a place here in the Brotherhood. You have a place," he says fiercely, "and you have no idea how important you are, how every minute of the day God beams with pleasure that you are doing his work. God is your father now and he is so proud of you. We couldn't have done this, we couldn't have saved our school from SNAKE's evil, without you, without anyone here. You must never forget that."

Martyn nods, sniffing, embarrassed by the tears he's shed. But a pride burns in his eyes and he nods again, bowing his head before our Great Leader.

NOON

As I enter the Hostage Room, carrying Padma's food, she picks up her glass and hurls water at me.

Her cuffs ruin her aim; the water sails past me in an arc, spraying me only softly. I wobble; her plate of baked beans nearly pitches to the floor. She glares at me as I put down her plate, right next to last night's plate: uneaten, the beans congealing in a pyramid of orange glop.

"I hate you," she seethes.

"Padma—"

"You didn't tell him, did you?" She tries to kick me as I sit down next to her. "You lied to me! You said you'd talk to Jeremiah about Martyn!"

"No, no, I did—I did! I told them and Jeremiah believes you, he knows you're telling the truth."

"So they're not going to kill me now?"

"No—I—" *Oh God, forgive me.* "No. It's okay."

She blinks several times, then breaks into tears of relief. My heart knots. I put my arm around her and she leans in and lets out a choked sigh. I run my hand over her hair. It feels like a sheen of black silk. I know I should stop; the others are waiting for me in the kitchen and they might come in at any minute. But I stay there, holding her, feeling her warmth seep into me. Ever since Martyn broke down this morning, I've been feeling strange . . . *tainted*. I stroke her hair over and over, and it's as though her hair is like Samson's, as though there is magic in it, not strength but softness, a healing, soothing softness; I feel human again. I remember the look on Jeremiah's face as he sneered at Martyn, but then I remind myself that Jeremiah did it out of love. He was showing compassion.

I make to move, but she clings to me. Suddenly the silence between us is alive, prickling and tingling like the air before a storm. She looks at me and I look down at her and then I pull away quickly and tell her I must go; I will be back later to educate her.

4:00 P.M.

Dear God, I'm sorry. I need to confess what just happened with SNAKE. I need to clear my conscience. I just hope you can forgive me.

I *kissed* her. Or she kissed me. I don't know how it happened; it never should have happened, but it did. And now I am sick with guilt.

It took place an hour ago. . . .

✝✝✝

Jeremiah and I go into the Hostage Room. I feel disappointed about him coming, which I guess is a bad sign; the *raptor* in me craves being alone with her. The moment we enter the room, he and SNAKE lock eyes. Poison dances in her retinas. Jeremiah walks right up to her and looks down at her with a sneer. He waits for her to speak first.

"I'm not a terrorist and you know it," she says, her back pressed tight against the wall. Her voice shakes slightly; I realize just how terrified she is of him. "We both know you twisted my words in the changing room. Come on—all I said was that I was going to leave a textbook in someone's locker and you make out I'm planting a bomb!"

Jeremiah continues to stare down at her, his eyes cold with disbelief.

"Come on, if I was white, I wouldn't be here, would I? I just happen to fit your nice little stereotype of a terrorist. That's why you assumed I was a Muslim. You're the type of guy who sees anyone who's Asian or from the Middle East with a backpack on a bus and immediately thinks they're carrying a bomb."

"Oh, am I?" Jeremiah looks ruffled. "Because anyone who wants to combat terrorism is a racist, aren't they? I'm racist because I want to live in a world free from terror? I'm racist because I want to live in a world of peace?"

"Look, I'm a Hindu, I'm the same as you. I love God, I love the world, I believe in peace."

"A Hindu." Jeremiah rolls his eyes. "So you claim. And I suppose you believe in reincarnation. I read all about how your last dying thoughts determine where you go in your next life because, hey, man, we all get recycled."

"Do you want to know why we belive in reincarnation?" she spits out. "Because we believe in karma. If you do wrong, it comes back to you, in this life or the next; if you do good, it comes back to you. And when you're free from karma then you get enlightenment, the ultimate freedom, but you wouldn't understand that because this karma is on your head, all that you're doing to me now—you'll have to suffer it yourselves, you'll have to pay for this!"

Jeremiah stares her down and says, "I'm not afraid."

"People like you—you're all devil worshipers!"

"Devil worshipers!" Jeremiah mocks her with a high, girly voice.

"It doesn't matter what words you use—if you kill me in the name of God, then it's not to please God, it's to please the devil. In fact, God does just become a name, a meaningless name, a word. You—you give religion a bad name. It can do so much good, but when people read about people like you they think religion can only do harm and bring more suffering into the world."

"It's not killing if you're stopping other people being killed!" Jeremiah says in a voice of ice. "It's our duty to help people live their lives in peace and freedom."

"Freedom!" Padma cries. "That's a joke coming from a fascist like you."

"I'm not forcing anyone to be here, SNAKE. Any of us can just walk out when we please. You want to go, Jon? You can just go, can't you?"

I nod quickly as Padma glares at me.

"Come on. In your cult, people aren't allowed to read, they're not allowed to think—it's fascism."

"No, we simply believe in a new democracy where people do as we guide them for their own good." Jeremiah shakes his head. "I suppose you disagreed with the war in Iraq? I guess you opposed the introduction of democracy there?"

"Yes," Padma hisses. Then, suddenly, she turns to me. "D'you agree with the war in Iraq, Jon?"

"I—I—no—"

"Not what *they* tell you to think, not their brainwashing—what do *you* think?" she cries.

"I—I don't know enough about it."

She grabs my hand and to my horror, right in front of Jeremiah, she pulls me down beside her and puts her hand on my heart. "Here. This is how you decide if something's right or not. This is how you know. No dogma, no politics, no crap. You just listen to your intuition and then you feel what's right!"

I stare at her, gaping, and then look up at Jeremiah, terrified that he will sense everything, will know how I held her just a few hours ago. But he kneels down on the other side of Padma and presses his hand to her heart. She shudders, curling away from him, but he holds her gaze and smiles.

"I can feel the most terrible *raptor* in the world in here," he says. Then he reaches into his pocket and pulls out a noose.

"No!" she cries. The color drains from her face. "No." She turns to me. "You said—you promised—"

"Hold her down while I put it on," Jeremiah says.

I grab her arms. I can't look her in the eye. I can't bear it.

She doesn't fight back. She doesn't scream. She freezes up. Jeremiah tightens the rope, checking it with scientific scrutiny. My whole body is clammy with sweat. My heart keeps screaming, *This is all wrong, I can't do it, oh God, I thought I would be able to go through with it, but I can't, I can't*—

"Good." Jeremiah takes the noose off and stands up. "It's ready."

He walks over to the door. "I'll leave you to educate her. We'll wait until the ten o'clock news to see if the government responds. In the meantime, try to save her soul, Jon. Remember, if she dies unsaved . . ."

He leaves us alone.

I turn to Padma. And then—she kisses me.

But that's a lie. And I cannot lie to you, God. Maybe I'm gripped by the fist of sheer lust. But it feels like more than that. I think it's the look of pain on her face. I want, simply, to make her feel better.

I kiss her. At first she doesn't respond. And then her lips move against mine and for a moment everything is forgotten, past, present, and place. Bliss leaps in my heart. I feel as though

I'm kissing this wonderful angel and I want to drink in her kisses like nectar. . . .

A little *zapor* climbs onto my shoulder and whispers: *You're kissing a terrorist. What are you doing, Jon?*

I break off and she gives me a look of such sweetness. . . . I don't understand, God—how can evil be wrapped in such beauty? Have you done this to test us? To torture us?

Then she says to me: "How can you believe all this Hebetheus shit, Jon? You seem so *nice*. So intelligent." I recoil, and she bites her lip and says more softly, "You used to be a Christian, right?"

"Yeah," I admit, "but only because my dad shoved it down my throat. I came to the Hebetheus out of choice, okay? I wanted to find the truth."

I tense up, waiting for her to argue, but instead she asks, "So how does your dad feel now that you're with the Hebetheus?"

I pause. "He left us to be with his mistress. And he doesn't care what I do."

"I'm sure he does," Padma insists, stroking my cheek. "Jon, I used to think my parents didn't care about me because they were always laying down rules—stay in, do your homework. Then one day we had this big fight and I realized they were doing it out of love. He might not be living with you now, but that doesn't mean he doesn't love you."

"No, no. It's not like that. Look, he can't even be bothered to visit me. We moved, and my mum told my dad he could come and see me on Sundays. So that first Sunday—" I break off, swallowing; I haven't even told Jeremiah this, but the sympathy in her eyes is so beguiling that I carry on. "The thing is, I told my mum I didn't want him to come, I told *myself* I didn't want the bastard to come, but deep down I couldn't help it. He is my dad, after all. And I sat there all day. I didn't go out on my bike, I wouldn't go out with my friends, I was just waiting, waiting for him. But he never showed. Later on my mum called him and he said he'd been at a conference and forgotten me."

"Well—I mean—did you ever see him again?"

"No. Every fucking Sunday I'd wait for him, but something always came up. He'd be busy with Harvest Festival. Or cleaning the church. Whatever. In the end—in the end . . . I kind of wondered if maybe my mum was lying to me, coming between us. I even started to hate her. So I decided to find out—I went to visit him."

"What happened?" she asks gently.

"I decided to surprise him and go to his house. I had all my essays in my backpack. I thought—I just wanted to show him I was *special*. He always used to say I was special—I just wanted to remind him. I'd worked really, really hard at school—got five A's for geography, math, physics, biology, and English. But when I rang the bell, his stupid piece of ass answered the door and said he wasn't around. She told me to go home. Then, when

I was leaving, I looked up at the curtains . . . and he was there, hiding."

"He's screwed up," Padma whispers. "But not because of you."

"But it *was* because of me," I cry, hearing anger in my voice. I fall silent, remembering how I felt the next day when I sat on the playground. I had bought fries from the canteen and a greasy nest sat perched in my lap. I wanted to eat to take away the pain in my stomach, but every time I looked down at them they looked like yellow worms. I kept trying to think of ways I might make him remember I was special. Maybe I could offer to build a new tree house, or maybe I could organize a new church group. And then I ran out of ideas. I stared into my chips, and a quiet voice said: *If your own dad doesn't want to see you, you can't be special, you can't be worth anything.*

That was the day I first approached Jeremiah.

"Jon." Padma interrupts my silent pain. "You *are* special. You don't need to belong to any religion to be special. Out of this whole group, you stand out the most."

"Really?" I turn to her, and she leans in and gives me a kiss of such deep reassurance that I pull her in tight and hold her close, kissing her cheek and hair, unable to let her go. "What about you?" I whisper into her ear. "How are your mum and dad?"

"Well, you know. I love them, and they love me. But sometimes they love me a little bit too much. They make me work hard and they're always saying, 'Have you done your homework?' They really want me to get into Cambridge and be a doctor. Everything was going so well until . . . God, they must be worried sick. I can't imagine what they're going through right now."

"Look," I say quickly, "I'm going into town tonight. Chris and I are going to get some medicine for Thomas, to help with his Soul Shift. Can I get you something—anything—to make you feel better? Some chocolate?"

"What—but—but—can't—can't I come? If you're going at night, I could sneak out, I could escape."

"Padma, I *can't*—"

She interrupts me with her lips. I kiss her back, electric with yearning, and suddenly I feel overtaken, I ache to feel her skin, and I slip my hands up her top, but she breaks off and whispers, "Please. You could find the key to the cuffs and hide it under a floorboard. Then when you go, I'll climb out of the window—"

"But someone will be on guard. They'll call Raymond and we won't get three feet before they catch us. I mean, there are five of them—don't you see?"

"We have to try! We're running out of time!"

The *we* makes me jump. What would Jeremiah say if he walked in right now? Then I look into her face. I'm the only one she feels she can trust. Her last hope.

"Look, we'll think up a plan," I whisper, hardly able to believe what I am saying. "I'll think it up tonight. I promise."

The Viper Within   173

"Okay." She looks so sad that I put my arm around her again. I kiss the smooth mahogany of her cheek, the edge of her lips, but then she shakes her head, pushing me away. I hear a creak outside in the hallway and I quickly recite: " 'Hebetheus is a true religion that will correct the mistakes of past religions. . . .' "

Padma fixes her gaze on the sunlight square that has formed a barred window on the boards.

Suddenly the door opens. I am too close to Padma. I stumble away.

"Jeremiah w-w-wants to see you," Chris says.

"Jeremiah w-w-wants to see you." Padma imitates his stutter perfectly. Chris flushes in outrage. For a moment I am taken aback. Then I realize what she is doing.

"Shut up, SNAKE, you stupid bitch!" I cry harshly. "Okay, Chris, I'll just be a minute. I'm on rule nine and I want her to understand it. If she can."

Chris leaves without closing the door properly.

"I have to go," I whisper, my eyes flitting from the door to Padma to the door.

"Please, when you're out, can you just call my mother?" she pleads. "Please let her know that I'm safe. Please. Please."

"I—" I am about to say *I can't* when Padma raises her eyes to mine. I see the pain deep in her pupils. What must it have been like during those lonely nights of terror, sitting here, wondering what we might do to her? I whisper yes, and then I sin again;

I lean in to take another kiss and this time she lets me and bliss burns through my body. Then there is a creak and I see Chris at the door and my heart turns upside down—*did he see?*—but his expression is neutral. I coldly inform Padma that next time I will expect her to be able to recite the ten rules of Hebetheus back to me, and she rolls her eyes very slightly, a tiny smile at her lips, before assuming a contrite expression.

Immediately, I flee to the Prayer Room.

It takes some time—too long—for the shame to come. Instead, I keep thinking about our kisses over and over and over. I know I ought to be panicking, but there's a halo of euphoria around my heart.

✝✝✝

You know, God, I am reminded of something that happened to me when I was thirteen. I was struggling with my Christian faith. People kept telling me about God; I'd grown up drawing sticky crayon pictures of Noah and Jesus at Sunday school and hearing my father expound a thousand sermons, but his words were just words. None of them ignited a spark, and I was worried there was something deeply wrong with me.

Then I woke up one morning and went into the garden. I wanted to check on the tree house I was building with Dad. It was dawn and the sky was a mass of clouds with moments of pure golden clarity. The light lit up green streaks in the grass stalks, glittered dew like diamonds on a spider's web, surfed off a bird's wing as it soared overhead. There was a stillness

n the light, a calmness in the trees, in the soft breath of the
wind, as though the landscape was alive, alert but at peace. I
thought: *This is what Eden must have been like.* My heart filled up
with beauty until I was drunk on it. Just watching the light
travel up a leaf or shimmer on a glossy line of ants. I thought:
This is God.

The feeling lingered with me all day. That evening, when I
sang hymns in church, my new faith breathed life into the words
and they flew from my lips like birds that circled up to the heavens. Later, I tried to explain it to Dad, but he frowned and said,
"Don't go turning into a pantheist, Jon." And I realized I had
been mistaken. I pushed it aside and forgot it.

Today, when Padma kissed me, that feeling came back.

A taste of paradise.

✝✝✝

I force myself to read the third part of the Book of Hebetheus
again. Warning phrases war with my euphoria. *Women are snakes;
beware of them, beware.* Shame comes; doubts enter my mind and
my heart. What if she's deceiving me with her pleas about her
mother? What if her kisses carry poison? And the most crucial
thing I don't understand, God—why is it that Padma can make
me feel like that and Jeremiah can't?

Oh God, I feel as though she has wriggled into my heart and
is still writhing there. Please destroy her. Please save me. Please
keep me pure and forgive me.

10:00 P.M.

I give Chris a sidelong glance. Snow is falling: entire fields whiten before us as fresh flakes begin to billow from the night sky. The cold bites into my naked scalp with vicious teeth. Beside me, Chris squints at the little map Raymond drew when he stole into town earlier this afternoon. Raymond said it was straightforward—just follow the road down for two miles and then when it meets the big main road follow the signs to the town center.

The future feels jagged with what-ifs: traps, pitholes, and wrong turns we might take. What if CCTV picks us out? What if someone recognizes us and calls the police? Every so often I look back and peer at the cottage, watching it grow smaller and smaller until it is just a smudge on the horizon. And in the meantime the big wide world gets closer and closer.

I start to worry about Padma's request when suddenly something wet splats across my head. I jump and turn on Chris, who grins wickedly.

"Ow, you bastard, that really hurts!" I reach down and gather a ball and Chris yells and runs on. As I aim to throw, we share a nervous look: *Should we be doing this?* But we have to do this. I toss the ball at him and cheer as it explodes against his sweater.

From then on, all the way into town, we fight. We pass

houses, woods, yelling and screaming with hysterical laughter, and for half an hour it's as though we're just two guys walking home from school together, having fun.

Then we hit the first main road into town. That sobers us up. Even though all the shops are shut, there are still a few people about—mostly our age. I quickly pull my hood up over my face. It feels as though we've been locked away for months and months. The world seems a Technicolor dazzle; we pass shops, drunkenly feasting on commerce; horns and screeching tires scrape our senses.

And every so often we see someone.

An elderly tramp, his face graffitied with life's sorrows, trudging past with a bottle of gin. A girl with a bouncy walk and a nose ring and red hair like a fox. I stare at her and she bugs her eyes at me as if to say, *What are you staring at?* I quickly look away. I feel strange. Something is wrong, something is different.

For the last few months I have viewed people as though I'm behind a glass cocoon, pitying their doomed and silly souls. But now I feel almost . . . a sense of kinship with them. Like an echo of the feeling I had earlier today when Padma kissed me. Has my lust corroded my spirituality? Is she turning me into one of them?

"When w-we get to B-Boots, c-c-can you be the one to smash the glass?" Chris stammers as we pass a newsagent's.

"I—" I stop, wheel back to the billboard outside. "Hang on,

that's us!" I point at the headline: "Hostage Deadlock with Teen Boys."

Across the road, a newspaper is lying on a bench. I flip through the pages frantically.

"W-w-we should go, w-w-we don't have m-much t-time," Chris says.

Celebs . . . drugs . . . footballers . . . where are we? I feel a strange twist of disappointment. So nobody's noticed us; nobody cares. A risk of jail—all for nothing.

I turn to the front page of the *Mirror.*

"We Will Kill Her," another headline screams. Underneath there is a photo of Martyn, a grainy black-and-white smear cut from the video.

"Jesus!" Chris cries.

I scan the article, phrases leaping out: "*None of us can understand what these boys are doing. . . . We all know Padma Laxsmi is a kind and innocent girl. . . . These teenagers are deluded and dangerous. . . . Padma Laxsmi is the victim of an insane mistake. . . .*" It feels as though I'm reading about other people, a version of our story where everything has been simplified, like a movie: six evil boys and one victim.

"Here—listen to this!" Chris jabs the page. "It s-s-says they are tr-trying to tr-track us d-down from o-our computer and e-mailed v-video threats but they c-can't b-because one of us must be a c-computer genius! I'm f-famous."

"We're going to end up in jail," I say, my voice breaking.

Then I look at Chris quickly. "Only we won't, our God will save us. Let's just go to Boots."

We slip down a dingy side alley to the back of the drugstore. Chris passes me the crowbar. We're doomed anyway, so what will a robbery charge matter? I wield the crowbar and crash it against the window. The smash shocks me out of my numb state. As glass tumbles to the floor, my heart yells: *What are you doing?* But there's no going back now. I watch Chris pry open the doors. His face looks vivid with adrenaline; as he yanks them open, he whoops with pride.

Earlier today, Raymond came in and cut the wires to the alarms. But I don't trust him; I steel myself, waiting for their blare.

A safe cocoon of silence. Chris and I stumble in. A shelf of chocolate bars sings to us. All we've eaten in the last few days is toast, or beans on toast, or beans. We grab handfuls of them—Twix, Mars, Flake, Caramac, Topic, Lion Bar, Twirl—shoving them into our pockets. Chris dives for a six-pack of Coke.

"The pharmacy—it's over there."

The pharmacy is cool and gray, a toy shop of colored boxes with fancy Latin names. Chris starts panicking, pulling out cough cures and flu elixirs, tossing them onto the floor. A bottle of cough syrup spins over and breaks, emitting a sickly cherry smell.

"Chris, calm down! Just try—"

"H-here is it!"

"You've got it?" I run over to him. "No—that's not it, Chris, you're panicking."

"I don't know where the h-hell it is!"

"Look, this medicine is serious stuff. They'll have locked it up at the back, okay? Let's try these cabinets."

Minutes squeal past. My eyes burn; it gets to the point where I am reading a label without reading it.

"We could just take some Valium!" I cry, picking out a box. "Just give him a double dose."

"I-I've g-got it—"

"Yes. *Yes.* Come on! We have to get out of here!"

As we leave, Chris knocks against the door and suddenly an alarm screams.

"I knew Raymond would—"

"J-just *go!*"

We slip through the alley and dash back onto the main street. A man walks by wearing a neat gray overcoat and an eccentric black hat, the sort you see in old gangster movies. He spots us and roars: "STOP!"

Chris tugs my sleeve, wheeling behind me. I grab him and we run.

"I'LL CALL THE POLICE!"

Shops and benches streak by. My hood flies back off my face with a blast of freezing air. The ground is thick with snow, my sneakers skid all over the place. I look back; he is gaining on us. His hat flies off and he lets out a bellow, then leaves it behind. I notice his head is entirely bald; this suddenly, irrationally, strikes me as hysterical, and laughter bubbles in my torn lungs. Then Chris stumbles, half falling in the wet snow. I yank him up and yell, "COME ON!"

Oh God, please don't let him catch us, Oh God, please don't let him catch us, I cry inwardly to the rhythm of my thudding feet. My legs tremble as though the muscles will snap; my lungs swirl with acid. We hit a main road, looking left right left right—which way?—and then Chris lets out a yell and I turn and suddenly the man is right behind us and he reaches out, yanking my hood, and I cry out and he slips forward into the snow. Chris and I stare down at him. Then we run.

Across the road, horns blare and tires screech to a halt. We run down one suburban street, then another. Chris is wheezing desperately. We plow through yards, tumble down a side path, and crouch behind a fat green recycling bin. Chris pulls out his inhaler and gulps it in, shaking violently.

We wait another ten minutes. We share a Twix, cramming the chocolate into our mouths, gorging ourselves on the comfort of sugar. Chris smudges chocolate on his cheek and I want to tell him to dab it off but I don't.

I peer out from behind the bin. No sign of the man.

We get up and slink to the edge of the yard, creep from car to car, winding back to the main road, where we pause behind an illegally parked Fiat.

"We're l-lost," Chris stammers.

"We're not—we just head down the main road and then it goes back into the country, right? Look, we'll get up on the count of three and then we RUN, okay?"

We streak down the main road, looking back every three seconds. Still no sign of him. The road thins and we stop outside a pub while Chris sucks on his inhaler. A drunk woman comes stumbling out and I duck my head.

"W-w-we sh-should go through the w-w-woods," Chris says. "I kn-know the w-way."

"Are you sure?"

"Y-yeah. I w-w-went w-walking th-there with Martyn y-yesterday—we j-just w-went for a w-walk."

"Okay—" I break off, for a few feet down the road is a phone box. An old-fashioned red one, quaintly preserved.

We walk on, right by it, and I tell myself I'll just explain to Padma about the man who chased us and how there wasn't time to stop—

And then I remember the feel of her lips against mine.

"I have to make a call."

"What?" Chris cries.

"Just wait here. I'll be one minute."

Chris stutters some more, but I ignore him and run.

Earlier, when I was on a guard shift, Padma breathed on her window and wrote her mother's number in the mist. I memorized it, too nervous to write it down. I pick up the receiver, fumble in my pockets, slot in thirty pence. Chris bangs his fists against the glass, shaking his head in astonishment. I wave, mouthing, "Wait!" *0 . . . 2 . . . 8 . . . 6 . . . what was it—yes, 44, my mum's age . . . 7 . . . 71, 7 for the seventh of May, the date I first spoke to Jeremiah, then 1 . . . and was it 389 or 839? Oh God, what was it . . . ?* Chris walks off, turns, throws up his hands. *Wait, wait. It's 839.* It rings. *What am I going to say?* I push the door ajar with my foot and cry, "Wait!" But Chris keeps going. Finally, someone picks up.

"Padma?" I cry without thinking.

"Padma? Padma's not here. . . . She's . . ."

I know instantly that for days and nights to come I will lie awake and retaste the raw anguish of that voice: a voice more dead than alive.

"She's alive—she's okay, she's okay."

"Oh my God—oh my God—you've got my Padma, are you the boy who has my Padma—"

The stench of her anger is so intense that I cut in pleading: "Please don't worry, she's alive, I'm going to get her back to you, I promise—"

She bursts into tears.

"Oh my baby, oh my poor baby . . ."

I find I am crying too. I smear my face with my fingers and I can't see where Chris is now and I don't care.

"I'm so sorry, I'm sorry," I sob, "I'm going to bring her back to you."

"My little girl, oh please tell me you haven't hurt my little girl—"

Beeps. I shove my hand in my pocket: no change left.

I lurch out of the phone box and stumble down the road as though drunk.

"Oi, you!"

A cool car swerves past, boys and girls waving and whistling out of windows, bass line pumping—the night is still young. I stare at them as my tears dry on my face. I could be in a car like that right now. I'll probably never get to ride in a car like that again.

The car passes, the music fades.

Chris appears. He stops a wary two feet away.

"So." His anger steamrolls through his stutter. "You finished calling the police?"

"Chris, I'm your Brother. I was calling my mum, okay? I didn't tell her anything. I just wanted to hear her voice." It might be a lie, but my pain is palpable. Chris falls silent.

"Oh," he says quietly. "Okay." Then: "I won't tell Jeremiah. I think we sh-sh-shouldn't tell him about the m-man either."

"No, we shouldn't. Thanks," I say gruffly, and we gaze at each other as Brothers.

11:00 P.M.

We have five different symbols for God in the Religion of Hebetheus. The highest symbol is the circle. The circle, Jeremiah told me, is an image of pure, simple, divine perfection. No kinks in its smooth infinite curving. And in its center the empty space that God fills. Jeremiah, our Great Leader, is a human circle, allowing the messages of God to fill his space. *So God's message to Jeremiah can't be wrong, she must be a—*

I push the thought away, focusing hard. It is another hour until we will reach home. We walk in silence. The air becomes more and more pure, until finally the cold reaches a climax and bursts into another dizzy flurry of snowflakes. My eyes water and my nose stings with cold.

Padma Laxsmi has been kidnapped by a gang of ruthless criminals . . . are you the boy who's taken my daughter? . . . what have you done to her? I keep trying to push it down; I keep trying to squeeze it tight into the corner of my mind; my brow sweats, and inwardly I recite Hebethean chants frantically, but it bursts through them, finally: the truth. Padma Laxsmi isn't SNAKE. She's not a terrorist.

We've made a mistake.

We've taken a girl and we've locked her in a cellar and we've starved her and put cuffs on her and baited her and bullied her. And she's innocent.

We have become what we hate.

How could there be kinks in Jeremiah's circle? He can't be racist, like Padma said, and he can't be jealous of her high marks, and he can't be doing this for spite or for attention, so how, how can he have got it wrong?

I think of my father, the way he stood in the pulpit on

Sundays, endlessly lecturing. I would sit beneath him, drinking in his words. When I knelt down for prayers, the God in my mind was an older, more wizened version of my father. But my father is a stupid, pathetic fraud who pretended he was perfect when he was living a lie and fucking a whore. Jeremiah isn't a fraud, he can't be a fraud, he's divine. But—

Maybe God is testing him. Or . . .

Maybe God saw something Padma might do *in the future*. Maybe we still stopped the *possibility* of something, a kind of pre-emptive strike? And we've prevented that and actually saved her.

I mean—wouldn't it have been better if someone had killed the snake before it tempted Eve?

What will the headlines be the day they catch us? We'll pass from boys into myths. We'll stand in court and everything we say will be cut and pasted, stretched and shaped into legends. They'll never see I was a real person. They'll never understand that it was all more complex than just six youths who wanted to torment a girl, that there was good in the Hebetheus, that we meant well. We'll be sent to jail, lost in metal cages, when we should have been drinking beer and meeting girls and discovering sex and all that forbidden adult stuff that sounds so scary but exciting. We'll have to change our names, like those notorious teen killers who bludgeoned a baby to death a few years back. I remember the day Dad was driving me to school and it was on the radio. I remember the look of disgust on his face and how he shook his head. I could never have imagined then, never, that I might end up in the same boat.

"Hey!" Chris suddenly points. A horse appears, white as the falling snow. He neighs, snorting mist, before galloping off across the fields in lightning beauty.

I want to climb onto his back and be carried away forever.

"Let's go through the woods," Chris says. "I know a shortcut."

I follow him numbly. The woods are white with silence, stretching out like the land of Narnia before Aslan comes to redeem it. At one point Chris stops to scorch the bark of a tree with his lighter, telling me he's branding a Hebethean symbol. As the flame highlights his face, I wonder: *Doesn't he ever doubt? Hasn't it hit him?* But the Brotherhood *is* good. Even if we made a mistake, we are good.

Tonight my Brother and I will return to the cottage and the deadline will be up. My Initiation will begin and I will be asked to kill her.

I watch Chris carry on scorching tree after tree and I feel like tearing the flame from him and holding it against my own skin.

MIDNIGHT

"Jon," Jeremiah says, "I think you should narrate the video tonight."

"We're not—we're not going to kill her?" I stammer.

"Why—d'you think we should?"

"No—I—*no*—"

"Chris has given Thomas his medicine. Thomas is not well yet, though he'll join us. Tonight I would like to see the Brotherhood united as a group. I feel we owe the public one last chance. This is about their redemption as much as hers. We must be patient. So, Jon—your turn has come."

I see Martyn's face crumple with disappointment; he has been looking for ways to please Jeremiah all day. I look at Raymond, who is playing about with his steel bar, his favorite toy of late. I think of being in the phone box, Padma's mother pleading with me. Suddenly a deep weariness rises inside, filling me with black, choking smoke. I want to empty the Prayer Room and curl into a ball and sink into a bath of deep prayers. I want to wallow there and offer up my twisted heart to God and beg him to untangle it. But instead I have to stand here while a needle of a headache begins to prick my temples.

"I'm feeling a bit tired," I say, dropping my eyes.

"But not too tired to begin the first part of your Initiation, surely?" Jeremiah says in a very calm voice. "To narrate this video is an honor."

Five pairs of eyes home in on me, watchful.

"Yeah, of course," I say. "Sure. I'll do the video. It's an honor. Yeah."

I remember how desperate I once was to speak before the camera. To stand there and feel God's words flow through me.

I once imagined that when I looked into the lens, I would see a minute world, a blur of faces and minds my words might seep into. Now all I can see is the glint of glass and a big blue eye behind it. It feels as though I am standing in front of a loaded gun.

"We of the Hebethean religion are so compassionate that we are giving you one last chance." My voice sounds flat, and I try to buoy it up. "We will not kill our hostage tonight." I wonder what Padma's mother is doing now. Is she weeping? Is Padma's father holding her? "The Hebethean religion believes in peace . . ." And . . . what? What do I say next? I've forgotten the creed; I can't believe I've forgotten the creed.

The room has gone very quiet. I can hear the faint tap of Raymond's iron bar against his steel toe cap.

It's like I'm in an exam with a white sheet before me and a blank mind and everyone around is scribbling and oh God— thank God—the words rush back into place and I recite them by heart. My voice seems to detach from my doubts and take on a survival instinct of its own.

". . . in peace for all mankind and Soul Shifts for every soul. If our demands are not met by ten A.M. tomorrow, I will kill Padma Laxsmi." I hold up the coil of rope for the camera to zoom in on.

I think of my mother's face when she switches on the news tomorrow and sees me. I think of Mr. Abdilla. Of Padma's mother.

"That was good," Jeremiah says warmly, clapping me on the back. "But you stumbled a bit—it's natural to be nervous in front of the camera. Try again."

"Yeah, I guess I am a bit camera-shy," I say, feeling strange again, as though I am an actor and I have to keep remembering to slip into my part. "Cool. I'll do it better this time."

The headache begins to spread, its needle prick expanding and blurring into a temple thump. One of the candles flickers out, and dark shadows seem to gather in the corners as though listening to me too. I think unsteadily: *Is God really here, sitting in this room, listening? What does he really think of this?*

"We of the Hebethean religion are so compassionate that we are giving you one last chance."

My voice is stronger this time.

"We will not kill Padma Laxsmi tonight."

As I stare into the lens, it seems to spin like a white bird flying in a circle. I can see Padma's mother. Her fingers claw her cheeks as she breaks into a scream and she won't stop screaming and her screams knife my ears and I put my hands over my ears, folding in.

"Jon, are—are y-you okay?" I look up and see Chris. "It's o-o-okay, it was just a s-s-siren." He laughs nervously. "It w-wasn't for us."

"Don't worry, if they do come, we'll deal with them," says Raymond, caressing his iron bar.

"Sorry—I just—I panicked—"

"The stone circle outside will protect us; God will protect us," Jeremiah says coldly. "Have more faith, Jon. Try again."

It's all right, I keep telling myself, *just do it again. How many goes did Chris take? At least eight.* But a paranoid fear stings me. As Chris sets up the camera again, I feel my cheeks burn and my knees start to tremble and I'm certain they can see inside me, see every atom of fear and doubt. *Oh God, why did I make that stupid call, why did I do it? My faith is too fragile, I've broken its shell, oh why didn't I trust Jeremiah and listen to him?*

I glance beyond the camera. Through a crack in the curtains, I can see the dark silhouettes of falling snow. An urge grips me. *Run.* Push past them, head down the hallway, burst out of the door, and just run, pound down the road, into the open sky, into the snow. I half turn, then slap myself and stand up straight. *Just do it, just get through this, just get it over and done with. You have to do this, Jon. If you don't, what will they do to you? To her?*

"We of the Hebethean religion are so compassionate that we are giving you one last chance," I say. "We will not kill Padma tonight. . . ."

"Good one," Raymond says, giving me a thumbs-up, and I feel close to tears with relief.

"Nice," says Martyn, nodding, giving Jeremiah a cautious glance. "What do you think, Jeremiah?"

Jeremiah stares at me with a strange expression in his eyes.

"I think Jon should do it again," he says.

"What was . . . Okay," I say, shrugging. "It's cool. I'll do it again."

I speak more quickly this time, the words tumbling out, and as everyone stares at me they seem to come closer and closer until they are gathered about me in a circle, their breaths stifling my breaths, their eyes boring into mine.

Then it's over. Raymond says it's perhaps not as good as the time before, but it's still good.

"I think he should do it again," Jeremiah says.

I look at him; he looks back.

"Sure," I say very lightly. "I'll do it again."

I do it again. Every word feels as though it limps, staggering, from my heart and I have to push it up my throat with both hands. When I'm done, Jeremiah smiles and says to do it again. The room fades and it's as though I am hanging in white space, just me and Jeremiah, my voice floating above me, and he asks me to recite it again. I do it again and this time the space cracks and the room becomes too real and there is sweat sliding long fingers down my back and I feel as though I'm holding a table high above my head and my hands are shaking and I can't last much longer before my spine bends and breaks and I snap—and then Jeremiah says, "Enough," and turns away.

✠✠✠

I walk out into the hallway. Chris calls me, and I wave my hand: *Coming*. In the bathroom, I lock the door and break down. I collapse onto the floor, my head against the tile, as the sobs batter me like fists, punching my stomach until it is sore, wrenching wetness out of my ribs, bruising my eyes. I try to keep as quiet as possible.

I keep thinking they have stopped, but every time I try to rise they deal another blow. Finally, I stagger weakly to my feet. I flush the toilet just in case anyone is outside listening.

I turn to the sink, spin the taps. I look at my broken face and a curious voice whispers: *Who are you?* Then I cup the water and cleanse my face, over and over, until it is raw.

I find myself reaching down beneath the sink and yanking out the Bible. My hands are shaking violently; I flick through pages so quickly the paper tears. I read a passage from Proverbs, a parable, something from Revelation. I want it to fill me up and take away the pain, to tell me Hebetheus is wrong and this is right, but I only feel more and more desperate and empty and I find myself ripping out pages and tearing them into shreds. I open the window and throw the Bible out into the darkness and heave in breaths.

Back with my Brothers, I feel as though I am barely capable of speech. But I don't have to talk to anyone, for Jeremiah orders that I won't be getting any sleep tonight; Martyn has been released from his watch and I will have to guard the house for the next hour.

1:00 A.M.

I guess you're laughing at me now, aren't you, Dad? It's 1:00 A.M. and I'm sitting out here with Raymond in the freezing cold on watch, shivering, feeling sick inside, knowing this is all rot, all a waste of time—oh, I bet you're laughing at me now.

On impulse, I tell Raymond that I need the bathroom.

The others are all asleep. Padma must be asleep too, for when I pause outside her room the door is framed with a dark slit.

The key sits in the door. I twist it slowly, open the door very gently, step into the room, and close it behind me. It's so dark that her body is just a hump on the floor, like a piece of driftwood that's washed up from the sea. I can hear her snoring gently. The clouds in the night sky part and a shaft of moonlight washes over her face, lies in pools around her plump mouth. I sit down in the shadows and red thoughts slither into my mind, burning hot inside. I see myself crawling across the floor and lying down against her. Waking her gently with a soft, moist kiss. Tasting her sleep in her kiss. Her desire. A look of sweet surprise on her face. In my fantasy, her cuffs fall away by magic. She unbuttons my shirt and kisses my chest. I tear off her top and run my tongue over her nipples. I've never even touched a breast before. The thought electrifies me, hot charges gushing through my body.

And then—

A knife of shame slams down, cutting my snake desire in two. To lust is a sin. She is a female viper, luring me, tricking me. I remember those wicked words she spoke earlier: *How can you believe all this Hebetheus shit, Jon? You seem so nice. So intelligent.*

She can't be right, she can't be right. Can she?

I look up at the square of sky framed by the window. To imagine that the God of Hebetheus is only a product of my imagination, to accept that he is not a force singing through all things in this world, pushing the earth round, arranging the swing of the sun and the moon, suddenly knocks the air out of my chest. I feel cold inside; my heart goose-bumps in misery. How pale the stars look. And what is beyond them? Darkness, and more dying stars, and planets whose atmospheres are too cruel for life to exist. I stare out at the faintest twinkle of the distant town lights, where people are, this very minute, committing crimes and sins. The big bad world that I must now face without armor, without a shield.

My fist clenches in my lap.

"Jon?" she whispers. She is awake. Suddenly. "Jon? Did you call—"

I get up quickly and run out, locking the door behind me. I dash down the hallway and sit outside quietly beside Raymond while my heart freezes, by degrees, into a cold hard ball.

Guard duty ends; Martyn takes over. Inside, I lie awake for

hours, voices yelling in my mind, until finally a nightmare grabs me and pulls me under.

I am lying out on the front lawn, the snow seeping into my naked head. I am staring up at the stars and I am calling out to God. I am yelling at him, screaming at him, "Are you there, God, are you there?" I can hear my voice echoing around the stars, through the empty heavens and back to me. Echoing through emptiness. But I keep yelling, I keep screaming and—

I wake up hearing myself scream and I'm aware of a voice beside me, telling me, "It's all right, Jon, it's all right," and for a moment I think I am back home with my mum.

I lie there, shaking, and Jeremiah keeps telling me that it's all right, that I'm all right, to go back to sleep. He lies beside me, not touching but close enough so that the warmth of his body seeps into mine.

Every so often I wake up in the night and I am aware of that warmth close to me, a balm that soothes me and sends me back to sleep. . . .

DAY FIVE
8:00 A.M.

The next morning I wake up feeling tired. I'm aware of Chris and Martyn whispering across a mattress; I turn away to face the wall. If I was in the real world right now, I'd be getting up, getting dressed, Mum shouting at me to hurry up as she needs the bathroom, then on the bus to school and geography with Mr. Tims, who has a twitchy eye that always makes me laugh. I miss it all, even Mum's shouting.

This morning my heart is sad with acceptance. I don't believe in the God of Hebetheus anymore.

This isn't the first time I've felt like this. That's the worst thing: the repetition of it all. I remember what I went through when my belief in Christianity came crashing down: the sleepless nights, the tastelessness of food, the brick I threw through the church's stained-glass window, only luckily Dad didn't find out and blamed it on vandals. I thought I'd found the ultimate truth. Now I feel that I'm back to the beginning. I still sense there's someone, something, some divine force out there that we call God, but will I ever be able to know it?

In the hallway, Jeremiah's cheerful voice rings out, telling Thomas he looks much better, instructing him to prepare breakfast before prayers.

I decide I'll tell the others I'm ill. Yes, I'm just going to lie here and let the days disappear into nights, let my Brothers carry on with their crazy stupid stuff, let the world spin on with its wars and loves and highs and lows, let time go singing by. . . .

But then the godsend comes.

9:00 A.M.

Thomas calls out that we are on the news.

Chris jumps up, yelling, "Come on, Jon!" Martyn grabs my feet and pulls me across the mattresses, sleeping bags carpet-burning my back.

"Okay, okay, I'm coming," I mutter. Even speaking seems to take too much effort; my vocal cords feel as though they have been slashed.

Martyn and Chris exchange glances. Then Martyn turns to me and asks if I'm happy.

"Of course," I quickly reply. Then I look into his eyes and see an unexpected compassion. For a moment all my fears nearly come flooding out. I wonder: *Does he ever doubt?*

But no. I can't imagine Martyn or Chris ever do. Because to doubt, to take away everything you believe in, to leave your mind without a structure, is too unbearable. If only I could wind back the clock, if only I could walk back from experience to innocence again.

As I walk into the kitchen, I look round at my Brothers and they seem like strangers. Long before I joined the Hebetheus, I felt as though I never fit in anywhere. Even the Christian church felt slightly false, as though I was wearing my father's second-hand persona. At school I wasn't cool enough for the hard-asses or sad enough for the losers. The Hebetheus gave me an armor, a texture, a color that made me more than plain old Jon. Now, once again, I'm an outsider.

Mr. Abdilla appears on the screen. His face looks haggard.

"Boys—Jon, Jeremiah, Thomas, Martyn, Chris, Raymond—I have some good news for you.

"First, thank you for trying to make contact. We appreciate this and we would like to hear from you again."

Is he talking about the phone call I made?

Fear exhales an icy blast across the back of my neck. I look at Chris but he remains silent. I realize with shaky relief that maybe Abdilla's just referring to the video.

"I am pleased to announce that the police have taken your allegations about Padma Laxsmi very seriously and have investigated your claims. They have not found any evidence that she is a terrorist. Her home and locker have been thoroughly searched and we have not discovered any bomb-making equipment. Perhaps it is time for you to pass Padma over to the police, however, and let them question her fully at a police station. You also made some very compelling and interesting points about changing the laws and I am glad to report that last night I spoke directly with the prime minister himself and he has assured me that they are thinking very carefully about holding Commons debate regarding the length of detention of terrorists this very week.

"May I suggest, now that your demands are being taken seriously, that we could arrange to meet? If you telephone the following number, I can arrange for a safe place so that we can all meet to talk together. I can assure you that you will not be in any trouble and that we are merely anxious for your safe return and to see that Padma Laxsmi is returned to her family."

As he reels off the number, Thomas grabs a pen and hastily writes it down.

Oh thank God, oh thank God, we can leave now and Padma will be safe. I open my mouth. A squeak comes out. Chris turns and laughs. His face is such a bright red all his freckles look neon. Martyn does a monkey jump and punches me on the shoulder and I tussle with him and Raymond cheers and joins in.

"Wait!" Jeremiah orders. "It's a hoax."

"WHAT!" Martyn screams. "You heard him! Mr. Abdilla SAID they are taking our demands SERIOUSLY!"

"It c-can't be a h-hoax," Chris whispers, his freckles dancing back onto his face as the color drains away.

"It's a hoax," Jeremiah says dully, turning back to the TV and flicking it off.

"Oh yeah, right, come on, how would you know?" Martyn yells. "You just want to stay out here forever telling us what to do!"

Martyn walks up to him, eyes blazing. Jeremiah stays very cool, his fingers slack by his side, but his eyes become slits.

"He's right," Thomas says suddenly. "Jeremiah's right. If they were really *seriously* debating the terrorist act, we'd hear it on the news. The prime minister himself would be commenting on the new Commons debate or saying he felt the law needed to be changed. Since when does Mr. Abdilla make any laws? He's just been given a script to lure us in so we all can be arrested."

"Oh, what would you know anyway!" Martyn cries. "You're on crazy pills!"

There is a stinging silence. Thomas flushes red. Chris bites his lips as though forcing back a terrible laugh; Martyn looks at him and giggles as if they are sharing a private joke.

Jeremiah looks uncharacteristically angry. His eyes flash and his fists clench.

"And what about Mr. Abdilla saying we've made *contact*? What's that? Was that you, Martyn?"

"How the hell could I have contacted him? Jesus, Jeremiah. If Mr. Abdilla's just winding us up, then he's an asshole and we should stop standing around talking about it and just do it now. Well? Are we going to release SNAKE's soul or not? Let's show these fuckers that we are for real."

Jeremiah stares at him coldly and then says, "You and Chris will now go to the Prayer Room and paint the Redemption Symbol on the floor. Thomas, guard the house. Raymond, please prepare a final meal for our hostage. And Jon, I suggest you pray. You need to purify yourself to prepare for your Initiation."

10:00 A.M.

My heart wakes up.

I'm going to help her, Dad. I'm going to help her. I know my future's over, I know I'm going to end up in jail, I've ruined my life, but I will do this to save hers. I will do something good, one last good thing before they catch us. Oh God, help me, I'm going to save her.

The pressure racing through my mind squeezes out sharp, precise thoughts.

What can I do?

I can't dial 999. It would take me an hour to reach the phone box.

Jeremiah took my knife when he performed my Initiation ceremony.

There are knives in the kitchen, but Raymond is in there, preparing her last meal.

I could— *Yes!* An idea!

And even though I don't know anymore whom I'm praying to, I beg whatever God is out there to help me make this work.

11:00 A.M.

One hitch: Thomas is outside on guard duty.

"Can you take over?" he asks as I stroll outside. "I need to use the bathroom."

Perfect.

The moment he's gone, I bend down, pretending to tie my shoelace. It seems so long ago that we made the stone circle. I pick up a stone and slide it into my pocket. Then another. Then another. They jostle clunkily and a faint wet patch seeps through my pants. *Oh God, is this a stupid idea?* David may have slain a giant with a single stone, but who knows what bits of the Bible are true and what bits are stories to inspire us, not meant to be taken literally?

The front door opens. I jump up guiltily.

Martyn and Chris stride out, with Padma sandwiched between them. My eyes flit to hers. We flash a Morse code of irises. *Padma, I will save you, I will, I will.* I look away quickly, checking their faces, seeing if they saw our glance, translated it. Martyn is blank, preoccupied. But Chris has noticed . . . something? A tiny smile trembles on his lips, then passes away. Or is it just my imagination?

I stuff my hands in my pockets, frowning hard, hiding my inner panic.

"Where are you going?"

"Jeremiah told us to take SNAKE for a walk," says Martyn. There is a smudge of black paint on his face from painting the Prayer Room. "Before she—you know."

Martyn had better not lay one finger on her, or I'll kill him.

"That's a bit risky, isn't it?"

"Jeremiah said w-we should just take her round the house. We're k-keeping an eye on h-her," Chris says.

"Jeremiah is so compassionate," Padma interjects.

A ghost of a smile flickers on my lips and Chris gives me another strange look.

"Well, okay, I'll go inside. I'm going to be busy praying for a bit," I say.

I hurry down the hallway. Raymond is in the kitchen, preparing Padma's final lunch: burnt toast. I can hear Jeremiah in the bathroom. Then Raymond looks up at me through the doorway. I give him an innocent grin and slip into the Hostage Room.

The corner where Padma normally sits looks strangely bare without the glint of her cuffs and her brave smile above them. A plate sits, from her breakfast this morning, with a half-eaten apple, now browning at the edges. I take a bite, my lips brushing apple skin her lips have brushed, and it feels like a secret kiss.

Now for the catapult. Chris brought it along as his weapon. I go to the bedroom, figuring he must have hidden it under his pillow. And then another idea hits me. *Come on, Jon, hurry up, come on.* I hurry to the Prayer Room. If I use the window to escape—they wouldn't expect that! I'll fire stones at them, shock them, grab my few precious seconds, take Padma out through the window. But can that work? Oh God, if only I had more time—

I open the Prayer Room door and stop short.

Martyn and Chris have painted an image onto the floor: a

cartoon of Jeremiah looking like a menacing angel, taunting a disciple, with the caption: "The joys of a Soul Shift."

"Jon!" Jeremiah bursts into the room.

I move in front of him, desperate to hide the cartoon from him. But he pushes me aside, gaping in shock.

"Where is she?" Jeremiah demands. He breaks off and does another double take at the cartoon, drinking it in. He spins back to me. "Where IS she? For fuck's sake, SPEAK! Where's SNAKE?" He comes up to me and shakes me. *DID YOU LET HER GO?*

The force of his anger blazes through me, leaving me stunned.

"Where is she?"

"She's with Chris and Martyn, just like you told them. A nice little walk to cheer her up before you—you make me—make me—"

"*WHAT!* They took her? And you let them? What direction were they going?"

"I don't remember—"

"Oh God—can't you see? For days Martyn's been brewing something, and now *this*—"

"What—what are you saying? That they've taken Padma?"

"Yes, you idiot. Yes." Jeremiah throws up his arms. "They've taken SNAKE. They've stolen our hostage!"

2:00 P.M.

I forget my anger for Jeremiah; I forget the cartoon; I forget my dreaded Initiation. My desire to bring her back blots them all out.

Jeremiah pulls me into the kitchen. He tips over the table, sending five plates of beans on toast crashing to the floor in a scatter of china and slop of sauce.

"Hey!" Raymond shouts.

"They've run off with our prize!" Jeremiah screams. "They went for a walk—"

"Oh shit—I gave them permission. I thought they were just—"

"Get the weapons! Get them all! Now!"

Raymond runs out, shoving past me. I grab hold of the door frame and steady myself. Jeremiah is breathing in and out rapidly, smoothing his fingers over his chin, blinking hard.

"What do they want with her? What will they do with her?" I cry. "Maybe they just want to save her from being killed. Maybe they've just taken her to the police."

"No." Jeremiah looks at me blankly. "They won't do that. If they go to the police, they get themselves arrested. No. It's Martyn."

"But why would he—"

"Because he's a son of a bitch, that's why! He's jealous of me

and he wants to bring me down, and if he thinks he can get away
with it, well, then he can't—"

He breaks off as Raymond enters with Thomas by his side.
Their arms are groaning with the weight of the long plant boxes
from the bathroom, the ones that hold the seeds for spiritual
plants. They dump them on the table. Thomas looks quizzical
but Raymond flings up handfuls of earth, drawing out a plastic
grocery bag. He rips it away to reveal . . . a rifle. From the next
box, he unearths two guns wrapped in cellophane. He hands
one to Jeremiah, one to me.

I stare down at it.

"This is a toy, right?"

"What we do is this," says Jeremiah urgently. "We spread
out. We'll go down the road—no, wait." His eyes narrow. "They
won't have gone down the road, not to where people are. . . ."
He snaps his fingers. "They'll have gone to the forest. Right,
now we go, go, go—"

"But—the spiritual seeds . . ." The gun is still lying flat in
my palm in a spray of dirt. I flex my hand wide open, balancing
the gun there, afraid to curl my fingers around it. I look at
Thomas, who stares back at me with dazed eyes.

"Give me the gun back," Raymond cries. He nods at Jeremiah. "I told you he wouldn't be able to handle it."

"We were meant to stand for peace!" I cry. "What the hell
are we doing with guns?"

"Listen," Jeremiah hisses, "we brought them along only in

case of the worst emergency. Like if the police invaded and tried to steal SNAKE."

"But—"

"They're purely for defense."

"I can't take this," I say, holding the gun out to him.

"We don't have time," Raymond interrupts. "Just leave Jon behind—take Thomas instead. We have to *go*—"

"No. I want Jon to come and I want Jon to understand," says Jeremiah fiercely. "Look, I'm not asking you to shoot anyone. We're just using them *in defense*, to scare Martyn and Chris. D'you want them to get away with SNA—with Padma?"

"N-no," I stutter. "No—God, no—"

Jeremiah comes up to me and takes the gun. Then he takes my hand. He slots the gun into my palm.

"This is how you put the bullet in, see?" He looks at Raymond, who nods reassuringly. "You can put up to six bullets in. This is how you cock it. And you pull the trigger like this. It's simple." He curls his hand around mine, fusing my skin with the cold metal. His eyes hold mine. The desperation in them shocks me.

"We have to get her back," he says. "We have to. You don't want Martyn to get his hands on her, do you?"

I shake my head slowly.

Jeremiah holds my gaze. The warmth of his hand becomes an insistent heat.

"Okay?" he whispers softly.

"Okay," I whisper back. "Okay."

"Should I come?" Thomas asks in a trembling voice. "I'm sorry I wasn't on guard duty—I just needed the bathroom—"

"No," Jeremiah spits out, "you stay here and guard the cottage."

Jeremiah grabs me, dragging me toward the door. Then he swings back to Thomas.

"If Martyn and Chris come back here—with SNAKE—then keep them here. Act as though you're on their side. But whatever you do, don't let them leave the cottage, okay? They're traitors.".

"Okay." Thomas still looks stunned.

"Okay," Jeremiah cries, hitting me, "come on, let's go!"

2:30 P.M.

They could have gone anywhere. Into town, to a farmhouse, out across the fields. It's only the snow that gives us a trail: a jagged trio of footprints leading across the road, over the field, and out toward the woods. Just by the rim of the trees, Jeremiah stops us, frowning, bending down and examining with intense concentration. The footprints are smeared into a muddy confusion; Raymond asks worriedly if they might have called the police and been caught here.

"No," Jeremiah says in a low voice, shaking his head, "I think maybe they just had a tussle here."

My fingers clench tight around the gun. I hear Jeremiah's

voice: *You don't want Martyn to get his hands on her, do you?* I hear Padma's voice: *He told me that if I didn't tell the truth, he'd rape me—*

Bang! I fire without even realizing. The shot knocks me back, and my arm burns with a twisted pain.

"Jesus!" Raymond shrieks. "What the fuck!"

"I'm sorry! I'm sorry!"

Jeremiah stares into my eyes and I push my hatred down and stare back.

"I'm sorry," I repeat.

"Are you on their side?" Raymond asks suddenly.

Jeremiah's eyes narrow.

"Of course I'm not," I cry desperately. "I just want to find her! Please, *please,* can we just get a move on before it's too late?"

Raymond looks at Jeremiah.

"It's okay," Jeremiah says softly. "Jon would never betray me. He is the most loyal of them all. His devotion to the God of Hebetheus is eternal."

And despite everything that's happened, I find myself dropping my eyes in guilt.

3:00 P.M.

The forest is our enemy. As we go further in, the undergrowth thickens. The footprints become finer and finer, like those of a ghost, until finally they disappear altogether beneath a heavy bush.

"Shit!" Raymond curses. "We'll never find them now."

"God is on *our* side, Raymond, not theirs!" Jeremiah snaps sharply. "Look!"

He points to a clump of black hair, snared by green thorns. I curl my palm away, resisting the urge to claim it for myself.

Then my eyes fall upon a nearby tree: a burn mark flushing up its trunk.

"Keep going," Jeremiah whispers. "Just keep going!"

We move on a few more feet. The forest seems to stretch out forever: black trunks in endless rows of mocking pillars. Even though it's only afternoon, the heaviness of the undergrowth creates a veil of murky gloom.

And then divine inspiration strikes.

"Hang on," I whisper.

"Shh—"

"No, I know—I've got it. I know where to find them!" I cry in excitement. "Look, just follow me."

My heart screams with gratitude for God. I draw them back into the clearing and show them the scorched trunk.

"Look—look—" I compress my voice into a highly strung whisper. "This mark—Chris made it on the way back from the phone—"

"From what?" Jeremiah asks.

"The town—we went—the medicine—I mean, on the way

back, we came through the woods—and—and—Chris kept lingering for ages, making marks on the trees—I thought he was just messing around but he must have made them to—to—"

"To mark an escape route?" Raymond whispers.

"You see?" Jeremiah whispers breathlessly. "I said that God was with us! Our Hebethean Savior has answered our prayers."

I open my mouth, stung with outrage. *Not* your *stupid god,* I want to say. My *God, who is* real, *who doesn't give false dreams about innocent girls.* I bite my lip. Jeremiah pauses for a moment, looking pale and creased with worry.

"To think," he muses, "they've been plotting against me for days."

3:30 P.M.

We find another marked tree; another; another.

"Shh—listen!" Jeremiah suddenly hisses.

Martyn's voice:

"I can't get the bloody thing open." *Thump, thump.* "You didn't tell me there was a lock."

"I d-didn't kn-know—I'm s-sorry—"

"I want to go back." *Oh, Padma!* "I want to go back now."

I run ahead to save her, but Jeremiah pushes me back.

He glides forward stealthily. I try to jerk into second place behind him, but Raymond shoves me back, forcing me to follow him.

"H-h-hurry up, th-they'll be h-here s-s-soon, oh G-God—"
Chris breaks off as he sees us.

They are gathered outside a rickety shack. As we scatter
into the clearing, Martyn wheels around. He drops the hammer
he was using to pry open the door. I look at Padma, my heart
flowing with love and apology. But she's staring in horror at the
guns. Chris turns pale; Martyn bends down as though to pick up
his hammer, then stops. Jeremiah sneers and points his gun
right at him.

"What the fuck do you think you're doing?" Jeremiah asks
quietly.

Martyn looks at Chris, who looks at him. Then they both
look at the guns.

"We were just—" Martyn bursts out. He puts his palms up
flat, but the gesture seems theatrical, cartoonish. "It was just a
joke, that's all—we were going to bring her back."

"You think this is funny?" Jeremiah asks, holding the gun
steady.

Martyn gives a nervous laugh, then gulps it back.

"Don't you realize"—Jeremiah's voice rises—"that you're
standing before the judgment of God? And if you don't tell the
truth, then, by God, you will be sorry!"

Martyn looks over at Chris again. They both start as though
to speak, then lose confidence. I feel Padma's gaze on me and I
stare back at her with eyes of hope. There seems to be a desperate signal in her gaze. She flashes it again, but I can't translate
it. *What, Padma, what?*

"We were going to bring her back," Martyn repeats.

Padma stares at me hard. Then, suddenly, she lets out a scream that slices straight through my gut.

The shock causes Raymond to fire by mistake—up into the sky.

"Fuck!"

Padma runs; Martyn grabs her and they disappear. Chris flees in the opposite direction. As Padma and Martyn escape, Padma glances back with a swish of dark hair, and even though their bond is formed on the spur of the moment, a collusion of desperation, a fierce jealousy stabs my stomach.

"After them!" Jeremiah roars.

For a moment, nothing makes sense. We've got guns; they haven't. They have no advantage on us. But a cartoon moment saves them: Raymond and I make to follow Chris, and Jeremiah makes to follow Martyn, and we all bang together. My nose hits Raymond's chest; my elbow jabs Jeremiah's ribs. We recoil, stung.

"For God's sake!" Jeremiah yells.

"Jesus, you!" Raymond cries at me. "You pointed that thing right into my stomach just now! Don't you know what you're doing with that thing!"

"Come on!" Jeremiah yells, starting to run and then stopping and waving at us.

"You shouldn't have that gun!" Raymond cries to me, holding out his hand for it.

"No." I need this for Padma, for us.

"Just give it, hurry up, they're getting away, you wanker—"

"No!"

"COME ON, GUYS!" Jeremiah screams in fury. "*NOW!*"

"Sorry—"

"YOU TWO GO AFTER MARTYN AND SNAKE! I'LL CHASE CHRIS!"

"You shouldn't have that gun," Raymond repeats as we run across the mud. He slips on a patch of snow and I catch him, heaving with his body weight.

"Thanks," he mutters. He shoots my gun another furious glance, but he knows there is no time for arguing. We run, following flashes of color and cloth ahead as they flit through the trees.

The trees thin out. Their camouflage is blown. We see them slow, pause, Martyn whisper in her ear. Then they split. Padma to the left, Martyn to the right.

"I'll go after SNAKE, you—"

"No, I'll get SNAKE!" I run before Raymond can stop me.

4:00 P.M.

Why is she running from me?

"Padma," I wheeze desperately, my voice hissing from my lungs. "It's me!"

She glances back, sees me—but she keeps on running. I follow the black swirl of her hair. Maybe she just wants to find a place where nobody can see us?

Finally, she gives in. She bends over, her cuffed palms flat against her knees. She heaves in air, shooting me terrified glances. I run forward, calling her name.

I am dismayed when she starts, ready to run again.

"Padma! Padma!" I call. "I'm not with them!"

I run up, panting. She takes a wary step backward. Then I realize: the gun. I place it down on the forest floor.

"Look—see? You don't need to run." I can't get my words out, there's so much to say to her and no time to say it. "Look, I know—I know you're right. You're right about Hebetheus—it's all wrong—it's crap!"

She starts at the word, and I repeat it.

"It's *crap*. You're not a terrorist. We're idiots—oh God—I just—I just—"

A smile of wonder comes over her face and she lets out a breathless hiss that is almost a laugh.

Then she says: "I need to run. You have to let me go."

"Yes, run—that's what I mean. Just ignore me and run. Go that way—it goes into town. You'll be safe there—you can find a phone. I called your mother, by the way—I spoke to her—"

"You did?" Her face lights up in exquisite shock.

"I did. She—she—misses you. . . . You should go—you should go—"

I run forward to kiss her goodbye, but she turns away from me. She runs about a foot, then turns back, runs up, and clashes her face against mine in a clumsy, messy kiss. I cling to her; I want to breathe in her taste and bottle it forever—but she wrenches away from me.

"I'm sorry!" she cries.

I stand and watch her run until the forest devours her.

4:30 P.M.

Footsteps crunch behind me.

"Did you get her?" Raymond demands.

"No—I—" I swallow thickly, terrified my face and voice will betray me. "No."

But Raymond looks almost pleased that I didn't succeed where he failed.

"Me neither. That little bastard Martyn—I had him, then one minute he was there and the next he'd vanished into thin air. I just—I mean, I just don't know how the fuck he did it."

"Shall we go back after him?"

"No, we'll go back to Jeremiah."

We run in silence. The closer we get, the more the dread begins to mount. Even though we have guns and the so-called Hebethean God on our side, we still let them get away.

As we enter the clearing, we find Chris lying on the ground; Jeremiah's boot pins down his shoulder.

"Did you get them?" Jeremiah demands, eyes flashing.

"No, we lost them. They split up."

"Right. You—Jon—guard the hostage, Chris. C'mon, Raymond. We're not letting them get away."

"Okay," Raymond says. "Jon—keep him under control." He grins at me and I start at the unexpected moment of solidarity, the rapidity of swing from me versus Raymond to us versus Chris.

Chris starts to scramble up. I point the gun at him. It feels strange, almost ridiculous, as though I am an actor in a movie playing a part. I feel relieved when he lies back down, writhing and wheezing. *Good,* I say silently, *good. You tried to steal Padma, you bastard, you deserve to suffer.* I try not to notice that his breaths are becoming shorter and shorter. I stand still, listening intently: my heart dreads the pound of footsteps, the swish of leaves, a shrill scream. I close my eyes and pray. *Oh God, please don't let them find her. Please let her make it in time.* I glance into the sea of trees, tempted by their freedom. But I can't leave without knowing she has got away.

"I've lost my inhaler. . . . I've lost it. . . ."

"You'll have to wait until Jeremiah gets back."

"Please . . . please . . . ," Chris gasps.

What am I doing, watching one of my Brothers writhe in front of me in pain? What am I becoming?

"Where did you lose it?"

"I dropped it by the tree," Chris gasps. "When Raymond—when Raymond—"

"Okay, okay. . . ."

I kneel down, scrabbling desperately through leaves. I begin to panic. What if I can't find it? What if Chris is lying? What if I go off to look for it and he runs and I lose him?

"It's by the tree—the tr-tr-tree . . ."

Here.

I grab it and kneel down and press it into his hand. Chris sucks in grateful gasps. I stare at his face and the wall between us crumbles: the labels of traitor and enemy. For the last few days, Chris has probably been running through the same mazes of worry and torment that I have.

"Why did you run?" I ask. "What were you going to do with her?"

"M-M-Martyn wanted us to form—" Chris breaks off and takes another hissed sip. "A new r-r-religion wh-wh-where there w-w-would be n-no leaders, no h-hierarchy, and we'd all b-be equal. J-Jeremiah's just l-lying to us, you know he is."

"Oh, and Martyn's the Dalai Lama?" I cry. "Jesus. And Padma . . . what were you going to do with her?"

"A-a-ask h-her m-mum and dad for some m-money and then give her b-back."

"Don't you think her parents have been through enough? God, you just wanted some fucking money so you could buy yourself a new Game Boy—"

"No—*no!*" Chris hisses. "N-not for u-us—t-t-to f-f-fund our

n-new r-r-religion. It's b-because w-we c-couldn't b-bear to
s-see her hung that we did it. W-we don't want to m-murder
anyone, even if she is a t-t-terrorist. We don't want to be
m-murderers. . . ." Tears fill his eyes. "I w-w-w-want to believe,
I really want to believe, but I can't anymore. . . . We wanted
to make a religion of p-peace, where nobody is killed. We
wanted to save her—e-even th-though sh-she didn't b-believe
us—b-but we w-were!"

My hand drops to my side. I feel cold and numb.

"What will Jeremiah do to me?" Chris whispers fearfully.
"What will he do to us?" We have crossed a line. We no longer
respect Jeremiah; we are afraid of him.

"We could run," Chris whispers. "We could both just r-r-run
now."

I open my mouth to speak when we hear voices.

Jeremiah and Raymond come rushing into the clearing with
Padma.

5:30 P.M.

"Where? Where did you find her?" I ask shakily.

"In the forest. Where else? You should have looked harder,"
Jeremiah adds tersely.

I see a flash of gratitude in her eyes.

Jeremiah orders Chris to get up and tells me to keep the gun trained on him. He commands Raymond to keep his gun trained on SNAKE.

"We're going to get Martyn," he says. "We're going to search through these woods until we find him. I don't care how long it takes."

Jeremiah makes us walk in file: him leading, followed by Padma, followed by me, followed by Chris, followed by Raymond. Hostages sandwiched between believers, as he puts it.

Every so often, Jeremiah gets out his lighter and marks a tree. As he leans over to defile an oak, Padma twists her head and gives me a desperate pleading glance, nodding at the gun in my hands.

I want to do it, Padma, I say silently to the back of her head as we carry on, *but if I hold the gun to Jeremiah's head, he'll turn his gun on me. He knows I won't be able to shoot him. And I think he would shoot me; I think he would. I've never seen him act like this before—he's out for blood. And Raymond's right behind me with a gun. . . . If I could just signal to Chris—but Raymond will see. Oh God, there must be something I can do. . . .*

Padma is tired; I can see her pushing through it bravely and I want to hold her and kiss her, give her my last drops of energy.

We come to a clearing and Jeremiah stops us. He lifts his head. His eyes narrow and a cunning smile creeps across his lips. I shiver.

"Martyn," Jeremiah sings lightly. "Oh, Martyn, won't you come down?" His voice thins into an insidious whisper. "Martyn, Martyn, Martyn."

"I'm not coming down," Martyn bellows.

Jeremiah turns to Chris.

"Call him down," he orders.

"B-b-but—" Chris stammers.

Raymond points the gun at him.

"O-okay. M-M-Martyn!" Chris calls. "They've—they've got me. Pl-pl-please come down."

Silence. I stare up through the crazy paving of green. All I can see is a white sneaker sticking out over a branch. I look over at Padma. She gazes back. A snowflake floats down and kisses her hair: my dark angel.

"Fine," Jeremiah calls up. "We're going to wait here. We can wait all night if you like." He turns to me. "Go and get some sticks."

Padma automatically moves to follow and help.

"Hey." Jeremiah's eyes narrow. "SNAKE. What are you doing? This isn't Girl Scout camp."

Padma moves back quickly and bows her head.

I gather the damn sticks. Not for Jeremiah; only for her, for her warmth, her comfort. I make a pyramid and ask Jeremiah to borrow his lighter. He passes it over distractedly, his eyes still on Martyn. The look on his face confounds me. It's as though a demon has taken over our leader. Was it always there, lurking in the shadows of his soul?

I sit down in front of the fire and shut them all out: Jeremiah catcalling up to Martyn; Raymond wielding his tough-guy gun; Chris whimpering. I shut out everything but her.

Suddenly it becomes unbearable not to touch her. I stretch out my leg until I feel it brushing her ankle. I look around furtively. Millimeter by millimeter, I shift my leg. As I do so, my pant leg rides up. My bare skin touches the thrilling scratch of her trousers. I shift closer and find a tiny patch of bare ankle so that our skin connects in a flow of warmth. She looks up at me and a trace of a smile forms on her lips.

I have to lower my face quickly to swallow back the smile, swallow it and push it back down into my heart, where it breaks in a bubble of bliss.

Oh God, I love her.

"We're all very cozy down here, Martyn," Jeremiah calls up. "Let's just hope the fire doesn't spread into your branches."

"If I come down, will you shoot me?"

Jeremiah ponders.

"I don't know. Maybe."

Padma's eyes widen and flicker with panic; I hold her gaze steady until she looks away in relief. I will protect her; I will protect her always.

The more I look at her, the more everything else seems to drop away until there's nothing left but this curious sensation in my heart. Like the ice on the streets after winter is seeping into spring. Full of slush and gray dirt and cool running water and sparkling light. I feel as though I want to dance and run a long, long way and climb a tree and stand on its uppermost branch with the world waving nervously beneath and whoop out how much I love Padma.

Is this what God is? If you take all these moments, all the love beating in people's hearts all over the world, the love of a boy for a girl, a man for a woman, a kid for a parent, a brother for a sister, a friend for a friend—if you put it all together and roll it into one big ball, is that God?

Maybe God isn't the man I have thought him to be, the elderly stern man who sits in the clouds above like a headmaster ready to give cosmic detentions or gold stars. Maybe he is a man, a woman, a thing who loves you always and doesn't even care whether you love him because he just *is* love, so he'll simply wait for you forever until you find him and all the time he'll just love you. I feel dizzy and strange and like crying and laughing and kissing Padma all at once.

I look up at Jeremiah with wet eyes and I can't even feel any hate for him; I want to jump up and shake him and tell him my revelation: he's just as weak as any of us. He just puts on a better act. I have to keep remembering that.

Then Jeremiah splashes the tree with lighter fluid, sets it alight. And reality comes crashing back in.

7:00 P.M.

Within seconds, Martyn screams and comes slithering down the tree. We jump up, exchanging glances. I stand by Padma's side. Martyn edges back to the tree trunk, shoulders hunched, eyes darting, a fox cornered by his hunters.

"Thanks for coming down," Jeremiah says, then punches him in the face.

Shit. Even Raymond blinks and curses under his breath. I feel Padma edge toward me and with her little finger she takes hold of my jacket.

Martyn clutches his cheek, staring at Jeremiah with shocked eyes. Chris starts to cry. I move closer to Padma. The crack of Jeremiah's fist connecting with Martyn's cheek echoes raw in my stomach.

"For God's sake!" I cry.

Jeremiah carries on staring at Martyn, his mouth thin. This is all wrong, this is all wrong. I thought that Martyn would come down from the tree and Jeremiah would order an Advanced Super-Sacred Cleansing or something like that and we would all return home for another session. I thought Jeremiah was a leader who believed in compassion. And I want to open my mouth and say all of this, but I'm scared that if Jeremiah doesn't beat Martyn up, he'll beat me up. But I don't want to see Martyn hurt either; he might be stocky and a good fighter, but he is no match for Jeremiah and his cold, leonine strength. *Oh God*, I pray, *please calm Jeremiah, please calm him down.*

"I'm sorry," Martyn says quickly. "I'm sorry." He gets down on his knees. "I'm sorry, I'm really sorry. . . ." He bows until his nose is in the mud.

I wince and lower my eyes.

Jeremiah stares at him and his face softens.

"Get up," he says. "Get up and take off your clothes. And you—" He points a finger like a bullet in my direction and I say, "What? Me?"

"Not you. Her. Let go of your loverboy's jacket and take off your clothes."

Padma shrinks back toward the trees, but Chris grabs hold of her.

"No," I say. "Chris—let her go. Chris! For fuck's sake—a minute ago you were trying to get me on your side."

Chris stares at me, shaking his head. His tears are dry now and I see the desperation in his face: desperation that he doesn't cross the line and become the victim.

I turn back to Jeremiah. My heart is pumping and my head is spinning with prayers. *Keep cool. Keep very cool. It's the only way you might win.*

"You said I was going to be the one to hang her. For my Initiation. You promised."

"I'm not going to hang them," Jeremiah says. "Now. Get SNAKE. Over here. *Now!*" His voice rises to a shout.

Martyn takes off his jacket. Padma stands next to him, staring at me wildly. I turn to Raymond. Even he looks uneasy.

"Raymond!" I cry. "You can't let this happen."

"It's all right," Raymond snaps. "Jeremiah?" he addresses his brother softly.

Jeremiah turns.

"It's okay. I've got this under control. It's just a little divine punishment. Nobody's going to die. Well, as long as they do what I say."

He takes the gun from Raymond, who lets it go with a slight tug. He points the gun at Padma's skull. Martyn begins to undress with greater haste.

"Come on, then," Jeremiah says, looking her up and down.

Padma stares into his eyes. And then a look comes over her face.

"No."

"Do as I say." Jeremiah's voice is ice. "I am the leader here."

"And I am your hostage," Padma says. "If you shoot me, what else do you have to bargain with? You'll all just go to jail."

"Our God won't let any of us go to jail."

"Well, I won't undress." She shrugs.

Jeremiah fires.

We all flinch.

Padma clutches her head, shaking. The bullet missed her by inches.

She gulps, then takes off her pants.

Her panties are frilled with sprays of folded toilet paper, and I remember that she told me she had her period. She manages not to cry, but her face is crumpled with defeat.

Suddenly I snap. I fly at Jeremiah, knocking him sideways. He turns in surprise. And then I feel arms locked around my shoulders and Raymond grabs my gun, flinging it into the snow for Chris to pick up. I lash out, thrash about, but Raymond holds me tight. Jeremiah laughs, shaking his head, then trains his gun back on Padma. I turn away, refusing to contribute to her humiliation. I hear her clothes drop into the snow. Hatred burns inside me—whether good or evil I don't know and don't care. I am ready to grab the gun and kill them all. I struggle again and cry inside: *Oh God, stop this, you can't let them touch her, oh God, you can't let this happen, I can't believe this can happen if you really exist, I can't bear this evil, you can't allow this to happen—*

"Okay," says Jeremiah lightly. "Now. You—put on her clothes. And you—put on his clothes."

Padma looks bewildered. Martyn picks 'p her knickers, shaking out the blotted toilet paper, and pulls them on. Their red hearts look absurd against his hairy thighs. Padma picks up his yellow Y-fronts and pulls them on with great disdain. Jeremiah looks at them and starts to laugh. He turns to his brother and Raymond gives him a confused grin.

"Come on, come on," he says. "Put on her bra. That's it. And her sparkly top."

Padma reaches down to pick up Martyn's gray vest. As she does so, her long hair parts, revealing her breasts. Raymond's grip softens in distraction; I hear Chris draw in his breath sharply. Without even thinking, I turn to Chris. *Wham!* I punch him across the face. Chris stumbles, blood pouring from his mouth. Jeremiah turns and then grins at me.

"Hey, hey, steady." Raymond takes hold of me again and I

don't protest. Suddenly I am limp and weak. My knuckles ache. I feel dirty, spent, useless.

Padma and Martyn are now fully dressed. Padma's black sparkly top stretches across Martyn's chest; Martyn's hooded top hangs over Padma's wrists in ghostly fronds and she has to hitch up his jeans around her waist.

"Well, Martyn, you look divine," says Jeremiah. Martyn tries to grin but it ends up a snarl; he is close to losing it.

Jeremiah seems to sense this. He pauses, frowning, watching the snow for a few minutes. And then in a flash he is the old Jeremiah again, the cool, calm leader.

"Okay. We're going back. The punishments are over. We'll return to our holy base, and Martyn and Chris will be judged before God."

9:00 P.M.

The day is over. The coup has failed. We just want to get back to the cottage, to fall into a black pit of forgetful sleep. But Jeremiah orders Martyn to show him where the shack is.

"I'm tired," Jeremiah declares. "I need a horse. Martyn, be my horse."

Martyn sinks to his knees and carries Jeremiah with awkward waddles. Jeremiah picks up a twig and thwacks him from time to time.

Jeremiah suggests that Raymond should use SNAKE as a horse too but he declines, quietly muttering that she wouldn't be strong enough.

I want him to bend down before all of us and admit that he lied. Tonight I have seen the real Jeremiah, stripped of his layers of guile and charm, his fancy words about miracles and dreams and compassion. He is—what do adults call it?—a megalomaniac. He wants us to worship the cult of Jeremiah, and if we don't then we will all suffer the whip. Hatred burns in my heart. He is just like my father. He is worse than my father. He made us kidnap an innocent girl all because she came from a country he doesn't like, has a tone of skin that doesn't fit into his color scheme.

I want to tear him into pieces. But Padma walks ahead of me, her spine rigid with tension and anger, and every ripple of her body reminds me of the danger she is in. There is no knowing how far Jeremiah will go. One part of me feels terrified for her, but another voice inside me whispers with relief that she didn't escape, that she's here with me, helping me to survive this nightmare. And I hate myself for thinking it, but it's the truth.

We come to the clearing and wait while Jeremiah gets off his horse, kicks him, and examines the shack. He inspects it with a scientific curiosity, oblivious to the cold. I step closer to Padma. She turns and scowls at me with flashing eyes.

"Okay," says Jeremiah, "we can now return. Horse. Come

on, get up. Tired, are you?" He kicks and Martyn whines. Jeremiah sighs. Padma takes a step back. "I shall have to walk, then. Pathetic."

Raymond stares at his brother, his jaw set; Chris hovers with a tense fist. For one curious moment I sense that we would all like to pummel Jeremiah, cut ourselves free from the net of fear he has thrown over us, and if only one of us would do it, then all of us might stop him. But we keep on walking.

The night has reached its rawest point. We stumble, drag ourselves on in stunned misery. I walk behind Padma, staring at the dark tangle of her hair. Why is she angry at *me*? For not protecting her better, for my pathetic punch at Chris? Yesterday I tasted love in her kisses. Our love feels so precious, so fragile, and perhaps tonight Jeremiah has thrown it to the floor, smashed it into irredeemable pieces. Suddenly I am panicking and desperate to feel reassured by her kisses; suddenly knowing she still loves me seems more important than anything, even escaping.

I could turn on them. I could knock Chris sideways, grab my gun back. I could point the gun at Jeremiah and I could shoot him. I would do it for her. But then what? Raymond shoots me? Raymond shoots Padma? We all die? I have to come up with a better plan. We won't hang her tonight; I'm certain we won't. Jeremiah seems more intent on punishing Martyn than her. *Oh Padma,* I whisper silently to her back, *please forgive me. I won't let you down again.*

As we go back into the cottage, the smell hits us. We hadn't noticed it before because we'd become immune to it, but the freshness of the forest highlights it: the old woman, still lying in her bed, slowly decaying.

11:00 P.M.

Jeremiah summons me to the Prayer Room. Chris, Martyn, and Padma are all cuffed and tied down in the Hostage Room. Thomas is guarding them at gunpoint. Raymond is guarding Jeremiah's door with a crowbar and a gun. He actually has the nerve to feel me for weapons. My temper flares up; my dislike of Raymond, which I tried to repress in the Brotherhood, now biles into hatred. He is not my Brother, not my friend.

"Are you crazy?" I spit out. "You know I'm on your side. Just let me in, okay?"

Jeremiah is lying on the floor, his cheek nestling against a Hebethean symbol, eyes lowered. I look down at him, searching his face. There ought to be a wicked glint in his cool blue eyes, a nasty scar slashing his smooth skin. Just some sign, some warning of the viper within. The innocence of his appearance suddenly seems inhuman. I can't understand him, his morals, his ethics. The cogs of his mind don't work in the usual way normal people's do; they belong to another culture, another country he has created inside himself.

I carefully sit down next to him.

He glances up at me, his eyes filmed with tears. I look away in embarrassed surprise.

"I knew they'd betray me," Jeremiah says softly. He sniffs. "I had a dream—God warned me they would betray me. I didn't take the warning seriously. I trusted you all, I thought you were all my Brothers."

"They just—" I break off, confused. My feelings swerve toward pity. Why is it so difficult to hate him? "We all just feel—"

"*We?* So you're on *their* side?"

"No! No! I didn't know anything about the coup. It's just—things feel out of control. We were meant to stand for peace. But now people think we're criminals. People actually hate us, Jeremiah." I break off, knowing he will only tell me that that is their weakness, not ours.

But instead Jeremiah sits up, blinking.

"I'm just trying to do *good*," he cries. "Why can't they see that? Why can't you see that? I just want everyone here to be happy and find their Soul Shift. That's all I came here for. I never wanted to hurt anyone."

"But you did!" I cry back, hardly able to believe my nerve. "You did hurt—" I break off, about to say, *Padma*. I glance back through the ajar door to Raymond, note the black tip of his gun, and rein in my words. "You hurt Martyn. I know he did wrong, but you—"

"Martyn?" Jeremiah winces. "I refuse to hear his name spoken aloud. From now on, his code name is BLACK. And Chris's code name is DEMON. Tonight I'm going to get to the bottom of this. We need to interrogate BLACK together."

"But I thought you said before that we use code names for terrorists!"

"Exactly."

"Come on, Chris and Martyn aren't terrorists!" I cry. "They're just—I mean—they wouldn't be out here with us if they were terrorists."

"They tried to undermine us and steal our hostage." Jeremiah's tears are gone now. His face is stern. "Look, I'm speaking to you in black-and-white terms, Jon, because there's no room in our world for gray anymore. People are either with us or against us. They're either Brothers of the Hebetheus or they're terrorists."

"Matthew," I say without thinking.

"I'm sorry?"

"That's from Matthew. In the Bible." I flush. " 'He that is not with me is against me.' I just—just remember from . . . before . . ."

"Well, whatever. I'm talking about those who stand in our way. Okay, I'm not saying they're planting bombs. But the definition of a terrorist is really much wider than that. It's becoming wider every day. It's someone who doesn't want to save the world and bring peace, and anyone who doesn't want to do that in this age of war and chaos can only be a terrorist."

"But what if the rest of the world doesn't want to be in

Hebetheus? What if the only people who believe are just us? What then? Does the rest of the world have to die?"

Jeremiah shrugs.

"What—you're saying that, like, entire countries, millions of people, should just be wiped out if they don't agree with us?" I cry.

"Look at Eden. There was only room for two people there. For God's sake, Jon, you have to see that your mind has been warped by society. No—don't interrupt me—just listen. *Listen.* Listen to me with an open mind and heart. Who says the world is suited to a population of millions? It clearly isn't. There's a lack of resources everywhere, so most of the world starves. And let's look at those who aren't starving. If you walked up to the average person on the street in this country—this privileged country where people think they're poor if they only have one TV set, for crying out loud—and asked if they were generally happy or unhappy with their lives, you know what they'd say? Unhappy. They'd say life doesn't feel quite right, life isn't satisfying them, giving them what they want. This world just isn't working. That's why we're driving it to destruction by killing the trees, the ozone, turning the sea levels topsy-turvy. The experts are telling us, day by day, that we're heading for disaster, but does anyone listen? No. Why? Because deep down we want to push that self-destruct button. Maybe the world is suited to just a few very select spiritual people, living in harmony together."

For one wistful moment I want to believe him. I remember Chris, lying in the forest, whispering from the bottom of his soul, *I really want to believe, but I can't anymore.* I feel the same pain stab my heart. I thought I'd found an ultimate truth; I thought I knew the answers that people spend their lives searching for; I thought I was the luckiest boy in the world. Now I feel as though I'm floating in a womb—lost, white, shapeless.

Jeremiah watches me carefully. I try to hide my thoughts, but I know he has sensed a crack he might pry open wider.

"Come on, Jon, you know there's sense in my words. Even if you might not say yes to every detail, can't you feel in your heart some beat of truth?"

"Jeremiah," I say more firmly, "I don't believe that Padma is a terrorist. I know you . . . I know you believe in what you're doing and God talks to you, but I think maybe you got that wrong . . . maybe you misheard that conversation . . . maybe . . ."

"Oh you do, do you?" Jeremiah pauses, eyes narrowed. "Have you forgotten the sixth part of the Book of Hebetheus?"

I blink at the change of subject and then quickly recite: " 'God made woman first and he made her imperfect. Then he shaped man and he improved on woman and made man perfect.' "

Jeremiah nods, wets his lips, and looks at me slyly.

"Women are a dangerous sex, Jon. They are made to lie. They're snakes that weave and slither and sidle into your consciousness, and just when you least expect it, they bite."

I look down sullenly. I don't want to listen. My love for

Padma feels like a flickering flame that I must shield with both hands.

"Just be careful," he says. "SNAKE trusts you. Which could be useful for us. Just don't allow yourself to be useful to her. Remember, she has nothing here. No God, no hope, no weapons. She's desperate. Believe me, if we weren't in this cottage, Jon, she wouldn't give you a second glance. I remember the night we brought her here, when she was in the nightclub . . . but maybe I shouldn't tell you this."

"No, what?" I cry.

"She was standing in the queue and this guy had his arm around her and he was kissing and licking her neck—it was gross."

"*What!*" I tell myself to calm down; I tell myself he is only lying. But even so, jealousy squeezes my heart into pulp. "Well, maybe," I say quickly. "I mean, she is SNAKE."

"Exactly. All women are sluts at the end of the day. You see, they can't reach God as easily as men can. Women aren't as naturally spiritual as we are. They have babies, their place is in the home, at the cradle, that's their role. Whereas we . . ."

His voice fades; I won't allow him to pollute me. I close my eyes and think of Padma, her lips like a rose, of brushing my finger along the silk of the petals. The image is broken open by an image of her in a smoky club, of her—but I smash it. *Don't let him get to you,* I tell myself. *Oh God, protect my love for her. Keep it pure, keep the dirt away from it, keep it clean.*

And then his words make my heart stop.

"From now on you are forbidden to speak to SNAKE. I am laying down this rule for your own good."

"Okay," I say, struggling to keep my face a smooth mask. "Sure."

I go to rise, and then he says: "When did you last have something to drink?"

"I—I don't know," I say, caught off guard, my words stumbling into each other. "Um—before the betrayal."

"Good. Then you won't drink anything for another twenty hours. Not one drop of water."

I picture myself sneaking into the bathroom and—

"I shall inform Raymond. He'll be in the hallway so he'll be able to see if you enter the bathroom or the kitchen. When you do, you must keep the door open so he can see what you're doing. And if you do dare to take just one sip, then—well, SNAKE will suffer on your behalf."

"But—but—why?" I cry.

"It's your punishment."

"But I had nothing to do with the betrayal! I told you!"

"Jon, you don't have to betray God with your actions. You can betray him inside, in your heart, and in many ways it's worse. Fast without fluids, feel the pain, and purge her from your heart. Let God back in. Because I'm warning you, Jon, if you don't deal with this now, then the evil will fester. And I might not be able to save you from the wrath of God. There may be one way you can prove yourself, however."

"How?"

"We will now interrogate our hostage Martyn. I may need your assistance."

"Of course," I say quickly.

"When I give the signal, put Martyn's head in the water."

What? To do what? The words don't quite sink in, but Jeremiah is already out in the hallway and Raymond is tugging Martyn.

"Ow, you're hurting me!" Martyn cries. His hands are cuffed behind his back and Raymond has a fistful of Padma's sparkly top. He opens the bathroom door and throws Martyn in.

Outside the door, I pause. My hands begin to tremble. I have a terrible feeling that I am about to walk into a nightmare. I don't want to go in; I want to run, I want to grab Padma and run and run into the cool freedom of the night.

Then Jeremiah looks at me and I nod dully, knowing I must play along until the time comes.

MIDNIGHT

Thomas comes into the bathroom too. He doesn't look sick anymore, but it's as though his medication has stripped away some essential spark, some essence of him. His eyes are dull, his voice is flat.

Jeremiah nods. Thomas spins on the taps. Jeremiah kneels down next to Martyn and nods at me. I am not sure what the nod means, but I kneel too.

"So, Martyn, when did you first conspire against the Brotherhood of Hebetheus? When did you first feel you could challenge God?" Jeremiah dips his fingers into the water and splashes some onto his cheeks. Martyn recoils in terror. But Jeremiah's touch is soft; he washes away the dirt and sweat on Martyn's face.

"It was just a whim," Martyn gabbles. I've never seen him look so scared, and I feel an odd, cruel sort of pleasure that his cockiness has finally been stamped out of him.

"I mean—it was Chris," Martyn goes on, "it was just a dare— we just thought . . . it would be . . . a dare . . . We didn't really think it through. We just came up with it this morning."

My eyes flick uneasily to the water, slowly filling up the bath. Is Jeremiah preparing some sort of warped cleansing baptism?

"Oh really?" Jeremiah's fingers close around Martyn's chin. "Just this morning, you say?"

"Yeah, this morning."

"And it was your idea to defy God?"

"No—no—it was Chris's!"

Jeremiah nods at Thomas, who turns off the taps. Martyn struggles, sensing trouble. Then Jeremiah nods at me. I sit paralyzed. Jeremiah nods again. I raise my hands slowly to Martyn's head. Jeremiah nods once more. I can't move. Martyn whispers, "I'm sorry."

Jeremiah says to me, "Are you with us or against us? Because if you're against us, we'll interrogate you next and find out the true color of your mind."

I push him down. Martyn kicks against me, but his hands are cuffed and Thomas moves forward to pin down his ankles. I hold him under the water for just a few seconds—though the horror of the moment seems as though it goes on for hours—and then let go.

"Jesus—I'm going to drown, you're going to drown me," Martyn shrieks in panic. "Jon—you have to help me—Jon—"

"Just tell the truth and we won't drown you and we'll let you go," Jeremiah says. "How long have you been plotting against me?"

"Like I said, this morning—"

"How long?"

"A day! It was after my Sacred Cleansing—all that stuff you said about my dad—I was upset—"

Jeremiah nods at me. I pause, my hands jelly. Jeremiah nods again. I can't move, so Jeremiah reaches over, puts his hands on top of mine, and forces Martyn back down into the water. Martyn thrashes about. Water licks into his hair and spills over the back of his neck. I feel blank. I feel strange. And then for one electric moment I feel powerful. I almost want to shake away

Jeremiah's hands, to show him I am tough, I am mighty, I can administer this judgment.

Then as I lean in against him I breathe in Padma's scent, lingering on her blouse. Suddenly I push against Jeremiah, but Jeremiah holds my hands down tight. The white walls spin. How long has Martyn been under the water? A surge of panic shoots through me, and I shove Jeremiah away so violently he knocks back against the bath.

Martyn bursts up from the bath, vomiting water. He quick-gasps air. Tears pour from his crimson face. He whimpers, "Please, enough, no more, enough, please," and he crashes onto the floor and lies on his side, his rib cage heaving in, out, in, out. His fingers twitch like a butterfly's wings. I look up at Jeremiah, who gazes down at Martyn with the eyes of a scientist testing out a new and dangerous experiment.

"Don't disobey me or the God of Hebetheus ever again," he says. He doesn't bother waiting for Martyn to reply.

I watch Jeremiah undo his cuffs and think of Padma. I tell myself I can go to her now. I will get her alone; I will kiss her; I will feel the sweet purity of her breath entering my body, cleansing this blackness in my heart, bringing me back to life. But she seems too distant—like a character in a book I read long ago. I close my eyes and search my heart.

Later that night, when I lie awake desperate for the relief of sleep, my mind keeps playing the scene over and over. I ache to bathe, but the thought of going anywhere near the bathroom terrifies me. I realize then that it can feel worse to inflict violence than to receive it. No pain to throb and no bruises to heal; it is the nothingness that is the pain, to have become less than human. To feel a mark branded forever on my conscience, to feel a little bit of my heart chipped away. To know too that I might have to pay that karma back and suffer it myself. Was Jeremiah punishing me most of all? Was he trying to kill the love in me?

Surely this is not the work of God.

That moment of power when I nearly wanted to drown Martyn. Was that really me? Is that human nature? To feel compelled to tip the seesaw against others so that their weakness supports our rise? Maybe this urge for power is the root of all evil. In order for one person to gain something in life, someone else always has to miss out; we can't all get A's or win football matches or medals. Someone always has to lose, and that's the way society works. Maybe in murderers, the weakest people of all, this urge for power is a hunger so acute they have to take a life in order to gain a double life: their own and someone else's shadow. So when I pushed Martyn under the water, for that moment when I enjoyed his torment—does that make me evil? Does that mean I might be capable of murder?

I was close to killing Padma.

I want to pull this evil from my heart by its roots.

My mind scrambles desperately for images of goodness. I think of St. Teresa, St. Francis, Jesus. None of them ever needed to use violence. St. Francis had a father who was worse than mine; when St. Francis sold his clothes to give money to the poor, his father beat him, took him to court, and disowned him. But St. Francis loved him still. I remember how my dad told me the story of the wolf who terrorized the people in the village of Gubbio by eating their animals. Every villager who tried to stop the wolf perished. Then St. Francis went into Gubbio and the wolf appeared. St. Francis made the sign of the cross and the wolf bowed his head and lay down at St. Francis's feet, meek as a lamb. St. Francis asked the wolf to make a pact, and the wolf put his paw into St. Francis's hand and agreed to leave the people alone. In return, whenever the wolf came into the village, the people would feed him. All these saints, these people who loved God, none of them ever said, "We must kill in the name of God." They never tried to fix the world by stamping on evil, by bombing nations; they just shone a light into the darkness, washed away the evil with pure compassion, with love.

I try to think of good things I have done. But they seem so puny. Once, before Dad left, I delivered food baskets to old people during Harvest Festival. Dad gave me the last basket to deliver. The address was in a run-down housing estate, graffiti crawling like neon ivy across the walls. The old man who opened the door smiled toothlessly, spread out his arms, and cried, "Won'tyoucomein?" I thought he was drunk. I wanted to run, but I was scared he might complain to Dad, so I crept in.

Then he explained to me, "I'vegotcancerinmythroat," and when I gave him the basket his face lit up and he danced around the room and then made me play Scrabble with him for an hour, and despite the fact that he kept cheating, it was the best game I'd ever played in my life. When we said goodbye, even though he was a stranger, I felt I loved the man as though he was family. As I walked home, I felt my body singing with sunshine, blazing with love for life. I promised the old man I'd visit him again, only the next week I had too much homework. Then Dad left and I never did go back.

I promise myself that if we get out of here alive, I'll go back and see him.

At last, I feel the relief of tears and weep quietly until dawn comes.

DAY SIX

9:00 A.M.

I am prodded awake by a gun in my ribs. Raymond's face leers above me.

"Get up. It's time for prayers."

The cartoon that was in the Prayer Room now lies hidden beneath a fresh coat of white paint. And yet still it seems to linger, sniggering quietly. Every corner of the room has been cleaned to a pitch of desperation. The few tiny specks of dust glint against the desert of white. I wonder sleepily if it's possible to ever remove every speck of dust or whether the moment you thought you'd achieved pure whiteness a speck would always appear somewhere.

Chris and Martyn are uncuffed, sitting in a new black circle that must have been painted during the night. I cannot see what the symbol is beneath them.

I kneel down quickly. Thomas and Jeremiah enter. I look at Jeremiah, but he doesn't look at me. He gives Chris and Martyn a pained gaze, then sits down, cross-legged, eyes closed, while Thomas stands up, unfolds a sheet of paper, and declares that some new rules are being introduced for our Brotherhood.

"Prayers will be said at 8:00 A.M., midday, and 6:00 P.M. All shall attend.

"Nobody is allowed to open a window, leave the cottage, or use the bathroom without asking for our leader's permission.

"Nobody will be allowed to speak directly to our leader. If you need to ask permission to open a window, leave the cottage, or use the bathroom, or if you have any other queries, then you must ask the second in command, the seer Thomas, who will then consult with our leader."

Raymond shifts; Thomas flushes slightly.

"There will be a curfew at 9:00 P.M. every night.

"Nobody is allowed to read anything or write anything down.

"The guard shift will continue twenty-four hours a day. Please consult Raymond every morning for your shift."

Thomas pauses and coughs slightly, the paper shaking in his hands.

"The penalty for breaking these rules will be severe.

"All traitors will be punished. Martyn and Chris have apologized for their treacherous behavior and are now pardoned in the eyes of God, provided they abide by the new rules of the Brotherhood."

Chris and Martyn shift and nod solemnly at Jeremiah.

Thomas folds up the sheet of paper and kneels down without looking at any of us.

Jeremiah half opens his eyes and nods.

We all bow down to pray.

Our prayers are just words; we're gripped too tightly by fear's fist to think of God. I feel sad, remembering how only a few days ago we sat in such deep prayer we no longer felt six but one. Funny how when we were Brothers together, our rules were there to gently guide us; our strength lay in our love for God and for each other. It's only now that we're individuals, now that our chains are slack and weak, that we need rules.

And I realize: *It's all over.* Our God has cracked and crumbled into pieces of dead stone. My heart quivers with a pang. Once it was all real to me; it changed my life; it gave me hope, gave me a vision, explained the mysteries of the world to me. I feel as though I am looking through closed gates, catching glimpses of a beautiful garden I will never walk in again.

How can it be so easy for faith to slip away?

Just six days. Where did our fall begin? The woman at the door? Martyn's doubts? Just little breezes that began to blow gently at our house of cards. Is that the danger of evil—that it poisons in the tiniest doses, a little here, a little there, until one day you wake up and something that was once beautiful has rotted and shriveled?

Maybe the only way for faith to last is to love God from within, so that it's just between you and him, so that every day a prayer binds a thread between you until there are so many threads they can't be snapped. A private love that nobody from the outside can look in at, or shape, or have any say in. But how long might that take to grow?

For a moment I am full of despair. Then I remember Padma. She is all I have left.

I close my eyes and remember that moment in the forest when Padma showed me the God of love. But too much pain has blurred the memory. I can't quite pin down exactly how I felt then; it was as though I was in an exalted state, tasting a heaven on earth. Maybe the God of love is the answer; maybe I should pray to him even though no religion defines him, even though no prophet on earth is shouting his message, even though I feel him more than I understand him.

I start to pray once more. But my soul fumbles blindly. In the end, I give up on prayer and simply hope, just hope that I will find a plan to help Padma and that she will help me, that everything will come out good in the end.

NOON

We have just finished prayers when there is a knock on the door.

"Who's that? Who's on guard?"

"Martyn was meant to be, but now that he's on probation, there—"

"There weren't e-e-enough p-people—"

"Who is it?"

"Go and look!"

"Shit, it's that woman again!"

"Jon, go speak with her. Be calm. Remember, God is with you."

"But who the hell is meant to be on guard? They should be hung, drawn and quartered—"

"Quiet! Let Jon go." Jeremiah narrows his eyes and picks up his gun. "Jon has yet to prove himself. Careful, Jon, careful. Be very careful. All now depends on you."

I open the door.

"Ned!" she cries. "Hello, my love. Is Brenda better yet?"

"Er, no. Not really." My face burns despite the raw air. "Can you come back another time? She's kind of busy. . . ."

"Well, I brought her some eggs." She proffers a box, her own stencil sketch graceful on the lid. "I'll just come in, if you don't mind. I know Brenda won't mind a jot. I expect she's sketching again; is she—"

"No—no—you can't! You can't come in! Brenda's in a very delicate state."

She starts, staring at me. It's a fatal moment. She notices me. My features, previously an impersonal blur to her, now come into focus.

"You . . . you look . . . like . . ." She trails off. "You look like those boys on the— Where's Brenda? You're not Ned, are you? I *thought* you looked too young." Very slowly, she pushes her eggs back into her bag and risks a look at me again. Her shoulders seem to shrink back into her coat, and she drops her eyes hastily.

"Well, now, I ought to be going. . . ."

"Yes," I say brightly. "I think you should go." *Oh thank God: we're going to be saved. She'll call the police. Careful now, Jon, don't give away a single clue, let Jeremiah think you played your part.*

"Hey!" Martyn suddenly cries, coming up behind me. "Hey, don't go!"

The woman swings round. My heart crumples.

"If you're looking for Brenda, she's just in here," Martyn says cheerfully. "She really wants to see you." He punches me on the shoulder, hard. "Ned, you spacehead, you should have let her in."

The woman steps in cautiously, lost in confusion. Now she's thinking: *Did I get it wrong? Are these boys just boys?*

"She's in here," Martyn says, spreading open his hand as though inviting her into a friendly hotel.

Martyn opens the door to where the dead old lady lies.

Martyn beams as though he can already hear Jeremiah praising him for his ingenuity, for his fucking *improvisation*. The woman enters the room, crying, "God—the smell in here! You should have opened some windows!"

Then there is a long, long silence. And then her voice, like a little girl's.

"What did you do to her?"

"It wasn't us," Martyn giggles nervously.

"You monster!" she shrieks.

Raymond appears, tinkling cuffs. I listen to the sounds of him silencing the woman. Then he leads her into the Hostage Room to join Padma. Jeremiah sidles into the hallway, nodding. A moment later, Raymond steps out, slamming the door behind him.

Now we have two hostages.

3:00 P.M.

As Thomas and I walk down the hallway to the Hostage Room, I feel as though I am floating above myself. I can understand why Moses and Daniel and Elijah fasted; there is a strange, black euphoria to my dizziness. It acts as an anesthetic, muffling the outside world into a woozy haze.

But when we enter the Hostage Room—when my eyes fall on Padma—my body sings awake.

Padma and the woman are sitting side by side, handcuffed. The woman looks bedraggled, and the bruise on her cheek is like a ghostly apple imprint. I feel embarrassed by the look she gives me. As though we're animals. I want to protest, *I'm not one of them, I love her, I'd never hurt her.*

Thomas turns to me. He doesn't look me in the eye—I assume because I am supposedly too inferior.

"Jeremiah has instructed you to recite the Book of Hebetheus in order to soothe the souls of our ignorant hostages."

I sit down, cross-legged. Thomas stands behind me. Padma's eyes are soft; I am forgiven. But then they gleam with some urgency I can't translate.

Thomas lays a hand on my shoulder.

" 'Imagine for a moment that human beings are in a cave.' " *You will not drink, you will not drink until after she is dead. Take one sip and you will be found out—I guarantee it. And then SNAKE will pay for your sin.* " 'From childhood, they have their legs and necks shackled so that they can only stare straight ahead of them at a light reflected on the wall—which comes from a fire burning far above and behind them.' " Each word sucks the last dregs of saliva from my mouth; each word becomes heavier and heavier, a boulder I roll up my throat and force from my lips. " 'On the wall, they see dancing patterns of life like shadow puppets—' "

"You stupid little boy!" the woman suddenly bursts out.

"Sorry?"

"I mean—honestly! What on earth are you talking about?

You're sixteen years old, for God's sake! What are you doing sitting here and quoting Plato at me? If I wasn't wearing these handcuffs, I'd take you over my knee and give you a jolly good spanking!"

"I—" I look back at Thomas, who suddenly looks sheepish.

"And are we to sit here without food or drink?" the woman demands.

"Your meal is set for later," Thomas says firmly.

"Well, we're thirsty!" the woman booms. "You might have guns and we might be your victims, but if you really believe in God, you'll give us something to drink."

I feel a dizzy rush of laughter inside. But I also feel relieved. As though I've been wanting someone to tell me off for some time.

"I'd like something to drink too," Padma says loudly. She gives me an urgent glance again. "And I'd like some paper and a pen. I think the rules of Hebetheus are so interesting I'd like to write them down. Can you get them for me, Thomas?"

Thomas stares at her, looking sweaty and tense. The woman crimps her lips furiously.

"But—the new rules." He frowns, muttering to himself, then pulls a piece of paper out of his pocket. "Rule number five—nobody is allowed to read or write anything down. I'm sorry. It's not allowed."

"But these are the rules of Hebetheus we want to write down," Padma objects. "They're obviously the exception. As the new deputy, you ought to be able to allow this without wasting Jeremiah's time. He might be angry if you bother him."

"Yes—well—yes." Thomas looks uncertain. "Well. Jon should go," he says at last, running a trembling hand through his hair. "And you may get the water too."

In the kitchen, I twist on the taps, filling the cups. I think of waterfalls, of flowing rivers that trickle clear over shiny stones. *If you do dare to take just one sip—well, SNAKE will suffer.*

I am about to turn away when I suddenly see the glint. I put down the glasses. There, by the sink, sitting on a plate, is a razor blade. The one Jeremiah used to shear off my hair. Beads of water glimmer on it as though it's been freshly washed for some new purpose. I picture Padma's hair falling in sheafs to the floor and my heart clenches. I grab the blade, wrap it in a piece of tissue, and shove it into my pocket.

Back in the Hostage Room, I pass them their water and give Padma her pen and sheet of paper. She scrawls something on the top and flashes her eyes at me again.

"I don't know what the matter is with you boys." The woman breaks off from spilling most of her water down her front. "You boys with your knives and guns, you take it all for granted, how good your lives are. This would never have happened in my day."

"Um, Jon, can you just help me? I can't quite remember rule three," Padma asks, patting the floor. A tremble flickers through the veins in her hand.

I kneel down next to her, peering over her shoulder. I give

Thomas a nervous glance and then look. Her writing zigzags across the top: *The woman has a mobile just now when we were alone she pressed 999—*

My eyes flit to the woman, who gives me a stout glance. I picture her, hands struggling in her cuffs like crabs, easing her mobile out of her pocket, tapping in the number for emergency services with one finger, bending down, whispering into the phone, "I'm in Suffolk, I've found the boys, they're here with the girl, come quickly. . . ."

"What is that?" Thomas suddenly asks. "What's she written?"

"Nothing!" My heart is screaming in shock. "Nothing—she just wrote down a rule and she got muddled."

"Run," Padma hisses. "Before they get here—run, Jon!"

"What is it?" Thomas asks. He holds out his hand. "Show me." His voice turns to ice. "Show me or I will get Jeremiah now."

I stand up, shakily, looking round. They could be here already, creeping up to the house.

"It's nothing," I try, but Thomas wrenches the piece of paper from me. I stand in helpless, heart-hammering pain as his eyes moon.

"Jesus," Thomas cries. "The police—"

"It's too late now," the woman crows. "I had a feeling something funny was up, I knew it in my gut—and I was right! They'll be here any minute, and it won't be any good reciting more Plato."

Plato? The word lingers in the periphery of my shocked mind. What does she mean by Plato? Something inside tells me there is some obvious connection . . . something . . . that I have read about the philosopher—but there's no time—

"Run," Padma cries. "Jon, just go—I'll be all right now that the police are here—go!"

I make for the door, but Thomas slams against me, knocking me to the floor. I lie there, winded, tears burning my eyes. *Oh God, oh God, please can they just get here, please can this all be over with—*

And then the sirens start to scream.

"*Jeremiah!*" Thomas yells.

4:00 P.M.

We are standing in a line in the hallway: a winding snake of nerves, of bitten nails wrapped around guns, of jerky whispers and flitting eyes and desperate prayers. When we heard the sirens, the Brotherhood flew into a panic, but Jeremiah calmed us down. He announced that it was time to leave our holy base. He ordered Thomas to bring Padma into the hall with us, adding, "We will leave the woman behind. Give her this." He passed Thomas a copy of the Book of Hebetheus. I am waiting for Thomas to inform Jeremiah of my betrayal. But he has not said a word.

Come on, come on, come on, I silently beg the police. The two sirens play a duet: an undercurrent, a repetitive shriek of *wee-ah, wee-ah,* and a soprano that swells and retreats over the top. Sometimes back home I'd be in my bedroom, flicking through a book, and I'd hear a siren and idly wonder: *Who's it for? A robbery? A murder? Will they come onto our street?* But the sirens would fade away and the mystery would pass. I never imagined I'd be in a situation where the sirens would be a war cry for my blood.

Then, suddenly, they stop. An eerie silence stretches out. Jeremiah peers through the front door and mutters that he can't see any police cars. We whisper in bewilderment. Have they parked the cars down the road to fool us? Maybe they are slipping through the fields, creeping up behind trees, pacing toward us. . . .

"Shouldn't we go out through the back?" Martyn whispers.

"No—we'd have to cross two entire fields without cover. This way is risky, but we can be under the shelter of trees much quicker," Jeremiah hisses.

Oh so slowly, Jeremiah eases open the door. Raymond slips out, yanking Padma with him. The sight of his meaty fingers curled around her slender brown wrist sickens me. We keep the door open a slit, watch them creep across the road, climb over a stile into the small field, dart to the clusters of trees. I feel my heart banging; I can hear Thomas's heart too, his lips moving in prayer like mine. Our prayers must be enemies that clash and fight in the heavens above.

Raymond and Padma make it safely to the woods. A pale sweat washes over me. Why are the police still at the bottom of the road? Is this a game?

Jeremiah's eyes narrow in confusion. Then he says, "Okay, we go. We go quickly. Thomas—you keep your gun trained on Jon."

"Why?" I bluster, my cheeks flaming. "I'm—I wasn't the one who tried to—"

"There isn't time for this," Jeremiah hisses. "We go—now."

How has he seen into my heart and detected its true color? To my fury, Martyn nods at Thomas, whispers, "Yeah—watch him," then sneers at me with a smug smile. Only yesterday he was a so-called traitor; now he is desperate to bind himself back to Hebetheus.

We head out into the front garden. Our Sacred Circle of stones lies jagged, like fallen statues of gods broken into pieces, half covered with forgetful snow. The air is bitingly cold. At the gate, Jeremiah hisses, "Wait!" and we cower behind the hedge. If I had a gun, I could fire it into the air. One shot would do it. I eye Thomas's gun, but he is clutching it tightly, with both hands.

Jeremiah watches the faint flash of a distant siren.

"I do believe," Jeremiah says with a chuckle in his voice,

"that the police have cornered the wrong house! How very inept. Well, God has protected us once again. Let's move."

I watch my sneakers rise and fall on the road, an echo of another night here. If only I had run then.

At the stile, I hang back, but Jeremiah waits for me to climb. In the field, I stand up, raising one arm to wave at the police—who are too far away to see it, but who knows, they might, they just *might*—but Martyn thwacks me hard on the back and I lurch down, my spine shrieking.

We go into the woods.

And then the sirens scream once more.

5:00 P.M.

"Look at them," Jeremiah sneers in a whisper. "This is why the world needs us. They shoot a Brazilian man on the tube thinking he's a bomber. They act as though *we're* the terrorists, and then they get our hideaway wrong and now we've escaped. Idiots." He shakes us. "This is why the world needs us to fight evil. Only we can do it."

We peer at them through the trees.

The scene before us feels as though it's being shot for a movie. Cars pull up. Policemen tumble out. They have megaphones and fancy big black bulletproof jackets. They creep behind the hedge, they call out threats, they cajole, they warn, words ringing like metal through the cold air. I could call out to them, but they wouldn't hear; we're too far.

I look at our faces. Raymond looks determined, Martyn shocked, Chris frightened, Thomas blank. Jeremiah looks thrilled, his eyes gleaming.

So as the police invade, as they discover the dead woman and release the living one, as they enter the room full of strange symbols, we are hustled further into the forest. Every so often, I slow down and feel Thomas's gun in my back. I'm terrified he will slip on a branch and set it off by accident. Martyn is ahead of me; he keeps glancing back to check that I am at his heels. Only yesterday he was against Jeremiah; fear has persuaded him back. Is he just going along with this? Can I change him? Mostly I sense he just wants revenge for last night; he is scrambling to become Jeremiah's golden boy again, to be the one who inflicts rather than receives pain. I shoot a look back at Thomas, who nudges me sharply with the gun: *Keep going.* I want to grab him and shake him and yell, *Can't you see? We've lost! The police will find us sooner or later. Can't you see how stupid this is?* But Thomas is lost in doctrine, in fear, in devotion.

Padma's cuffs are slowing her down, slowing the group down. On the fringe of the forest, Jeremiah stops and orders Martyn to unlock them and tie her wrists loosely with rope. Martyn fumbles and Jeremiah yells at him to hurry up, *hurry up.*

We are zigzagging through the trees, slithering and slipping on the snow, branches and bushes tearing our hair and faces. I fall back in line with Padma, but Raymond comes up behind us, pointing his gun and yelling, "Keep going, you guys, keep going!"

As I run I feel the lethal blade in its tissue cocoon gently banging against me.

8:00 P.M.

It's dark in the shack. There's a lawn mower propped up against the wall, with rusty blades and a handle splattered with bird shit. A hole in the corrugated roof frames the darkened sky, and the wooden walls are filled with holes like gaping eyes. It feels both hot and cold, our warm breaths mingling to form a collective fog against the cold blasts that the wind blows in. My body is weak, my mind exhausted from lack of food and drink.

There's only just enough room to pack us in. Padma is sitting between me and Chris; Chris's pistol nudges her thigh. Raymond and Martyn guard the door; Raymond wields his gun. Thomas is hunched up. Jeremiah stands in the center, looking up through the hole. Then he turns and looks at us with glazed eyes.

"I have just received a message, O Brothers, a message from God. The world is coming to an end. And it is coming to an end soon."

I see Padma's shoulders shake with a brief ripple of laughter; she quickly represses it.

"A man who has not experienced a Soul Shift is, from God's point of view, a worm. Worse, he is a worm trapped inside a golden palace—and that palace is the mind of a human. He fails to use his divine nature. Instead he is trapped in a small, petty wriggle of desires, fears, and worries.

"Our world is full of worms, and they offend God! Unless more Soul Shifts take place, God will show his anger with punishments! People foolishly believe that the ice caps are melting and holes are forming in the sky from the use of aerosols, believing with typical egotism that their trivial actions dictate the shifts of weather. No! That is not the case! They fail to understand that the weather is a representation of God's mood. The sun is his happy smile. The wind is his frustration. The rain is the tears he weeps. As God waits for more Soul Shifts and people fail to respond, to turn to the message of the Hebetheus, disasters will begin to become more frequent: hurricanes that eat up millions of homes, typhoons that eat up races in one easy gulp. And God, expelling warm breaths of anger, is slowly destroying the world—slowly because he is giving us a chance to experience a Soul Shift in time—breathing on the ice caps and melting them, sending tidal waves flowing to drown entire countries. England will soon sink beneath the waves and become a forgotten land, a myth people will speak of in one thousand years' time.

"God has had enough. I can feel his rage! We have only hours left before a terrible disaster will strike us all down and change life on earth forever. Now, before it is too late, we must pray, pray, and pray again." He raises his hands, staring up through the hole.

Heads bow. I keep my lips whispering false chants while my hand slips into my pocket and gently eases the blade out through the tissue.

I wait, body clenched, the blade cool against my steaming palm.

Jeremiah shifts, turns. All eyes fly to him. In that moment I pull my hand out of my pocket and curl it down by my side.

I close my burning eyes. I wait for the shouts, for someone who spotted the glint. But there is silence.

I open my eyes, muttering. Jeremiah is looking directly at me. I bow my head and shift slightly, my thigh pressing against Padma's. She looks at me. I ignore her. But she deciphers my silent signal, for her eyes drop and I feel her thigh quiver against mine and I know she's seen the razor, hidden between our thighs. She yawns and shifts, stretching out her arms, and then brings her knotted hands onto her knee. I lift the edge of the razor to them and, behind the shield of her leg, I gently begin to saw.

As my fingers move, my eyes scan the others quickly. I picture a scene in my mind: *I undo her ropes and then stand up. Then I cry, "Look, her ropes are undone!" Everyone will be shocked, diverted.*

I grab Raymond's gun and then I've got them. Can that work? Oh God, can that work?

I hear my father's voice in my head, sneering at me, and I shove it away. *I'll show you, Dad, I'll show you that I can do this, I can.*

Out of the corner of my eye I flash Padma a glance. Our eyes burn for one raw second and I feel the God of love beating brightly in my heart. I know that I will be her savior, I will.

Almost there now. The rope holding her is nearly nothing but a wisp—

And then I make a mistake. Maybe it's a flash of fear or a brief flicker of guilt that causes me to look over at Jeremiah.

"Jon," he says. My fingers freeze and the blade cuts into my skin.

"Thomas will now go on guard duty. You will join him, and he will keep his gun trained on you at all times," he says.

I quickly push the razor away from me, and Padma shifts so that she's sitting on it as I stand up. As Raymond escorts me to the door, I open my mouth to say, *Her ropes are*— but the moment doesn't feel right. Jeremiah is watching me; it's too dangerous. My heart clenches into a fist of angry frustration. *Be patient, Padma,* I tell her silently. *We'll get our moment, we'll find it, and then*—

MIDNIGHT

Thomas grips his gun tightly. His eyes flit nervously between me, his hostage, and the outer world, as though he's not sure which holds the greater threat.

The snow has eased off now, but the air is still frosty and our teeth chatter in time with each other. The police must have finished going through the cottage by now. Surely they will be here soon, God, surely? My mind reels, drunk with hunger; my body keeps convulsing with shivers.

If I could just get Thomas on my side. And if Thomas could persuade Martyn, Chris would follow. . . . Raymond is hopeless, he'll always be on Jeremiah's side, but it would be four against two. I wish I could determine the color of Thomas's mind: how much has been stained by Jeremiah, how much of his own pigment still remains. If only I had the gift of gab. I need to be like Jeremiah—to pull my words out of hats like colored scarves, to make them whiz and bang like fireworks.

I look back at the shack. Can they hear us?

I whisper: "Thomas?" *Go in gently,* I decide, *go in gently.* "Do you really think the world is about to end?"

"Well, Jeremiah says so," Thomas whispers back.

Silence. The snow is settling now, glimmering crystal in the moonlight.

"Maybe it's the Apocalypse coming—maybe it's a sign," Thomas whispers.

Did I just catch a note of sarcasm? Or is it feigned sarcasm? Is he testing me?

"But d'you really believe it?" I whisper.

"I suppose," Thomas whispers, "that we have to think the Apocalypse is coming."

"Do we?" I whisper uncertainly.

"Well . . ." Thomas looks back at the shack, then drops his voice so it is a whisper of a whisper. "Don't you think that every religion has to have a story? And that story has to end somehow, doesn't it?" His words gabble as though he's been holding them in for some time, churning with them. "I mean, why is the end of the world so appealing? Maybe because it gives our lives a richer meaning. You know—we were the last ones on earth, God saved us for the end, we were the ones who saw it out. Because if life does go on forever, millions of years unrolling from millions of years, then our lives, so important in our minds, are really just tiny blinks in time. We're all nothing in the end. . . ." He trails off, swallowing, staring into the distance.

"We can do something about this," I whisper breathlessly, and Thomas's eyes widen. "We could—" A faint noise comes from the shack and I break off.

Then comes the sound of Hebethean chanting floating across the forest: strangely beautiful, almost eerie.

I turn back to Thomas.

"You know, Jon, I've got to say this, I've been meaning to . . . it's just . . . you're stupid if you believe that she loves you, Jon," he whispers.

I blink in bewilderment at the swerve of subject.

"Yeah—only I don't love her, she's a terrorist, right?" I whisper brightly. I swallow, a weak saliva washing down my parched throat.

Has Jeremiah told him to grill me? Is this all a trick?

"The thing is . . . ," Thomas whispers.

"What?"

"Oh, nothing." He looks back at the shack quickly, then looks away. "Nothing."

My heartbeat begins to quicken. He doesn't seem interested in interrogating me. Something tells me that the shadow of Jeremiah is absent. I sense that I'm on the edge of a dark abyss. Though I'm screaming at myself not to ask, I do.

"So what information do you have about SNAKE? I should know. I mean, I'm the one who's going to kill her. I need to be prepared."

Thomas glances back at the shack. The chanting is rising in pitch, coming to its climax.

"She . . . when she first got here, when I went in to interrogate her, she asked me to kiss her. Jeremiah says it's because she's an evil vixen, but I think she's just desperate. All she has is her female charm."

"*Asked?*" I pounce on the word. "Are you sure she *asked*? Are you sure you didn't threaten her like Martyn did—"

"Shh!" Thomas hisses. "Keep your voice down."

"Okay, okay, I'm sorry," I whisper.

Thomas glances at me sharply.

"Of course I didn't torment her. She asked me to kiss her. That's all."

"Yeah? And did you?"

"Of course I didn't."

A long pause.

"The thing is—" I force the emotions rising in my chest back down into my stomach, where they swirl and howl. "The thing is, she was desperate, I guess."

"Did she try that with you?"

"No! No, she didn't."

Thomas raises an eyebrow. "Well, maybe it was just me, then."

"But—but—did she ever ask you to kiss her again—ever?"

"No, but sometimes . . . there was a vibe. But she's just desperate. That's why I'm warning you. If she had a chance to wind any of us round her little finger, she would." A pause. "So you're not in love with her, then?"

"Don't be stupid!"

"Look, I'm sorry . . ."

"She trusts me, that's all, and I guess—" My voice cracks, and I swallow and mend it. "I guess it just goes to show that we need to be on our guard."

We sit in silence. Thomas takes a bottle of pills from his jacket pocket. He shakes one out and spins it up in the air, catching it, then throwing it, catching it, then throwing it, until he drops it and it lands somewhere in the earth.

"I'm so sick of being here," Thomas whispers dully. "I'm so sick of everything here."

Silence.

"Did you hear that?" I whisper.

"What?"

"A noise—I heard a noise."

"It's just Martyn." Thomas points. "He's gathering sticks. Jon, Jeremiah told me you have to stay by my side—"

"I'm on your side. No—I think it was something else. Over there. I'll just go and check."

As I rise, I am amazed that my legs can carry me and hold me up; my body feels like a machine where a cog has snapped and all the parts are about to fly apart. I wait for Thomas to tell me to sit down, to point his gun at me. But he just looks at me with sad eyes and lets me go.

1:00 A.M.

I pause. The shack is a hump in the distance; Thomas cannot see me.

I could run. I could leave her in the hands of jackals.

I step away.

"Jon?"

Martyn's eyes gleam in the moonlight. His face looks haggard, middle-aged.

"Jeremiah wants to talk to you. Now. For a private discussion. In his Sacred Space." He pauses, frowning. "You're not meant to be on your own. Thomas shouldn't have let you walk out here."

I search my mind for arguments to bring Martyn onto my side. But what *is* my side, anyway?

"Come on," Martyn says impatiently. "He's waiting."

DAY SEVEN

1:15 A.M.

I stagger into Jeremiah's Sacred Space—a small patch in the woods by the shack, warmed by a freshly burning fire—and collapse. Martyn stands by with a rifle; Jeremiah nods at him, and Martyn leaves.

I stare into the fire. The flames blur into a red haze of anger. I want to spring up, run back, demand that Thomas repeat the whole story again. What if he was mistaken? What if he misheard her words?

I tremble, ready to rise. Then I notice Jeremiah and slump back down again.

Did you know? I want to yell. *Did you know all about it all along?*

Were you laughing at me, telling me to fast, telling me not to speak to her? I look up at the sky through the knives of branches. I feel God laughing at me from behind the stars; I can feel his mockery in the moving clouds, hear his chuckles in the play of the wind and his giggles in the rustling leaves.

Jeremiah drones on about how the Hebetheus is a special religion, about how I am special, about how even special people make mistakes, can wander from the path and find themselves pricked by thorns, thorns that in fact are blessings from God, reminders of how we have strayed. I want to scream at Jeremiah to shut up. My mind keeps spinning back through the past, remembering phrases, kisses, looks, rewriting phrases, kisses, looks. Was she wincing in disgust when my lips touched hers? Did she ever mean what she said about me being different from the others?

"How do I know that you didn't just get Thomas to say it?" I burst out. "To lie to me?"

"Say what?" Jeremiah asks.

I shake my head, dangerously close to tears.

"You know what I mean. She tried to kiss me. She tried to kiss Thomas."

Jeremiah sits up very straight.

"She's a lying whore," he spits out. "She did it to weaken your faith, to make you question. And while I have told you, Jon, that yes, you should question, sometimes doubt can be a worse tyranny than faith. Sometimes you just have to trust, Jon.

Trust God. Trust *me*. She planted seeds of doubt in your mind. She manipulated you, she turned you against me."

"Well, I guess she was desperate . . . ," I mutter miserably.

"*Desperate!*" Jeremiah's voice is barbed with disgust. "She nearly succeeded in tearing apart our group, in turning you from God, in condemning your soul to hell! All for her own selfish aims! All while she was using you to escape so she could go out into the world and kill innocent people. . . ."

Jeremiah's rhetoric falls from his lips like snowflakes, melting instantly into emptiness. Betrayal weighs heavily on my heart. First my father, now Padma. Is this the end of my journey for the truth? To find that I know less than when I began? That everything I've believed in is ashes and lies, that everyone has let me down and used me?

Suddenly I am gripped by a fierce determination to know the absolute truth about Padma, to have some understanding as to how we created this hell.

"I know I've asked you before about the conversation you heard about the bomb plot . . ."

"Yes?" Jeremiah stares deep into my eyes. "You can ask me anything you like about it, Jon. I want to bring you back to God, to Hebetheus. Ask me whatever you need to to heal your soul and restore your faith."

"I want to come back, I do." I manage to sound convincing. "But . . . the conversation . . . I know I've asked you this before, but it always seemed . . . well, it seemed odd that you would have overheard her in the changing room on her own. . . . There're always other people about, all through the lunch hour. I mean, maybe there's someone who could back you up, who could back us up to the police. . . ."

"No," Jeremiah says firmly. "There was nobody else in my dream."

"Your dream?" I cry. "You're saying you based your accusations on a dream?"

"I—" Jeremiah breaks off and a brief panic shadows his face. He shakes his head. "Yes, well—there was a dream and then in real life my experience echoed it!"

"But . . . what was the dream and what was real life?"

"In the dream I heard the details. I saw her, Jon, I saw her in the changing room, and I heard her speaking about her plot. And then the very next day, she was in the changing room, she was whispering. I couldn't hear *precisely* what she was saying, but I heard the word *locker* and then—well, I knew the rest; I'd already dreamt it. If I am wrong, if I—then God will judge me in heaven, but I know this cannot be so."

A few stray snowflakes fall and melt against my burning face. Jeremiah frantically repeats his story, reminding me that he dreamt about me before I met him, that all his dreams have always been accurate.

My hand curls into a shaking fist. I nearly rise and run to the shack. If I pounded open that door and yelled the truth, though, would they listen? They believe Jeremiah's dreams are divine. And Jeremiah would persuade them against me. In a war of words, Jeremiah will always win. His weapons of rhetoric are far sharper than mine.

Frustration claws me. In a flash I can understand why it happens: why governments lie, why the strong can manipulate the weak. It's words, not weapons, that are dangerous in their chameleon colors, their ambiguities and veils. Words are the true bombs and knives and cannons of aggressors.

"Perhaps you doubt my judgment?" Jeremiah pleads. "I feel, Jon, that despite your finding out she's a whore, despite everything, I'm losing you to her."

"No." I turn back to face him. It takes effort to push down the hatred roaring up and say in a steady voice, "I just want to understand why you have such faith in your dreams, how you can be so sure they're real."

"I know because . . . you see . . . I know what it is to suffer, Jon. I know what you're going through now, ten times over. When I lost my parents, that was when the dreams came. . . ."

"That's when you came to God?"

"Yes. You know—I haven't told anyone else in Hebetheus this, Jon. I'm confiding in you now, letting you see the side of me that's human. I killed my parents. When I was fifteen I started getting into drink and drugs and smoking, just like all the other fallen souls out there. One night I left a joint burning in the living room and drifted off to sleep. I woke up smelling smoke and hearing Raymond's screams. The whole house went up in flames. Raymond saved me, but my parents . . . it was too late. Raymond wanted to go back in for them, he wanted to, but the firemen wouldn't let him. For weeks I could hardly live with myself. But now I feel glad they died."

"Glad?"

"Because that's when the dreams came," Jeremiah cries. "God made me suffer in the most terrible way. He did it so that I would be driven into such a deep hole that I had to look for a hand to pull me up and out! D'you see, Jon, d'you see now why this has happened to you? God has broken your heart so that he may heal it again. . . ."

I stare at Jeremiah and my clenched fist slowly slackens. For the first time in my life, I feel sorry for him.

"And in the first dream, did you—"

But Jeremiah interrupts me, his tone hardening. "We don't have time for talking, Jon. God is becoming impatient. She nearly escaped just now, you know. Raymond noticed that her ropes looked loose and went to tighten them. She nearly slashed him in the face. Somehow she'd got hold of a razor."

I jump.

Once again, Jeremiah is three moves ahead.

I will regain his trust only if I take the risk.

"I found it," I say, dropping my head in shame. "I . . . I

found it in the kitchen and I gave it to her to help her escape. I thought she loved me. I've behaved like a *raptor,* and I'm so, so sorry."

"You were foolish, Jon. She has used you and played you like a puppet," he says. "And by giving her that razor . . . God, if she had—"

"I know, I know," I cry. "Now I know her true colors, I'm only with you, Jeremiah. From now on, I'm going to become a true monk," I splutter thickly. "I'm—I'm never going to speak to a woman again. I'm going to give all my love to the God of Hebetheus. . . ."

Jeremiah pauses for an agonizing length of time. Finally, he says: "You have turned your back on the God of Hebetheus. You need to ask his forgiveness. Your faith is so fragile that you must make it firm before the world breaks it apart. But I am warning you, Jon, that God will only open this door to you one last time. If you do not do your Initiation, then your soul will be lost. Forever."

He pauses.

"You must hang her. You must do it now. You must prove to me and God that you have truly returned to your faith."

A false smile burns pain across my lips.

"Of course," I say. "Of course I'll do it."

Jeremiah smiles and then reaches out and unexpectedly pulls me into a tight hug. My mind is racing. How do I get out of this? I could just make an excuse, say I need to pray and then run and run and run. Leave her to suffer her fate, pay the price for using me.

But I can't. All this tragedy, all on the basis of an ephemeral dream. And in my understanding, forgiveness flows. I still love her, and my heart still feels raw, but I can understand why she did it. Her life was at stake. And to her we can never have seemed anything other than sheer crazies.

I have to save her. I owe it to her. The police will be here soon. My life will be over. But this is my last chance to do something good.

4:00 A.M.

Jeremiah calls me back into the shack. After the cold of the night, it feels lurid: a wooden fug of collective breaths and sweat. Everyone is silent, heads bowed, lips moving. Everyone knowing what we are about to do. The air feels thick with prayers, molecules clotted with their frantic intensity.

Jeremiah tells me to say my final prayers. The police may find us soon, he says urgently, but we have just enough time; God will protect us for just a little longer.

I kneel down in the center of the circle. I won't look at her, I won't; if I see the fear in her eyes, it will infect me too. I have to hold my nerve.

After fifteen minutes of prayers, Jeremiah says, "It is time."

We stand up, put down our prayer books. Our silence becomes self-conscious in its solemnity, amplifying the clatter of guns. Everyone is aware of the last grains slipping through SNAKE's hourglass.

Martyn comes up and gives me a hug, whispering, "This is your time, Jon, this is your moment." Even Raymond shakes my hand. Chris smiles and Jeremiah nods, his eyes vivid with pride.

I feel her eyes on me, feel the hunger of her pleading, but I dare not fling her a crumb of a glance. Jeremiah is watching me too closely.

As Jeremiah passes me the noose, she hunches up in the corner, whimpering softly. Jeremiah looks weary, his face pale, his eyes pockets of black. He warns us to hurry, we have little time left.

I turn to go, and without thinking I look in her direction.

Our eyes lock.

✝✝✝

A few seconds later, Thomas and I walk out into the forest. Her look keeps singing in my retinas. The love in it; the unexpected love.

My eyes fall to the gun that Thomas is carrying. For all Jeremiah's assertions that he still trusts me, he has not given me a weapon.

The forest is beautiful, the darkness fading, waiting for the first streaks of light to break. Rain falls, so light it feels more like breath than mist.

"Here," says Thomas. "This tree will do." He pats the trunk of an ancient oak.

I pass the noose over to Thomas.

"You do it."

Thomas shrugs and begins to climb.

He has chosen the tree well: there are two branches running parallel. Thomas paces along the lower one, tying the rope to the upper. He ties it very tightly, winding the rope over and over, tying knot after knot, testing for strength. I look out into the forest. Through the pillars of trees, a tiny glitter of dawn shimmers like a distant torchlight. I flick Thomas another glance and then lean down and, very casually, pick up the gun. I expect him to start shouting at me at once to put it down. But when I look up, he hasn't noticed.

"Do you believe in the God of Hebetheus?" Thomas asks, pulling the noose over his head, testing it.

"Yes."

"I don't."

He tightens the noose and steps off the branch.

5:00 A.M.

Thomas's body lies on the floor of the shack.

"We are happy that Thomas has chosen to release his soul from the cage of its body."

His neck is bruised purple; his head slants strangely from his body, propped up at an angle. Jeremiah ordered Raymond and Martyn to carry him into the shack and place him below the hole in the roof. Then Jeremiah lifted Thomas's eyelids.

"Thomas is staring up to Manu; his soul is hovering behind his forehead so that it is ready to depart upward."

Thomas's school shirt lies rumpled on the floor. Black paint gleams on his chest, for Jeremiah knelt down, trembling, tears clenched behind his eyes, and painted a Hebethean symbol on his chest.

"Thomas knew that the Apocalypse was nearly upon us. He had visions of ruined stars, burning bodies, the sky an ocean of smoke, and he chose to pass to Manu early, where he will wait for us all to join him."

Beside me, Chris starts to weep. Padma's shoulders are hunched, her face buried in her bound hands.

All I feel is a yawning wind in my chest, arctic cold. I keep seeing myself in the forest. Scrambling up the branch, tugging at the rope, feeling his pulse. The purple of his face, the bulge of his dead eyes. Letting his body down. I bent over him, stunned, begging him to wake up. *Why did you do it, Thomas, why did you do it?* Black smoke blew through my soul. I looked up at the sky and saw no light, just endless darkness, as though the outside world, beyond this forest, is a mother who might have forgiven us before if we had said sorry but now would never take us back.

"AND WE *MUST* PRAY. THOMAS'S SOUL IS SEARCH-ING, SEARCHING FOR THE LIGHT."

I watch Jeremiah's mouth moving, forming false syllables, words as meaningless as noise. Oh God, how did all our good intentions come to this?

"THE LIGHT! THE LIGHT! HELP HIM FIND THE LIGHT!"

What will we say to his mum and dad? Why did he do it? I know why he did it; we did it to him. *Oh, Mum, I want you here. Dad, I want you here. I want you to take me home, I want to say sorry. Oh God, what am I doing here?*

"THOMAS, OH, THOMAS, FIND MANU, FIND THE LIGHT! FIND THE LIGHT!"

It's then that Padma reaches out for me.

Her little finger brushes warmth against mine.

A tear spools out of my eye and slips down my cheek.

She slips her hand into mine and I grip it tightly and the tears start to pour.

I weep for her, for Thomas, for Jeremiah, for all that we might have been, for the stars we never reached.

The warmth of her skin cracks me open, tears down my shields like paper. She binds me back to the world, to every-thing I've left behind: school, home, my teachers, my mum. I want it all back, all of it. I want to be the Jon I was.

"AND THOMAS'S SOUL IS FINALLY REACHING MANU—OH YES, HE HAS FOUND THE LIGHT!"

The dawn light breaks in a halo and rain falls gently, pitter-pattering on Thomas's face like the tears of God.

"AND WE ARE ALL GREATLY BLESSED, FOR NOW IT IS TIME FOR JON'S INITIATION."

Padma squeezes my hand oh so tightly. I retaste that moment in the forest when I looked at her and saw the God of love. And I know that even if she never loved me, my love is the end of my journey.

Jeremiah turns to me.

Padma drops my hand.

"Now, Jon, it's time."

"After this—after Thomas!" I cry in shock.

"It's what Thomas would have wanted," Jeremiah says earnestly. "Do it for him."

"Jeremiah," Raymond says, "I think I just heard someone outside."

Martyn breaks off and kneels down, peering through a wooden eye.

"I can't see anything," he says. "D'you want me to go and search?"

Jeremiah shakes his head.

"No. We will continue honoring God, though if our enemies are near, we must hurry." He turns to Padma and gently strokes her hair. "I'm afraid it's time."

6:00 A.M.

Padma stands on the makeshift gallows. The rope swings gently above her head. Raymond discovered an old hook driven deep into the ceiling of the shack, perfect for supporting a noose. Her platform is a few blocks of wood that Martyn assembled.

She bows her head, weeping quietly, shoulders slumped, resigned. The Brothers' faces are hollow-eyed, shadowed with exhaustion, hunger, dirt. Their guns sit on the floor in front of Raymond, like extra spectators.

Thomas's gun was taken from me. If I try to grab one now, Raymond will get there first. The only weapon I have left is words.

"This is your moment of greatness, Jon," Jeremiah says. "This is your moment to save the doomed soul of a terrorist. This is the moment that you can pass from being human to being divine, from being ordinary to being special. To being truly one of us."

Think, Jon, think! What can you say to them to make them believe you? Think, think, you're running out of time.

"This is a deed of great compassion. Her soul is poisoned— you have tasted its poison when she betrayed you. Now is the time to intervene. It is a humane act to intervene. This is not murder, Jon, this is an act of compassion. You are giving her soul true freedom! I can feel God's energy in this room. At this moment in time, God has taken his eyes off the world and is looking at you—just at you. He is astonished by you, by this great gift you are about to offer him. He has marked you out as a chosen one, as one of his most precious sons. Now he looks down on you like a father, knowing that in return you are about to make a great sacrifice, an act of true love."

Jeremiah passes me the noose. I stare down at the weave of the rope. I look up at the group. Chris looks wide-eyed, a little fearful. Jeremiah looks firm. The expression on Martyn's face shocks me: there is a kind of savage hunger in his eyes. Raymond too looks hungry, as though relishing the moment that her neck will break.

For this is how she will die. We tighten the noose, kick away the wood, and then—

Crack!

I shudder.

"Now, Jon, *now.* This is your moment. Release the soul of the terrorist!"

"Jeremiah," I say, my voice shaking, "my Brothers, just now, when I was out praying in the snow, I briefly slept and had a divine dream."

Chris looks confused. Jeremiah stares at me with an expression of such deep betrayal that it's painful to hold his gaze.

"Don't be a chicken—just do it!" Martyn cries.

"I dreamt that Padma was innocent. I dreamt that Jeremiah wasn't really in the changing room—"

"Jon!" Jeremiah's face darkens. "I know she has seduced you, but you must fight the temptation! Remember, Jon, that you do not do this duty alone! You will act for all of us. You join us as a Brother! And you will always be protected, we'll always be here for you—*I'll* always be here for you. I'm never going to let you down. No matter what happens, from now until the end of your life, until we're together in Manu, I'll always be your friend. I love you, Jon! Be my Brother! Join me, Jon! Do it now!"

"Come on, Jon," Martyn calls out. "God is with you!"

"God is with you!" Raymond echoes.

"God is with you," Jeremiah cries, "and we are with you! Jon, hurry! Do it now! Kill her! Don't delay, do it! This is the girl who used you and betrayed you!"

I pause, letting the silence grow, and then cry savagely: "But what if he's made a mistake? You don't believe that I've had a divine dream—of course you don't—so why believe him? Because that's all his story is based on! He *never* heard Padma speaking about her plot in the changing room! He just dreamt it!"

Padma's eyes shine with wet relief and she nods fiercely. But the Brothers don't react with the shock I was expecting.

"Jeremiah's dreams *are* divine," Raymond says earnestly. "If he says she's guilty, we know it must be true."

"No, no, it's not true!" Padma cries.

"But what if he's made a mistake? A dream is just a dream! Do you trust your dreams, Martyn?" He stares back at me sullenly, confusion flickering in his eyes. I swing to Chris. "Do you

believe them, Chris? Do you really believe, one hundred per-
cent, that she's guilty? Because her life's at stake here. Her *life*.
And if we do this—"

"Jon, Jon," Jeremiah interrupts, shaking his head.

"—if we do this, and there's a shred of doubt, then we're
murderers, all of us! And it's like Padma once said—if we murder
in the name of God, we are only doing the work of the devil.
Chris? Do you believe me or him?"

"I—I—I—" Chris stutters. "I—d-don't think we sh-should—
k-kill her—"

"Enough!" Jeremiah cries. "She must die!"

"She must die!" Martyn echoes. He turns to Chris. "Don't
wimp out. She's the evil terrorist. Jon's just weak!"

"Please," Padma begs them. "Jon's right, I'm innocent, I'm
innocent."

I reach out and grip her hand tightly.

"Look," I try once more, "even if you can't believe her, you
should forgive her. We have a chance to do good, but this is not
the way. Because that's what God is, this is the God of love. I
mean, I've been confused, but everything is clear—the God of
love is the answer."

"The God of *what*?" Jeremiah's voice is like a whip.

"I think that's what God is. I just think God is . . . love." I
break off helplessly.

"That's so simplistic!" Jeremiah cries. "The world is
too dark for that sunshiny crap! What, we just love the

terrorists and let them carry on bombing us? For God's sake, Jon—*this* is love! To kill is love! If you really love her, release her soul! Set her free! Join her in Manu! We have to do this now, and if you're not ready, then we will do it! We have to kill SNAKE!"

Martyn takes up his cry: "Kill the SNAKE! Kill the SNAKE!"

"Kill the SNAKE! Kill the SNAKE!" Raymond joins in.

Their shouts fill the shack. Padma wails and I hold her tight. They try to pull her from me, but I cling to her. We lock together, sinking to the floor as they hammer us with fists and feet. I feel a punch on my shoulder and I curl in tightly. "I love you," I say into the darkness, not knowing if she can hear, "I love you so much."

They tear me from her. Raymond and Martyn hold me down. Chris stands to the side, arms dangling, gaping, shaking his head but doing nothing. I try to punch them away, but Raymond thwacks his gun against the back of my head. A wet warmth gushes through my head, and blackness spins. . . .

I open my eyes and see them. "Animals," I whisper, "you're animals." I'm aware of a presence beside me and I turn. Thomas's body, staring upward with glazed eyes. I sit up, tears falling into my mouth as I beg, "Stop, stop, this isn't God." But they have her. Martyn pins down her arms as Raymond pulls the noose over her head. Jeremiah smiles into her face, kisses her, and then kicks away the wood.

I duck my head, my hands over my ears, my heart screaming.

I curl into a ball and in the darkness I pray for her soul, I pray that she finds heaven, the God of love—but *oh God*—

I try to stand up but find myself falling. Then I feel warm hands around me, Jeremiah's hands, holding me up. His eyes are inches from mine. His breath cools my face as he whispers, "We have done the right thing, Jon, we have saved her soul, and though we acted for you, you are still one of us—"

"*MURDERER!*" I yell.

I push him away and look at her face. My heart gasps. She's still alive!

The rest of the group stares at her, stunned. The beast of anger lies flat; their eyes are glazed and frightened.

She's gasping. Swinging. Her hands claw desperately at the rope. I can hear Martyn whimpering, "The rope . . . We didn't do it right. . . . I told you if we don't do it right, her neck won't break and then—now look what we've done," and Chris's voice cuts through his, crying, "I need some air, I'm going to be sick!" and Raymond yells, "You can't be sick, you pussy, we haven't finished yet!" and she is still alive, still alive.

I leap up and tear the rope from the hook and her body falls to the ground.

Jeremiah gets up but he doesn't say anything. Nobody stops me, but nobody helps me. Even Raymond is still.

"We have to help her," I scream at them. "What are you, animals? Help her!"

Chris suddenly darts forward; Martyn tries to grab him, but Chris shakes him off. He kneels down by my side.

I clutch her face; my hands are shaking so violently her cheeks shudder against my fingertips. I tear at the rope. Chris passes over his knife, crying, "Cut it, cut it," but I can't cut it because my hand is shaking too much, so I pass it to Chris and then I cry, "Be careful, don't cut her, *DON'T CUT HER*," and he yells, "I WON'T—MARTYN, HELP ME," but Martyn stares down at us with blank eyes. The rope falls away, revealing a purple brand across her neck.

Outside a voice, magnified and metallic-sounding, orders, "COME OUT NOW AND LAY DOWN YOUR WEAPONS. COME OUT SLOWLY AND LAY DOWN YOUR WEAPONS."

"Shit!" Martyn curses.

"Nobody panic," Jeremiah orders. "We'll all stay here until we reach Manu. We'll all end as Brothers together." He holds out his lighter at arm's length.

A flame roars across the door of the shack, and Raymond screams, "*No!*"

"Padma, can you hear me, can you hear me?" I stare into the shell of her ear. Chris puts his fingers against her throat, but I push him away and bend over her mouth, listening. Nothing—*oh God*—nothing—but—

Something!

"COME OUT NOW AND LAY DOWN YOUR WEAPONS."

"SHUT UP!" I hear myself screaming. "I CAN'T HEAR

HER! OH GOD!" I yell up at the ceiling, through the hole in the roof. "LET HER LIVE! LET HER LIVE!"

"YOU ARE SURROUNDED. COME OUT NOW AND LAY DOWN YOUR WEAPONS OR WE WILL BE FORCED TO SHOOT."

Jeremiah lays his hand on my shoulder and I half rise, screaming, "You murderer, you murderer!" He looks stunned and I raise my fist, then drop back down by her side, hearing Jeremiah repeat firmly, "It's all right, it's all right, it's all right."

Chris tells me to do mouth-to-mouth. I lean down and try, then break off coughing, choking on smoke. Fans of flame erupt across the floor, competing to spread the fastest.

"No!" Martyn yells, his face ashen, waving his gun. "We have to get out of here!"

"We have to stay, we have to die—don't you want to go to Manu?" Jeremiah screams back. He flares his lighter against another wall, and a fresh volley of flames shoots up.

"Fucking get out of here!" Raymond tries to grab Jeremiah, but Jeremiah pushes him away.

"No, Raymond, this fire is holy, it is holy—"

Raymond runs to the door and kicks it open, yelling as his pant leg catches fire. Jeremiah gapes at his brother in betrayed shock. Chris gets up, grabbing Martyn, and they flee. Jeremiah glances at the flames with terrified eyes.

"Jon! Come on—just leave her—leave her!" Jeremiah cries. "God is telling me we should live, we should run!"

He grabs my shoulder and I punch him away. Flames fan and thicken; smoke steals the air. The door has been kicked flat into the snow, the doorway a burning arch of flames, as though a portal to hell. Bits of the frame fall and in one blurry moment it feels as though the shack is about to collapse in on itself. Jeremiah yanks me, but I pull back. I reach down and scoop Padma up in my arms. Jeremiah yells at me to hurry, and I run through the door and hear myself scream as we tumble out into the snow.

White flashes explode on all sides, catching the moment: a boy holding a ruined girl in his arms, his leg on fire.

Jeremiah thwacks my leg violently, throwing snow against my pants. I nearly lose hold of Padma; her arm and head swing dangerously, and I quickly put her down on a bed of snow.

I lean over her, my tears falling on her indifferent face, whispering desperately, "Oh God, please be alive, Padma, please, I love you, please—"

A figure behind me is groaning. Martyn. He's been shot.

Jeremiah holds out his gun, spinning about in bewilderment. Smoke fills the trees with black veils of confusion.

"Raymond?"

Chris. He runs toward us, followed by a figure who suddenly lunges forward through the smoke like some strange beast, wearing a black helmet and black padded jacket—a policeman?

"Jon, we have to get out of here *NOW, COME ON!*"

I shove Jeremiah away. Then—the shot. I lean down to breathe into her mouth but at the sound of the bullet my mouth freezes. Chris's eyes bulge; he crashes to the ground, his gun spinning into the snow.

"PUT DOWN YOUR WEAPONS, PUT DOWN YOUR WEAPONS, OR WE WILL BE FORCED TO SHOOT."

"They'll kill us, come on, come on!" Jeremiah screams, waving his gun.

I stumble up, reeling; he catches me. A man in neon yellow darts forward and kneels down by Padma.

"Come on—he'll take care of her. *They're going to kill us—*"

Fear screams through me. *I don't want to die; oh God, I don't want to die. If I try to say I'm innocent, they won't listen, they'll just shoot.* In my panic, I find myself running. I skid through snow and ice, trees grabbing out to meet me. Jeremiah's footsteps thud behind me.

"Go away!" I scream at him. *"Murderer!"*

And then I turn. I turn to run back and risk their bullets, to tell them I am not with the Brotherhood, I am not with Jeremiah. I turn to be with her, to tell her once more that I love her, to kiss her before it might be too late for kisses. It's my fatal moment, like Lot's wife, who got turned into a pillar of salt, for another black-helmeted figure yells and runs toward us—

Bang!

The policeman lets out a bellow, clutching his stained stomach. His face contorts: his veins become red snakes writhing beneath the skin. He falls forward, crashing across a bush, its spiky arms coming up to hold him, impaling him several feet from the ground. He groans, a foamy white-red river flowing from his mouth across the leaves.

Jeremiah clutches his gun with shaking hands. His face is green but he is smiling.

"I—look out!" he cries.

I spin. Another policeman running toward us. We both scramble to flee, and then—

Then—

The bullet slices through my skin, splitting open my stomach in a hot soup of pain. Then somehow, somewhere, the bullet hits muscle, bone, and comes to a halt, like a giant lead splinter, reverberating poker-hot. Pain: too much pain. I hear the cry from my lips like the yowl of an animal. Sky and ground tip like a seesaw. Cold snow on the ground. Pain: like a giant black dog taking huge bites out of me.

Above me, a voice: "Please don't shoot me. Oh my God, oh my God, please don't. I've thrown down my gun. Look. I've thrown it down. Please don't shoot me. . . ."

The voice fades away. Everything is going black. I feel myself sinking into that blackness, and suddenly the life instinct kicks sharply and I push the clouds aside, gasping for air, for life. . . .

"Oh, Jon, are you okay? Jon, are you okay?"

Above me, a face: Jeremiah. His fingers stroke my cheek; quiver paths of pain crack and splinter beneath my face. I try to speak to him, I need to speak to him, but all I can taste is a thick blood that soaks my teeth and drowns my tongue. I need to tell him to say goodbye to Padma for me, even though it might be too late. I feel a wetness soaking my cheeks.

Jeremiah's tears mingle with mine. He grabs my hand, sobbing, "Oh, Jon, please don't die, please don't die, Jon, I love you, God loves you, please stay with me, please don't leave me." I want to spit in his face; I want to say to him, *You bastard, you may have killed her, you may have killed her and it wasn't what God wanted and I die now hating you. Can't you see, Jeremiah, this wasn't what he wanted?* But I can't speak; no words will come out, too much pain. Here's his wrist: I press my fingers tight against the throb of vein. Pain draws me under again; sobs fall from my lips in shudders. Fast breaths. I flicker my fingers against his wrist, tapping out *You were wrong, you were wrong.* I squint into his eyes. What's he saying, his mouth is moving, what's he saying, oh God, I can't stand this—*pain*—

And then suddenly his voice, like poison honey dripping through my wounds: "Focus on Manu, Jon. Focus. Just look up, look up to Manu." I want to scream, put my hands over my ears, spit his words back out. I want Padma, I want her dying kisses, I want her by my side, whispering that we will be together in heaven. Blackness flowing over me. Where is my body now, where is this pain? It feels as though I am everywhere, like Padma says, I am Brahman, my body is a shattered mirror lying in pieces, and thoughts fly like dirt in a wind and *look up to Manu, Jon, know that you are my Brother, die knowing that you are a saint, that you helped to save this world, just a little, just a little,* I'm sixteen and I'm Jon and I'm dying and this is what it feels like to be dying. The whiz of bullets; more bullets; shouts and sirens screaming. Yes, I want the light; I crave it; not the light of Manu, not Jeremiah's false light, but a light, any light, to be with God; give it to me now, God, give it to me now. *Find the way, Jon, find your peace.* My resistance dies; I am desperate now. I push away Jeremiah's voice, I push away all the other noise and concentrate, very hard, using every last drop of sweat and blood in my leaking body to focus my eyes open until the pupils burn—

Beyond the curve of Jeremiah's head, beyond the policeman, past the leaves reaching up from the trees. Up to the dawn sky. A watercolor of pink and blue clouds. I want to drink that blue like a nectar to wash away the pain—

find the light, Jon, find the tunnel of Manu's light

—oh God I can't take any more of this pain take me God take it away. The sky is blue and I am Jon and this is what it's like to be dying and where is my light I need to grab it and let it pull me up

. . . where is the light God where is the light—

suddenly

a flash—so bright—so bright!

But fading,

fading softly . . .

As my eyes sink shut, one last vision: the white bulb of a reporter's camera, capturing me forever in the light.